Percy Bysshe Shelley

The best letters of Percy Bysshe Shelley

Percy Bysshe Shelley

The best letters of Percy Bysshe Shelley

ISBN/EAN: 9783337135553

Printed in Europe, USA, Canada, Australia, Japan

Cover: Foto ©Andreas Hilbeck / pixelio.de

More available books at **www.hansebooks.com**

THE BEST LETTERS

OF

PERCY BYSSHE SHELLEY

Edited with an Introduction

BY

SHIRLEY CARTER HUGHSON

CHICAGO

A. C. McCLURG AND COMPANY

1892

PREFACE.

THE year 1892 marks the one hundredth anniversary of the birth of the poet Shelley, and the English literary world has celebrated it in fitting manner. A splendid marble memorial has been erected to perpetuate his name within the precincts of the ancient seat of learning that once spurned him from her walls, and the Shelley Society has made the year the most memorable in its annals by its tributes to his genius. Bound as she is by all the ties of blood, of speech, and of tradition to the mother country, America holds the literature of England as somewhat of her own, and will not permit this occasion to pass unnoticed. Not that this little volume for a moment claims the distinction of being a memorial one, but it has occurred to the editor that no more appropriate time than the present could .be chosen at which to make an effort to arouse among American readers generally an interest in the prose writings of one who is chiefly known in the field of poetry.

In the preparation of this collection chief regard has been had to the literary excellence of the letters, without neglecting, however, their biographical value. All giving pictures of his time, and especially those which admit us into the inner circle of that distinguished coterie of English exiles with which Shelley was associated in Italy, are carefully retained. The object has been to give the " Best Letters " of the poet, and at the same time to make the volume a complete and ready work of reference for those who might desire to consult Shelley's records of his own life, and the lives of his poet-friends. Shelley was not a voluminous letter writer, and the present edition contains very nearly all that he left with the exception of the letters of his younger and more immature years. The editor is indebted to Professor Dowden's Life of Shelley for a number of letters which have never before appeared in any collection.

Some of the notes contributed to early editions by Mrs. Shelley, Lady Shelley, and Peacock have been retained, and are designated by their initials, — M. S., L. S., and T. L. P., respectively. For the other notes the present editor is responsible.

S. C. H.

September, 1892.

CONTENTS.

CONTENTS.

INTRODUCTION.

THE year before his death Shelley wrote in his noble "Defense of Poetry": "The jury which sits in judgment upon a poet, belonging as he does to all time, must be composed of his peers; it must be empanelled by Time from the selectest of the wise of many generations." To those who know the life and character of this remarkable genius, these words have a strange personal ring. He could not have applied them to his contemporaries save in a few instances. Byron, Scott, Southey, Wordsworth, Coleridge, his most famous coworkers in the realm of the Muses, heard the trump of fame while they were yet in the vigor of their intellectual youth. Shelley, on the other hand, was neglected by one half the world, and hated by the other half. Full of high hopes of elevating mankind, and believing poetry to be the loftiest mode of expression of the highest things, he sought to lure the world to nobler achievement by his sweetest strains. But the world turned a deaf ear to him, or denounced his music as the inspiration of an evil genius. Despite, however, the scorn of society, he felt that he might yet do something to raise his fellow-man, and, hoping against hope, he went forth as what Heine might have called "A brave soldier in the Liberation War of humanity." And he has been tried by the jury of which he spoke. "The selectest of the wise" of these latter days have rendered their verdict, and his genius has been vindicated. Probably no man so neglected by his own generation has been accorded so much praise and honor in after times, and it has been all in spite of Shelley himself. Death released his genius from its strange and unnatural surroundings, and when considered alone, apart from the man, there could be no doubt as to the position it should be accorded.

Just one hundred years ago Percy Bysshe Shelley was born in Sussex, England, and, as an eldest son, he was the heir presumptive to one of the richest baronetcies in that part of the kingdom. He was born in " the purple of the English Squirearchy," but his inherited honors received but little consideration at his hands. Gifted with a most untamable spirit of liberty, he had not attained his majority before he came to hate, with a hatred that lasted until the end, the empty show and paraphernalia of nobility. Filled with a sense of the equality of man, he despised the sentiment which arbitrarily placed one class above another, and which made one man better than his fellow by accident of birth. Living as he did in an age that boasted but little liberality of thought, it is not surprising that he met with scant sympathy. The terrors of the French Revolution were still fresh in the minds of men, and the world had not yet recovered from its first paroxysm of horror at the terrible school of free thought that was born of that period. But Shelley did not share this feeling of horror. He himself was of that French school, and he was ready to receive on their supposed merits any new ideas that might be presented. Holding such views, born in a period of anarchy and blood, and nurtured under skies red with the glare of Europe's blazing thrones, it is not surprising that he, the " Child of the Revolution," should have become an apostle of the new school, a high priest of iconoclasm.

In his desire to subvert the old order of things, his boundless enthusiasm spared nothing. Whatever merits an institution might have in itself, the fact that it was a part of the ancient economy of social or political life was sufficient for him to condemn it, and denounce it as a pernicious obstacle to the advancement of mankind. He knew nothing of discrimination, and just here lay the mistake which rendered his efforts of no avail, or, as it has been touchingly expressed, made him "a beautiful and ineffectual angel, beating in the void his luminous wings in vain." [1]

Shelley's youth was no less turbulent than his latter years. It seemed, indeed, that from his very infancy some strange destiny hung over him, forcing him into bitter opposition to everything with which he should have been identified. A brief and unhappy course at Eton was followed by a still briefer and more unfortunate residence at Oxford. As a student, he rebelled against the arbitrary curriculum of studies, and sought sources of knowledge which at that day were unknown to the ordinary undergraduate at Oxford, and known to the learned authorities only to be condemned in a manner more than characteristic of the bigoted age. Shelley, even as a boy, was a thinker, and his study of the French philosophical writers soon bore fruit. He had not been a member of the University six months before the ancient and orthodox seat of learning was startled by an anonymous publication — a mere leaflet — entitled "The Necessity of Atheism," which was scattered through the colleges. Shelley made no secret of the fact that he was the author of the remarkable work, and on Lady Day, 1811, he was summoned before the authorities and required to answer to certain peremptory

---

[1] Matthew Arnold concludes his essay on Shelley with this paraphrase of Joubert's comment on Plato.

questions regarding his connection with it. The spirit
of rebellion against anything like coercion was fired in
a moment, and he defiantly refused to answer. Without
any further formality, he was served with a notice of ex-
pulsion, which had been previously drawn up in anticipation of his refusal to submit to a formal examination
regarding his act.

Driven from Oxford, Shelley sought a residence in
London, and from there proceeded to open negotiations
with his father, with whom he had never been on good
terms, but in this business he had to deal with a Phi-
listine of a school as ancient as Goliath himself. Mr.
Timothy Shelley heard of his son's performance with a
horror that was indeed to be expected; but what does
surprise us is that never once did the stiff-necked old
English gentleman seek to win his erring son from his
error by the influence of that love which must have
come off victor in every case where he was concerned.
But he was a stern parent of the most pronounced
eighteenth century type, and his only thought was to
whip the rebellious boy back into the right path. Tact-
less almost to a degree of brutality, and bound hand
and foot by conventions which even the conservative
people of that day were beginning to disregard, it is not
surprising that his negotiations with his son ended in a
breach which was never healed, and that Shelley, at the
age of nineteen, found himself thrown on the world, and
in a position where he could with some color of justice
consider himself a persecuted man.

To Shelley's residence in London the keenest interest
attaches, as it was now that he met with one whose sad
career was to bring a strange tragedy into his life. His
sudden marriage with Harriet Westbrook, their brief
and checkered life together, their estrangement and
separation, are questions too lengthy and vexed to be
discussed in the narrow compass of this essay. The

immediate causes of their separation have never been accurately known, and probably never will be. The Shelley family promised them to the world, but Professor Dowden's Life of Shelley — two great volumes prepared under family auspices — have appeared, and the world is no wiser than before.

During the spring of 1813, while Shelley was yet living happily with Harriet, he became one of a little coterie of free-thinkers who attached themselves to William Godwin, the author of the famous work on " Political Justice." Some time previous Shelley had become acquainted with Godwin through a correspondence in which he invited the old philosopher of Skinner Street to become his guide in the devious paths of political and social philosophy. From this their mutual interest increased until now the young poet had become one of the most constant attendants on the frequent seances to which only the favored few were admitted. From this period date many of those friendships which exerted so much influence on Shelley's after life. It was here that he met Peacock, to whom his finest letters were addressed, and it was here, too, that he met Mary Godwin, the Mary who in after years filled so great a part of his life, — that daughter of illustrious parentage, who, while she brought Shelley the first and only happiness he knew, brought also into his life a dark tragedy, the only blot that has ever stained his fame.

Early in 1814 came the final break with Harriet, and a few weeks later he fled to the Continent with Mary, to escape the wrath of Godwin, who, although he was an opponent of marriage, was too weak to advance his theories into practice in the case of his daughter. With the birth of her second child, Harriet hoped for a reconciliation, but it was too late. Shelley saw her but once again, and they then parted forever. He went out into life, his heart filled with high hopes and aspiring am-

bitions; Harriet went back to her old friends, to drag
out a heart-broken existence, until, on a dark November
night two years later, the waters of the Serpentine
closed over her, shutting out from life one whose career
we must contemplate with infinite pity.

The following month Shelley was married to Mary
Godwin, and immediately set about to recover his children by a suit in Chancery. The notes to " Queen
Mab " were entered as evidence to prove that he was
not a proper person to rear his own offspring, and Lord
Eldon rendered a decision to that effect. The children
were placed in charge of a guardian, and the severest
restrictions placed on their father's visits to them.

During all this time Shelley had not thought of Italy
as a permanent residence. Although he hated the existing institutions of his country with all the strength of
his moral nature, still for England itself he had a love
which reminds us of the great love the exiled Heine
bore his down-trodden Fatherland, and it was not until
after the chancery suit that he thought of seeking freedom and peace in that "paradise of exiles." At this
time he was living at Great Marlowe on the Thames.
There he had the quiet of home, and the communion of
faithful and devoted friends. Leigh Hunt, Peacock, and
Horace Smith were his constant companions; there he
met Keats, his "Adonais"; and there he formed those
lasting friendships which infused so much of happiness
into his life. There, too, Shelley wrote. With his
ardent devotion to nature, most of his work was done
out of doors, under the spreading trees, in the fields
with only the blue English summer sky over him, or
while floating in some frail boat in the shadow of the
willows which bordered the picturesque Thames.

But these delightful, almost idyllic surroundings, could
not and did not bring happiness to Shelley. " The
Chancellor had said some words," wrote Mrs. Shelley,

"that seemed to intimate that Shelley would not be permitted the care of any of his children, and for a moment he feared that our infant son would be torn from us." This fear so haunted him that it soon became evident that he could have no happiness in England, and by the spring of 1818 he had fully determined to seek a home in Italy. April found him with his family at Milan, and from there he went from point to point, which inclination or his search after health prompted him to visit. For four years — "years," says Symonds, "filled with music that will sound as long as English lasts " — Shelley and Mary followed a series of delightful and uncertain wanderings through Italy. They had no settled abiding-place. All Italy was their home. Shelley wished for no roof save "the vault of blue Italian day"; the purple-peaked Apennines were the only walls and towers he cared to have above him; the Muses were his Lares and Penates, and their shrines he found everywhere, — in the flowered valleys, up the snowy mountain slopes, and on the bosom of the deep sea he loved so much. Wherever beauty was, there was his home. Like the ancient poets he found inspiration in all things; for him every fountain had its Nereid, every wood its nymph, and every mountain side its musical Pan. The riotous melody of Satyrs he heard in every wind, and the great forests were like vast Æolian harps upon which the powers of the air played the divinest music of nature. All the universe was filled with associations as dear to him as any that ever clustered around an humble hearthstone, or an ancestral hall.

But we will not linger over these Italian years. The only true account of them — and the most beautiful account that could ever be written — is found in his letters. So we will leave him to tell the story of his own life until we reach the last days. There we will pause.

It was July, 1822.   Lured by the sea whose music
ever had so subtle an influence on his spirit, Shelley had
found his way to Casa Magni, a little white stone cot-
tage on the Bay of Spezia, so near the water that in
times of storm, wrote Mrs. Shelley, "we almost fancied
ourselves on board ship."   Here, with Mary, Trelawny,
Byron, Edward Williams, and Williams's wife — the
"Jane" of so many of his short poems — Shelley passed
some Elysian days.   The water he loved so much was
at his feet, the breath of the warm south was pulsing
over the Mediterranean; on the east, across the blue
gulf, lay the picturesque town of Lerici, and far away to
the west shone the white villas of Porto Venere.   It
was summer in Italy, glorious season in a glorious land.
Late in June he wrote Horace Smith: "I still inhabit
this divine bay, reading Spanish dramas, and sailing,
and listening to the most enchanting music.   We have
some friends on a visit to us, and my only regret is that
the summer must ever pass."

One friend, however, was wanting to complete their
circle.   All through the years repeated invitations had
been sent to Leigh Hunt to visit them in Italy, and
now in this eventful summer he was on his way south.
During the early days of July at Leghorn the friends
clasped hands for the first time since Shelley had parted
from English shores.   The meeting was characterized
by that affection which in strong men is as touching as
it is beautiful.   "I will not dwell upon the moment,"
wrote Hunt, with inexpressible tenderness, in his Auto-
biography.

Hunt was established in Byron's palace at Pisa, and,
after a few days of delightful intercourse, Shelley
started on his return to Casa Magni, where Hunt was
to follow him in a few days.   On July 8, with Williams
and one seaman, he sailed from Leghorn in a small
yacht.   With a heart full of gladness at the anticipation

of his friend's companionship, there was no cloud on Shelley's sky that day; but waiting in the storm which crouched beneath the horizon was his fate. The afternoon was hot and sultry. There was a stillness in the atmosphere that boded no good to the sea-going mariner. "The Devil is brewing mischief," remarked the Genoese mate of Byron's yacht, as Shelley's little vessel beat slowly out to sea. A little later a fog shut out the sea view, and the storm broke. It did not last a short half-hour, but that brief space held woe enough for those who loved Shelley to tinge all after life with the sombre hues of an ineffaceable grief.

Trelawny had watched the storm from Byron's yacht, and when the skies cleared no sail was seen against the smiling horizon. Something told him that the worst had come. Summoning Byron and Hunt, the friends patrolled the beach for many miles, and not until ten days later was Shelley's body found washed on the sands near Via Reggio.

The quarantine regulations required that the remains be burned, and loving hands prepared them for the final rites. The body was placed in an iron receiver; over it was poured a vast quantity of oil and wine, and on the sea-shore, on August 8, it was consigned to the purifying flame. Only the heart refused to be consumed. It was rescued by Trelawny, and given to Mrs. Shelley, while the ashes were interred in the English cemetery at Rome, beside the grave of his son William, and near that of Keats.

Thus lived and died one of the strangest geniuses of the century; one who left behind him a deathless fame, but a fame that we scarcely know how to estimate. As a poet, as a man of intellectual power, as a man of almost transcendent genius, his position is not to be questioned. But he was more than this; he was the champion of those principles which were waging the bitterest warfare against the shams of the world, against that old idolatry which still remained from the Dark Ages; he was "the poetical representative of those whose hopes and aspirations and affections rush forward to embrace the great hereafter, and dwell in rapturous anticipation on the coming of the golden year, the reign of universal freedom, and the establishment of universal brotherhood."

His creed was that the truly good and the truly beautiful were one and the same, and in this he was much nearer to the highest truth than he realized. Holding to this belief, had he entered the right path at the beginning of his life, we cannot conceive of a career that would have been above his reach. With his intellectual power, combined with his intense earnestness and enthusiasm, his absolute fearlessness, and his limitless capacity for appreciating the lofty poetry which is interwoven like a thread of fine-spun gold through all the fabric of Christianity, he would have proved a splendid ornament to that religion, a blazing beacon whose rays would have shone down through future centuries guiding men to truth and light.

What we must admire most of all in Shelley is the great love he bore his fellow-man. However mistaken they were, his life was one continuous sacrifice to those principles which he conscientiously believed would elevate mankind, if carried out. He found man out of harmony with truth, with beauty. He recognized that the chords of his nature had not been torn asunder by the fall; they were only out of tune. He looked on humanity as some vast harp[1] from which could be drawn symphonies which could charm sin and depravity out of the world, but whose music was a jangling discord because the strings were not attuned one to another;

---

[1] See the "Defence of Poetry."

and he believed that it was his mission to find that key by which discord could be changed into music of a divine strain, and the harsh tones blended into an eternal harmony. This was his aim, and to it he sacrificed everything. But little did he realize the hopelessness of his task. In his enthusiasm, in his fearless warfare against every obstacle, he forgot that through a hundred centuries poets and prophets, priests and seers, had striven to bring about the same end, and that even in the face of divinely inspired effort the discord had swelled until human life had become a horrid Pandemonium. He did not know that the cause of the discord was human nature itself, and that the fingers of a god would have to sweep those strings before the music of which he dreamed could be brought forth.

Shelley's attitude toward his fellow-man he sums up in one of the grandest of his prose passages, in his eloquent note to that strange autobiographical poem, "Alastor." He says:—

"They who, deluded by no generous error, instigated by no sacred thirst of doubtful knowledge, duped by no illustrious superstition, loving nothing on this earth, and cherishing no hopes beyond, yet keep aloof from sympathies with their kind, rejoicing neither with human joy, nor mourning with human grief, these, and such as they, have their apportioned curse. They languish because none feel with them their common nature. They are morally dead. They are neither friends, nor lovers, nor fathers, nor citizens of the world, nor benefactors of their country. Among those who attempt to exist without human sympathy, the pure and tender-hearted perish through the intensity and passion of their search after its communities when the vacancy of their spirit suddenly makes itself felt. All else, selfish, blind, and torpid, are those unforeseeing multitudes who constitute, together with their own, the lasting misery and loneliness of the world. Those who love not their fellow-beings live unfruitful lives, and prepare for their old age a miserable grave."

The value of this declaration as an index to Shelley's position is enhanced by the fact that it was written at that early period when his opinions were but little modified, and when he gloried in the self-applied epithet of Atheist, " to express," as he said, " his abhorrence of superstition."

Mrs. Shelley, in passing judgment upon Shelley's prose writings, has said that he " commanded language splendid and melodious as Plato," and while we are not prepared to indorse to the fullest extent her naturally biased opinion, it is none the less true that the verdict of more than one eminent scholar has been that in splendor of expression and power of thought his prose more nearly resembles that of the ancient master than that of any of his contemporaries. Every true poet, as Wordsworth has declared, must be a writer of good prose. The genius possessed by the real poet includes in its scope the prose writer, and few men have ever attained a high plane in the realm of the Muses whose pens could not be used with singular force and effect in the more serious field of prose. But Shelley's power in this respect was not to be compared with the average of his fellow-singers. There was in all he wrote a melody, a subtle rhythm, which made his prose close akin to poetry. There was a depth to the current of his words as well as to the current of his thought, and his splendid imagery, and his wealth of metaphor, drawn from all that represented sweetness, light, love, beauty, and sublimity, in both physical and spiritual nature, has given to his writings so much of literary value that so distinguished a critic as Matthew Arnold has doubted whether Shelley's " delightful letters and essays, which deserve to be far more read than they now are, will not resist the wear and tear of time better, and finally come to stand higher, than his poetry."

In his prose writings Shelley covered a wide range.

When he entered Oxford, a stripling of eighteen years, he had already found a publisher for more than one novel of a distinct "blue-fire" type, and in 1812 he considered them serious enough to submit to Godwin for perusal. At an early age he began to put forth political tracts, which showed marked clearness of thought and directness of logic, and, what was most singular of all, considering the nature of the author, were models of tolerance and calm, dispassionate argument. Although the "Defence of Poetry" stands as Shelley's prose masterpiece, he rose to some of his most magnificent flights in the prefaces and notes to his poems. The extract already given from the note to "Alastor" is a striking instance of prose composed while the divine impulse was still upon the poet, while the fire of poetic enthusiasm was still aglow. The "Defense of Poetry" is an exquisite essay written as "an antidote" to Peacock's "Four Ages of Poetry."[1] This work is on the same lines as Sir Philip Sidney's famous "Apology," but contains much splendid and original thought, while the style and treatment are such as to secure for it a position as an English classic. Shelley intended to prepare the essay in three parts, but only the first was ever completed.

When one attempts to discuss Shelley's letters in any circumscribed space, he feels as hopeless as did the man in the Eastern fable who sought to imprison the giant in the flower. Nearly all of us at certain periods of our lives have conceived a passion for Shelley's poetry, which, in many cases, has been in a measure outgrown; but to outgrow a keen appreciation of Shelley's letters would be to lose a taste for some of the finest prose in the English tongue. In discussing them the temptation to discuss his poetry is wellnigh irresistible, for the reason that the two in so many instances are insep-

---

[1] See Letter LXXXVII.

arable. The letters often are the groundwork of his poems, and one famous letter has long since been included in every volume of his poetry that pretends to be either complete, or to be a selection of his best work. Shelley had a keen conception of the beautiful, and whenever he seized upon a beautiful idea he cherished it, and clung to it, and it imparted to him an inspiration which did not pass with the moment. First he would give expression to it in some letter of tender friendship to Peacock, or Hunt, or perhaps to the Gisbornes, and next we find it interwoven with other beautiful conceptions through the musical stanzas of some incomparable poem. This it is that so enhances the value of these letters. They cannot be divorced from his immortal works; each is the complement of the other. Reading them together, we find that he idealized and clothed in flaming verse the experiences and observations of his every-day life; that by the alchemy of his splendid genius he transmuted his restless, stormy life into a poem. There are few of his poetical productions that do not contain striking autobiographical passages, and by means of the letters we trace them with delightful accuracy. Idealist that he was, he knew no distinction between the common realities of his life and the higher things that were a part of his poet nature. To him poetry and all things beautiful were realities, and the sternest realities themselves he elevated and spiritualized.

Thus dwelling in an atmosphere of poetry, ever on the wing, Shelley transfused all life with a beauty that shines through everything he wrote, and most especially through the letters of certain periods. In those written to Peacock from Switzerland and Italy, more particularly, does he lose himself in the contemplation of the beautiful around him; and often does he pour forth periods as fresh and beautiful as the most unpremeditated song.

The descriptions he sends his friends of the paintings and statuary in the Italian galleries are no less artistic and inspiring, and the impressions he imparts regarding the ruins of "the capital of the vanished world," are in a style not inferior to any prose ever written. We have not space for long extracts, although the temptation to quote indefinitely is difficult to withstand. Take, for instance, a few lines from his description of the ruins of the Thermæ of Caracalla.

"There grow on every side," he says, "thick entangled wildernesses of myrtle and myrletus and bay, and the flowering laurestinus, whose white blossoms are just developed, the white fig, and a thousand nameless plants sowed by the wandering wind. . . . Around rise other crags and other peaks, all arrayed, and the deformity of their vast desolation softened down by the undecaying investiture of nature."

Pursuing this description he is overcome by the emotions produced by the contemplation of so much beauty, and breaking forth in words strikingly similar to those employed in the "Adonais," he cries: "Come to Rome! It is a scene by which expression is overpowered, — which words cannot convey!" We cannot but feel something of that intoxication that seized upon him as, winding through the "deep dells of wood, and lofty rocks, and terrific chasms" of this splendid ruin, he suddenly comes upon some little mossy lawn "overgrown by anemonies, wall-flowers, and violets, whose stalks pierce the starry moss, and with radiant blue flowers, whose names I know not, and which scatter through the air the divinest odor, which, as you recline under the shade of the ruin, produces sensations of voluptuous faintness, like combinations of sweet music."

Then comes the conclusion, tender, beautiful, and eloquent:—

"I walk forth in the purple and golden light of an Italian evening, and return by star or moon light through this scene. The elms are just budding, and the warm spring winds bring unknown odors all sweet from the country. I see the radiant Orion through the mighty columns of the Temple of Concord, and the mellow, fading light softens down the modern buildings of the Capitol, the only ones that interfere with the sublime desolation of the scene."

Aside from the literary value of these letters, nothing can be more delightful than the glimpses they afford of the life led by that strange band of literary Englishmen with whom Shelley was associated in Italy. Byron, Trelawny, Keats, Hunt, — the very names conjure up memories which will live for all time in the annals of English literature. Byron, "the pilgrim of eternity," is there seen at his best and at his worst; Trelawny, the strange adventurer, seems here, under Shelley's influence, to rise somewhat above his low nature; Hunt, who joined the exiles only at the last, appears through all the letters the gentle poet, the unyielding patriot; of Keats Shelley saw but little, but he watched his career with the keenest interest, and his criticisms in these records are among the best and most faithful the young "Adonais" ever received. The life we see here must ever be of the most intense interest to students of literature, because we know that from every phase of it were born works that gave immortalizing fame to their authors. How delightful to follow the evolution of " The Cenci," of " Epipsychidion," of "Adonais," to go with Shelley over the manuscript pages of his friend's " Childe Harold " and " Don Juan," to hear how Byron lived and worked, to learn of Shelley's strange erratic methods, and to read his own clear judgment on his own works ! In these letters the characters are their real selves; there is no false coloring, as by admiring biographers or unsympathetic critics of later times. Here we have the unvarnished truth, written, not for the public eye, but for those who understood him, to whom he could bare his whole heart, knowing that in so doing he was secure in their love and friendship.

A glorious life it was, that life in Italy, and a glorious reflection of it Shelley has given us in his letters. About them hovers the warm breath of that summer land; seen through the transfusing medium of his glowing descriptions, a double fascination seems to hover over its blue islands and crystal seas; its mountain peaks and crags seem loftier and more sublime, the emerald plains between them of a richer green; and while reading, one can almost imagine he hears the musical ripple of the water about the keel of his drifting boat as the exiled poet dreamed by the shores of that mystic country. There is a subtle charm about them like old-time music, which transports us out of ourselves and carries us far across the seas to that " Magic Land " which has been the birthplace of so much greatness and is the home of so much beauty.

S. C. H.

SEWANEE, TENN., *September*, 1892.

THE BEST LETTERS

OF

PERCY BYSSHE SHELLEY.

I.

TO LEIGH HUNT.[1]

UNIVERSITY COLLEGE, OXFORD, *March* 2, 1811.

PERMIT me, although a stranger, to offer my sincerest congratulations on the occasion of that triumph so highly to be praised by men of liberality; permit me also to submit to your consideration as one of the fearless enlighteners of the public mind at the present time a scheme of mutual safety and mutual indemnification for men of public spirit and principle, which, if carried into effect, would evidently be productive of incalculable advantages. . . . The ultimate intention of my aim is to induce a meeting of such enlightened, unprejudiced members of the community, whose independent principles expose them to evils which might thus become alleviated, and to form a methodical society which should be

---

[1] This letter was written on the occasion of Hunt's third acquittal of the charge of seditious libel. The charges were based on publications in " The Examiner."

organized so as to resist the coalition of the enemies of liberty, which at present renders any expression of opinion on matters of policy dangerous to individuals. It has been for the want of societies of this nature that corruption has attained the height at which we behold it; nor can any of us bear in mind the very great influence which, some years since, was gained by Illuminism, without considering that a society of equal extent might establish rational liberty on as firm a basis as that which would have supported the visionary schemes of a completely equalized community.

Although perfectly unacquainted with you privately, I address you as a common friend to liberty, thinking that, in cases of this urgency and importance, etiquette ought not to stand in the way of usefulness.

.   .   .   .

II.

TO WILLIAM GODWIN.

KESWICK, *January* 10, 1812.

.   .   .   .

You complain that the generalizing character of my letter renders it deficient in interest; that I am not an individual to you. Yet, intimate as I am with your character and your writings, intimacy with yourself must in some degree precede this exposure of my peculiarities. It is scarely possible, however pure be the morality which he has endeavored to diffuse, but that generalization must characterize the uninvited address of a stranger to a stranger.

I proceed to remedy the fault. I am the son of a man of fortune in Sussex. The habits of thinking of my father and myself never coincided. Passive obedience was inculcated and enforced in my childhood. I was required to love, because it was my duty to love : it is scarcely necessary to remark that coercion obviated its own intention. I was haunted with a passion for the wildest and most extravagant romances. Ancient books of chemistry and magic were perused with an enthusiasm of wonder amounting almost to belief. My sentiments were unrestrained by anything within me ; external impediments were numerous, and strongly applied ; their effect was merely temporary.

From a reader, I became a writer of romances ; before the age of seventeen I had published two, "St. Irvyne" and "Zastrozzi," each of which, though quite uncharacteristic of me as now I am, yet serves to mark the state of my mind at the period of their composition. I shall desire them to be sent to you ; do not, however, consider this as any obligation to yourself to misapply your valuable time.

It is now a period of more than two years since first I saw your inestimable book of "Political Justice" ; it opened to my mind fresh and more extensive views ; it materially influenced my character, and I rose from its perusal a wiser and better man. I was no longer the votary of romance ; till then I had existed in an ideal world, — now I found that in this universe of ours was enough to excite the interest of the heart, enough to employ the discussions of reason.   I beheld, in short, that I had duties to perform.   Conceive the effect which the " Political Justice " would have upon a mind before jealous of its independence, and participating somewhat singularly in a peculiar susceptibility.

My age is now nineteen; at the period to which I allude I was at Eton.   No sooner had I formed the principles which I now profess than I was anxious to disseminate them. . . . I went to Oxford. Oxonian society was insipid to me, uncongenial with my habits of thinking.   I could not descend to common life : the sublime interest of poetry, lofty and exalted achievements, the proselytism of the world, the equalization of its inhabitants, were to me the soul of my soul.   You can probably form some idea of the contrast exhibited to my character by those with whom I was surrounded.   Classical reading and poetical writing employed me during my residence at Oxford.

.   .   .   .

It will be necessary in order to elucidate this part of my history to inform you that I am heir by entail to an estate of £6,000 per annum.   My principles have induced me to regard the law of primogeniture an evil of primary magnitude.   My father's notions of family honor are incoincident with my knowledge. of public good.   I will never sacrifice the latter to any consideration. . . . These are the leading points of the history of the man before you.   Others exist, but I have thought proper to make some selection, not that it is my design to conceal or extenuate any part, but that I should by their enumeration quite outstep the bounds of modesty. Now it is for you to judge whether, by permitting me to cultivate your friendship, you are exhibiting yourself more really useful than by the pursuance of those avocations of which the time spent in allowing this cultivation would deprive you. I am now earnestly pursuing studious habits. I am writing " An Inquiry into the Causes of the Failure of the French Revolution to benefit Mankind." My plan is that of resolving to lose no opportunity to disseminate truth and happiness.

I am married to a woman whose views are similar to my own. To you, as the regulator and former of my mind, I must ever look with real respect and veneration.

III.

TO WILLIAM GODWIN.

KESWICK, *January* 16, 1812.

THAT so prompt and so kind an answer should have relieved my mind, I had scarely dared to hope ; to find that he, — who as an author had gained my love and confidence, whose views and habits I had delighted to conjecture from his works, whose principles I had adopted, and every trace of whose existence is now made sacred, and I hope eternally so, by associations which throw the charm of feeling over the deductions of reason, — that he as a man should be my friend and adviser, the moderator of my enthusiasm, the personal exciter and strengthener of my virtuous habits, — all this was more than I had dared to trust myself to hope, and which now comes to me almost like a ray of second existence.

. . . .

I know not how to describe the pleasure which your last letter has given me; that William Godwin should have "a deep and earnest interest in my welfare," cannot but produce the most intoxicating sensations. It may be my vanity which is thus flattered, but I am much deceived in myself if love and respect for the great and worthy form not a very considerable part of my feelings.

I cannot help considering you as a friend and adviser whom I have known very long; this circumstance must generate a degree of familiarity, which will cease to appear surprising to you when the intimacy which I had acquired with your writings so much preceded the information which led to my first letter. It may be said that I have derived little benefit or injury from artificial education. I have known no tutor or adviser (not excepting my father) from whose lessons and suggestions I have not recoiled with disgust.

. . . .

You say, "Being yet a scholar, I ought to have no intolerable itch to become a teacher." I have not, so far as any publications of mine are irreconcilable with the general good, or so far as they are negative. I do not set up for a judge of controversies, but into whatever company I go I have introduced my own sentiments, partly with a view, if they were any wise erroneous, that unforeseen elucidations might rectify them ; or if they were not, that I might contribute my mite to the treasury of wisdom and happiness. I hope in the course of our communication to acquire that sobriety of spirit which is the characteristic of true heroism. I have not heard without benefit that Newton was a modest man ; I am not ignorant that vanity and folly delight in forwardness and assumption. But I think there is a line to be drawn between the affectation of unpossessed talents, and the deceit of self-distrust, by which much power has been lost to the world ; for

> " Full many a flower is born to blush unseen,
> And waste its sweetness on the desert air."

This line may be called " the modesty of nature." I hope I am somewhat anxious not to outstep its boundaries. I will not again crudely obtrude the question of atheism on the world. But could I not at the same time improve my own powers and diffuse true and virtuous principles? Many with equally confined talents to my own are by publications scattering the seeds of prejudice and selfishness. Might not an exhibition of truth, with equal elegance and depth, suffice to counteract the deleterious tendency of their principles? Does not writing hold the next place to colloquial discussion in eliciting and classing the powers of the mind? I am willing to become a scholar, — nay, a pupil. My humility and confidence, where I am conscious that I am not imposed upon, and where I perceive talents and

powers so certainly and undoubtedly superior, is
unfeigned and complete.

    .   .   .   .

In a few days we set off to Dublin. I do not know
exactly where we shall be ; but a letter addressed to
Keswick will find me. Our journey has been settled
some time. We go principally to forward as much
as we can the Catholic Emancipation.

Southey, the poet whose principles were pure and
elevated once, is now the paid champion of every
abuse and absurdity. I have had much conversation
with him. He says, " You will think as I do when
you are as old." I do not feel the least disposition
to be Mr. S.'s proselyte.

    .   .   .   .

IV.

TO WILLIAM GODWIN.

Keswick, Cumberland, *January* 28, 1812.

    .   .   .   .

You regard early authorship detrimental to the
cause of general happiness. I confess this has not
been my opinion, even when I have bestowed deep,
and, I hope, disinterested thought upon the subject.
If any man would determine sincerely and cautiously,
at every period of his life, to publish books which
should contain the real state of his feelings and opinions, I am willing to suppose that this portraiture of
his mind would be worth many metaphysical disquisitions ; and one whose mind is strongly imbued with

an ardent desire of communicating pleasurable sensations is, of all others, the least likely to publish any feelings or opinions but such as should excite the reader to discipline in some sort his mind into the same state as that of the writer.

With these sentiments I have been preparing an address to the Catholics of Ireland, and, however deficient may be its execution, I can by no means admit that it contains one sentiment that can harm the cause of liberty and happiness. It consists of the benevolent and tolerant deductions of philosophy reduced into the simplest language, and such as those who by their uneducated poverty are most susceptible of evil impressions from Catholicism may clearly comprehend. I know it can do no harm; it cannot excite rebellion, as its main principle is to trust the success of a cause to the energy of its truth. It cannot " widen the breach between the kingdoms," as it attempts to convey to the vulgar mind sentiments of universal philanthropy; and whatever impressions it may produce, they can be no others but those of peace and harmony; it owns no religion but benevolence, no cause but virtue, no party but the world. I shall devote myself with unremitting zeal, so far as an uncertain state of health will permit, towards forwarding the great ends of happiness and virtue in Ireland, regarding as I do the present state of that country's affairs as an opportunity which, if I, being thus disengaged, permit to pass unoccupied, I am unworthy of the character which I have assumed. Enough of Ireland!

.   .   .   o   .   .   .

V.

TO THOMAS HOOKHAM, ESQ.

LYMOUTH, BARNSTAPLE, *August* 18, 1812.

.   .   .   .

You confer on me an obligation, and involve a high compliment by your advice. I shall, if possible, prepare a volume of essays, moral and religious, by November; but all my MSS. now being in Dublin, and, from peculiar circumstances, not immediately obtainable, I do not know whether I can. I enclose also, by way of specimen, all that I have written of a little poem begun since my arrival in England. I conceive I have matter enough for six more cantos. You will perceive that I have not attempted to temper my constitutional enthusiasm in that poem. Indeed, a poem is safe: the iron-souled Attorney General would scarcely dare to attack [it].[1] The Past, the Present, and the Future are the grand and comprehensive topics of this poem. I have not yet half exhausted the second of them.

I shall take the liberty of retaining the two poems which you have sent me (Mr. Peacock's), and only regret that my powers are so circumscribed as to

[1] "Queen Mab," Shelley's first serious effort. Contrary to his expectations, it was attacked in the courts, but not in the way he has reference to here. His children were taken from him on account of the views he expressed in the notes, although at the time he warmly repudiated the sentiments they contained.

prevent me from becoming extensively useful to your
friend.   The poems abound with a genius, an information, the power and extent of which I admire, in
proportion as I lament the object of their application.
Mr. Peacock conceives that commerce is prosperity;
that the glory of the British flag is the happiness of
the British people; that George III., so far from
having been a warrior and a tyrant, has been a patriot.
To me it appears otherwise; and I have rigidly accustomed myself not to be seduced by the loveliest
eloquence or the sweetest strains to regard with intellectual toleration that which ought not to be toler-
ated by those who love liberty, truth, and virtue.   I
mean not to say that Mr. Peacock does not love
them; but I mean to say that he regards those means
[as] instrumental to their progress, which I regard
[as] instrumental to their destruction.   (See Genius
of the Thames, pp. 24, 26, 28, 76, 98.)   At the same
time, I am free to say that the poem appears to be
far beyond mediocrity in genius and versification,
and the conclusion of " Palmyra " the finest piece of
poetry I ever read.   I have not had time to read the
" Philosophy of Melancholy," and of course am only
half acquainted with that genius and those powers
whose application I should consider myself rash and
impertinent in criticising, did I not conceive that
frankness and justice demand it.

I should esteem it as a favor if you would present
the enclosed letter to the Chevalier Lawrence.   I
have read his " Empire of the Nairs," — nay, have it.
Perfectly and decidedly do I subscribe to the truth
of the principles which it is designed to establish.

I hope you will excuse, nay, and doubt not but you will, the frankness I have used. Characters of our liberality are so wondrous rare, that the sooner they know each other, and the fuller and more complete that knowledge is, the better.

Dear Sir, permit me to remain, yours, very truly.

I am about translating an old French work, professedly by M. Mirabaud, — not the famous one, — "La Système de la Nature." Do you know anything of it?

VI.

TO HOOKHAM

February, 1813.

MY DEAR SIR, — I am boiling with indignation at the horrible injustice and tyranny of the sentence pronounced on Hunt and his brother; and it is on this subject that I write to you. Surely the seal of abjectness and slavery is indelibly stamped upon the character of England.

Although I do not retract in the slightest degree my wish for a subscription for the widows and children of those poor men hung at York, yet this £1,000 which the Hunts are sentenced to pay is an affair of more consequence. Hunt is a brave, a good, and an enlightened man. Surely the public, for whom Hunt has done so much, will repay in part the great debt of obligation which they owe the champion of their liberties and virtues ; or are they dead, cold, stone-hearted, and insensible, — brutalized by centuries of unremitting bondage ? However that may be, they surely may be excited into some slight acknowledgment of his merits. Whilst hundreds of thousands are sent to the tyrants of Russia, he pines in a dungeon, far from all that can make life desired.

Well, I am rather poor at present ; but I have £20 which is not immediately wanted. Pray, begin a subscription for the Hunts ; put down my name for that sum, and, when I hear that you have complied with my request, I will send it you.[1] Now, if there are any difficulties in the way of this scheme of ours, for the love of liberty and virtue, overcome them. Oh ! that I might wallow for one night in the Bank of England !

" Queen Mab " is finished and transcribed. I am now preparing the notes, which shall be long and philosophical. You will receive it with the other poems. I think that the whole should form one volume ; but of that we can speak hereafter.

. . . .

My dear Sir, excuse the earnestness of the first part of my letter. I feel warmly on this subject, and I flatter myself that, so long as your own independence and liberty remain uncompromised, you are inclined to second my desires.

---

[1] Hunt refused to accept any subscriptions, however.

VII.

TO HOOKHAM.

.   .   .   .

I SEND you my poem. To your remarks on its defects I shall listen, and derive improvement. No duty of a friend is more imperious than an utter sincerity and unreservedness [in] criticism, and none of which a candid mind can be the object with more inward complacency and satisfaction. At the same time, in spite of its various errors, I am determined to give it to the world. . . . If you do not dread the arm of the law, or any exasperation of public opinion against yourself, I wish that it should be printed and published immediately. The notes are preparing and shall be forwarded before the completion of the printing of the poem. I have many other poems which shall also be sent. . . . Do not let the title-page be printed before the body of the poem. I have a motto to introduce from Shakespeare, and a Preface. I shall expect no success. Let only 250 copies be printed. A small neat quarto, on fine paper so as to catch the aristocrats. They will not read it, but their sons and daughters may.

VIII.

TO HOOKHAM.

BANGOR FERRY, *March* 6, 1813.

IN the first stage of our journey toward Dublin we met with your letter. How shall I express to you what I felt of gratitude, surprise, and pleasure? Not so much that the remittance rescued us from a position of peculiar perplexity, but that one there was who, by disinterested and unhesitating confidence, made amends to our feelings, wounded by the suspicion, coldness, and villany of the world. If the discovery of truth be a pleasure of singular purity, how far surpassing is the discovery of virtue !

IX.

TO THOMAS JEFFERSON HOGG.

BRACKNELL, *March* 16, 1814.

MY DEAR FRIEND, — I promised to write to you when I was in the humor. Our intercourse has been too much interrupted for my consolation. My spirits have not sufficed to induce the exertion of determining me to write to you. My value, my affection for you, have sustained no diminution ; but I am a feeble, wavering being, who requires support and consolation, which his energies are too exhausted to return.

I have been staying with Mrs. B[oinville] for the last month ; I have escaped, in the society of all that philosophy and friendship combine, from the dismaying solitude of myself. They have revived in my heart the expiring flame of life. I have felt myself translated to a paradise, which has nothing of mortality but its transitoriness ; my heart sickens at the view of that necessity which will quickly divide me from the tranquillity of this happy home, — for it has become my home. The trees, the bridge, the minutest objects, have already a place in my affections.

My friend, you are happier than I. You have the pleasures as well as the pains of sensibility. I have sunk into a premature old age of exhaustion, which renders me dead to everything but the unenviable capacity of indulging the vanity of hope, and a terrible susceptibility to objects of disgust and hatred.

My temporal concerns are slowly rectifying themselves ; I am astonished at my own indifference to their event. I live here like the insect that sports in the transient sunbeam, which the next cloud shall obscure forever. I am much changed from what I was. I look with regret to our happy evenings at Oxford, and with wonder at the hopes which in the excess of my madness I there encouraged.

   .   .   .   .

What have you written ? I have been unable even to write a common letter. I have forced myself to read Beccaria, and Dumont's Bentham. I have sometimes forgotten that I am not an inmate of this delightful home, — that a time will come which will cast me again into the boundless ocean of abhorred society.   I have written nothing but one stanza which has no meaning, and that I have only written in thought :

> Thy dewy locks sink in my breast ;
> Thy gentle words stir poison there ;
> Thou hast disturbed the only rest
> That was the portion of despair.
> Subdued to duty's hard control,
> I could have borne my wayward lot ;
> The chains that bind this ruined soul
> Had cankered then, but crushed it not.

This is the vision of a delirious and distempered dream, which passes away at the cold, clear light of morning.   Its surpassing excellence and exquisite perfections have no more reality than the color of an autumnal sunset.   Adieu !

X.

TO MARY SHELLEY.[1]

[*October* 27, 1814.]

.   .   .   .

Know, my best Mary, that I feel myself, in your absence, almost degraded to the level of the vulgar and impure.   I feel their vacant, stiff eyeballs fixed upon me, until I seem to have been infected with their loathsome meaning, — to inhale a sickness that subdues me to languor.   Oh ! those redeeming eyes

---

[1] This and the two succeeding letters were written while Shelley was in hiding from creditors, who threatened his arrest.

of Mary, that they might beam upon me before I sleep! Praise my forbearance, O beloved one, that I do not rashly fly to you, and at least secure a moment's bliss. Wherefore should I delay? Do you not long to meet me? All that is exalted and buoyant in my nature urges me toward you, reproaches me with cold delay, laughs at all fear, and spurns to dream of prudence. Why am I not with you? Alas! we must not meet.

.   .   .   .

I did not, for I could not, express to you my *admiration* of your letter to Fanny; the simple and impressive language in which you clothed your argument, the full weight you gave to every part, the complete picture you exhibited of what you intended to describe, was more than I expected. How hard and stubborn must be the spirit that does not confess you to be the subtlest and most exquisitely fashioned intelligence! that among women there is no equal mind to yours! And I possess this treasure! How beyond all estimate is my felicity! Yes; I am encouraged, — I care not what happens; I am most happy. Meet me to-morrow at three o'clock in St. Paul's, if you do not hear before. Adieu! remember, love, at vespers before sleep. I do not omit my prayers.

XI.

TO MARY SHELLEY.

[*October* 28, 1814.]

My beloved Mary, I do not know whether these transient meetings produce not as much pain as pleasure. What have I said? I do not mean it. I will not forget the sweet moments when I saw your eyes, — the divine rapture of the few and fleeting kisses. Yet, indeed, this must cease ; indeed, we must not part thus wretchedly to meet amid the comfortless tumult of business, — to part, I know not how.

Well, dearest love, to-morrow, — to-morrow night. That eternal clock! Oh, that I could "fright the steeds of lazy-paced Time"! I do not think that I am less impatient now than formerly to repossess — to entirely engross — my own treasured love. It seems so unworthy a cause for the slightest separa-tion. I could reconcile it to my own feelings to go to prison if they would cease to persecute us with in-terruptions.

. . . I must return. Your thoughts alone can waken mine to energy; my mind without yours is dead and cold as the dark midnight river when the moon is down. It seems as if you alone could shield me from impurity and vice. If I were absent from you long, I should shudder with horror at myself; my understanding becomes undisciplined without you. . . . How divinely sweet a task it is to imitate each

other's excellences, and each moment to become
wiser in this surpassing love, so that, constituting but
one being, all real knowledge may be comprised in
the maxim Γνῶθι σεαυτόν (Know thyself), with infinitely more justice than in its narrow and common
application !

.   .   .   .

XII.

TO MARY SHELLEY.

[*November* 4, 1814.]

So my beloved boasts that she is more perfect in
the practice than I in the theory of love.   Is it thus?
No, sweet Mary, you only meant that you loved me
more than you could express ; that reasoning was too
cold and slow for the rapid fervor of your conceptions.   Perhaps, in truth, Peacock had infected me ;
my disquisitions were cold, my subtleties unmeaningly
refined ; and I am a harp responsive to every wind, —
the scented gale of summer can wake it to sweet
melody, but the rough, cold blasts draw forth dis-
cordances and jarring sounds.

My love, did I not appear happy to-day?   For a
few moments I was entranced in most delicious
pleasure ; yet I was absent and dejected.   I knew
not when we might meet again, when I might hold
you in my arms, and gaze on your dear eyes at will.

.   .   .   .

I expect to hear from Hooper to-morrow.   Thus it
is my letters are full of money, whilst my being over-

flows with unbounded love and elevated thoughts. How little philosophy and affection consort with this turbid scene, — this dark scheme of things finishing in unfruitful death! There are moments in your absence, my love, when the bitterness with which I regret the unrecoverable time wasted in unprofitable solitude and worldly cares is a most painful weight. You alone reconcile me to myself, and to my beloved hopes.

XIII.

TO THOMAS JEFFERSON HOGG.

BISHOPSGATE, *September*, 1815.

MY DEAR FRIEND, — Your letter has lain by me for the last week, reproaching me every day. I found it on my return from a water excursion on the Thames, the particulars of which will have been recounted in another letter. The exercise and dissipation of mind attached to such an expedition have produced so favorable an effect on my health, that my habitual dejection and irritability have almost deserted me, and I can devote six hours in the day to study without difficulty. I have been engaged lately in the commencement of several literary plans, which, if my present temper of mind endures, I shall probably complete in the winter. I have consequently deserted Cicero, or proceed but slowly with his philosophic dialogues. I have read the Oration for the poet Archias, and am only disappointed with its brevity.

I have been induced by one of the subjects which
I am now pursuing to consult Bayle.   I think he be-
trays great obliquity of understanding and coarseness
of feeling.   I have also read the four finest books of
Lucan's Pharsalia, — a poem, as it appears to me, of
wonderful genius, and transcending Virgil.   Mary has
finished the fifth book of the Æneid, and her progress
in Latin is such as to satisfy my best expectations.

The east wind — the wind of autumn — is abroad,
and even now the leaves of the forest are shattered at
every gust.   When may we expect you?   September
is almost passed, and October, the month of your
promised return, is at hand, when we shall be happy
to welcome you again to our fireside.

No events, as you know, disturb our tranquillity.
Adieu.

XIV.

TO WILLIAM GODWIN.

DOVER, *May* 3, 1816.

No doubt you are anxious to hear the state of my
concerns.[1]   I wish that it was in my power to give
you a more favorable view of them than such as I am
compelled to present.   The limited condition of my

---

[1] Godwin's interest in Shelley's affairs is explained by the
fact that he had been a pensioner on the latter's bounty for
many months. This letter was written on the eve of Shelley's
departure for the Continent, where he expected to find a permanent residence. He was in England again by the next
autumn, however.

fortune is regretted by me, as I imagine you well know, because, among other designs of a similar nature, I cannot at once put you in possession of all that would be sufficient for the comfort and independence which it is so unjust that you should not have already received from society.

    .   .   .   .

The motives which determined me to leave England, and which I stated to you in a former letter, have continued since that period to press on me with accumulated force. Continually detained in a situation where what I esteem a prejudice does not permit me to live on equal terms with my fellow-beings, I resolved to commit myself to a decided step. I therefore take Mary to Geneva, where I shall devise some plan of settlement, and only leave her to return to London, and exclusively devote myself to business.

I leave England — I know not — perhaps forever. I return, alone, to see no friend, to do no office of friendship, to engage in nothing that can soothe the sentiments of regret, almost like remorse, which under such circumstances every one feels who quits his native land. I respect you, I think well of you, better perhaps than any other person whom England contains ; you were the philosopher who first awakened, and who still as a philosopher, to a very great degree, regulates my understanding. It is unfortunate for me that the part of your character which is least excellent should have been met by my convictions of what was right to do. But I have been too indignant. I have been unjust to you. Forgive me : burn those letters which contain the records of my violence, and

believe that, however what you erroneously call fame
and honor separate us, I shall always feel towards you
as the most affectionate of friends.

XV.

TO THOMAS LOVE PEACOCK.

HOTEL DE SÉCHERON, GENEVA, *May* 15, 1816.

AFTER a journey of ten days, we arrived at Geneva.
The journey, like that of life, was variegated with
intermingled rain and sunshine, though these many
showers were to me, as you know, April showers,
quickly passing away, and foretelling the calm bright-
ness of summer.

The journey was in some respects exceedingly
delightful, but the prudential considerations arising
out of the necessity of preventing delay, and the
continual attention to pecuniary disbursements, detract
terribly from the pleasure of all travelling schemes.

.   .   .   .

You live by the shores of a tranquil stream, among
low and woody hills. You live in a free country,
where you may act without restraint, and possess
that which you possess in security ; and so long as
the name of country and the selfish conceptions it
includes shall subsist, England, I am persuaded, is
the most free and the most refined.

Perhaps you have chosen wisely, but if I return and
follow your example, it will be no subject of regret to
me that I have seen other things. Surely there is

much of bad and much of good, there is much to disgust and much to elevate, which he cannot have felt or known who has never passed the limits of his native land.

So long as man is such as he now is, the experience of which I speak will never teach him to despise the country of his birth, — far otherwise. Like Wordsworth, he will never know what love subsists between that and him until absence shall have made its beauty more heartfelt; our poets and philosophers, our mountains and our lakes, the rural lanes and fields which are so especially our own, are ties which, until I become utterly senseless, can never be broken asunder.

These, and the memory of them, if I never should return, — these and the affections of the mind, with which, having been once united, [they] are inseparable, will make the name of England dear to me forever, even if I should permanently return to it no more.

.   .   .   .

The mountains of Jura exhibit scenery of wonderful sublimity. Pine forests of impenetrable thickness, and untrodden, nay, inaccessible expanse, spreading on every side. Sometimes descending, they follow the route into the valleys, clothing the precipitous rocks, and struggling with knotted roots between the most barren clefts. Sometimes the road winds high into the regions of frost, and there these forests become scattered, and loaded with snow.

The trees in these regions are incredibly large, and stand in scattered clumps over the white wilderness.

Never was scene more utterly desolate than that
which we passed on the evening of our last day's
journey.

The natural silence of that uninhabited desert
contrasted strangely with the voices of the people who
conducted us, for it was necessary in this part of the
mountain to take a number of persons, who should
assist the horses to force the chaise through the snow,
and prevent it from falling down the precipice.

We are now at Geneva, where, or in the neighborhood, we shall remain probably until the autumn.   I
may return in a fortnight or three weeks, to attend to
the last exertions which L—— is to make for the
settlement of my affairs ; of course I shall then see
you ; in the mean time, it will interest me to hear all
that you have to tell of yourself.

.   .   .   .

XVI.

TO THOMAS LOVE PEACOCK.

MONTALEGRE, NEAR COLIGNI, GENEVA,
July 12 [1816].

IT is nearly a fortnight since I have returned from
Vevay. This journey has been on every account delightful, but most especially, because then I first knew
the divine beauty of Rousseau's imagination, as it exhibits itself in "Julie." It is inconceivable what an
enchantment the scene itself lends to those delinea-
tions, from which its own most touching charm arises.

But I will give you an abstract of our voyage, which lasted eight days, and if you have a map of Switzerland, you can follow me.

We left Montalegre at half past two on the 23d of June. The lake was calm, and after three hours of rowing we arrived at Hermance, a beautiful little village, containing a ruined tower, built, the villagers say, by Julius Cæsar. There were three other towers similar to it, which the Genevese destroyed for their own fortifications in 1560. We got into the tower by a kind of window. The walls are immensely solid, and the stone of which it is built so hard, that it yet retained the mark of chisels. The boatman said that this tower was once three times higher than it is now. There are two staircases in the thickness of the walls, one of which is entirely demolished, and the other half ruined, and only accessible by a ladder. The town itself, now an inconsiderable village inhabited by a few fishermen, was built by a queen of Burgundy, and reduced to its present state by the inhabitants of Berne, who burnt and ravaged everything they could find.

Leaving Hermance, we arrived at sunset at the village of Herni. After looking at our lodgings, which were gloomy and dirty, we walked out by the side of the lake. It was beautiful to see the vast expanse of these purple and misty waters, broken by the craggy islets near to its slant and " beached margin." There were many fish sporting in the lake, and multitudes were collected close to the rocks to catch the flies which inhabited them.

On returning to the village, we sat on a wall beside

the lake, looking at some children who were playing at a game like ninepins.   The children here appeared in an extraordinary way deformed and diseased. Most of them were crooked, and with enlarged throats ; but one little boy had such exquisite grace in his mien and motions as I never before saw equalled in a child.   His countenance was beautiful for the expression with which it overflowed.   There was a mixture of pride and gentleness in his eyes and lips, the indications of sensibility, which his education will probably pervert to misery or seduce to crime ; but there was more of gentleness than of pride, and it seemed that the pride was tamed from its original wildness by the habitual exercise of milder feelings.   My companion gave him a piece of money, which he took without speaking, with a sweet smile of easy thankfulness, and then with an embarrassed air turned to his play.   All this might scarcely be ; but the imagination surely could not forbear to breathe into the most inanimate forms some likeness of its own visions, on such a serene and glowing evening, in this remote and romantic village, beside the calm lake that bore us hither.

On returning to our inn, we found that the servant had arranged our rooms, and deprived them of the greater portion of their former disconsolate appearance.   They reminded my companion[1] of Greece ; it was five years, he said, since he had slept in such beds.   The influence of the recollections excited by this circumstance on our conversation gradually faded, and I retired to rest with no unpleasant sensations,

[1] Lord Byron.

thinking of our journey to-morrow, and of the pleasure of recounting the little adventures of it when we return.

The next morning we passed Yvoire, a scattered village with an ancient castle, whose houses are interspersed with trees, and which stands at a little distance from Nerni, on the promontory which bounds a deep bay, some miles in extent. So soon as we arrived at this promontory, the lake began to assume an aspect of wilder magnificence. The mountains of Savoy, whose summits were bright with snow, descended in broken slopes to the lake : on high, the rocks were dark with pine forests, which become deeper and more immense, until the ice and snow mingle with the points of naked rock that pierce the blue air ; but below, groves of walnut, chestnut, and oak, with openings of lawny fields, attested the milder climate.

.   .   .   .

We arrived at this town about seven o'clock, after a day which involved more rapid changes of atmosphere than I ever recollect to have observed before. The morning was cold and wet ; then an easterly wind, and the clouds hard and high ; then thunder showers, and wind shifting to every quarter ; then a warm blast from the south, and summer clouds hanging over the peaks, with bright blue sky between. About half an hour after we had arrived at Evian, a few flashes of lightning came from a dark cloud, directly over head, and continued after the cloud had dispersed, " Diespiter per pura tonantes egit equos," a phenomenon which certainly had no influence on me corresponding with that which it produced on Horace.

The appearance of the inhabitants of Evian is more wretched, diseased, and poor, than I ever recollect to have seen. The contrast indeed between the subjects of the King of Sardinia and the citizens of the independent republics of Switzerland, affords a powerful illustration of the blighting mischiefs of despotism, whithin the space of a few miles. They have mineral waters here, *eaux savonneuses* they call them. In the evening we had some difficulty about our passports, but so soon as the syndic heard my companion's rank and name, he apologized for the circumstance. The inn was good. During our voyage, on the distant height of a hill, covered with pine forests, we saw a ruined castle, which reminded me of those on the Rhine.

We left Evian on the following morning, with a wind of such violence as to permit but one sail to be carried. The waves also were exceedingly high, and our boat so heavely laden, that there appeared to be some danger. We arrived, however, safe at Meillerie, after passing with great speed mighty forests which overhung the lake, and lawns of exquisite verdure, and mountains with bare and icy points, which rose immediately from the summit of the rocks, whose bases were echoing to the waves.

We here heard that the Empress Maria Louisa had slept at Meillerie — before the present inn was built, and when the accommodations were those of the most wretched village — in remembrance of St. Preux. How beautiful it is to find that the common sentiments of human nature can attach themselves to those who are the most removed from its duties and its enjoyments, when Genius pleads for their admission at the gate of Power. To own them was becoming in the Empress, and confirms the affectionate praise contained in the regret of a great and enlightened nation. A Bourbon dared not even to have remembered Rousseau. She owed this power to that democracy which her husband's dynasty outraged, and of which it was, however, in some sort, the representative among the nations of the earth. This little incident shows at once how unfit and how impossible it is for the ancient system of opinions, or for any power built upon a conspiracy to revive them, permanently to subsist among mankind. We dined there, and had some honey, the best I have ever tasted, the very essence of the mountain flowers, and as fragrant. Probably the village derives its name from this production. Meillerie is the well known scene of St. Preux's visionary exile ; but Meillerie is indeed enchanted ground, were Rousseau no magician. Groves of pine, chestnut, and walnut overshadow it ; magnificent and unbounded forests, to which England affords no parallel. In the midst of these woods are dells of lawny expanse, inconceivably verdant, adorned with a thousand of the rarest flowers, and odorous with thyme.

The lake appeared somewhat calmer as we left Meillerie, sailing close to the banks, whose magnificence augmented with the turn of every promontory. But we congratulated ourselves too soon : the wind gradually increased in violence, until it blew tremendously ; and, as it came from the remotest extremity of the lake, produced waves of a frightful height, and covered the whole surface with a chaos of foam. One of our boatmen, who was a dreadfully stupid fellow, persisted in holding the sail at a time when the boat was on the point of being driven under water by the hurricane. On discovering his error, he let it entirely go, and the boat for a moment refused to obey the helm; in addition, the rudder was so broken as to render the management of it very difficult; one wave fell in, and then another. My companion, an excellent swimmer, took off his coat, I did the same, and we sat with our arms crossed, every instant expecting to be swamped. The sail was, however, again held, the boat obeyed the helm, and still in imminent peril from the immensity of the waves, we arrived in a few minutes at a sheltered port, in the village of St. Gingoux.

I felt in this near prospect of death a mixture of sensations, among which terror entered, though but subordinately. My feelings would have been less painful had I been alone; but I knew that my companion would have attempted to save me, and I was overcome with humiliation when I thought that his life might have been risked to preserve mine. When we arrived at St. Gingoux, the inhabitants who stood on the shore, unaccustomed to see a vessel as frail as ours, and fearing to venture at all on such a sea, exchanged looks of wonder and congratulation with our boatmen, who, as well as ourselves, were well pleased to set foot on shore.

St. Gingoux is even more beautiful than Meillerie; the mountains are higher, and their loftiest points of elevation descend more abruptly to the lake. On high, the aerial summits still cherish great depths of snow in their ravines, and in the paths of their unseen torrents. One of the highest of these is called Roche de St. Julien, beneath whose pinnacles the forests become deeper and more extensive; the chestnut gives a peculiarity to the scene, which is most beautiful, and will make a picture in my memory, distinct from all other mountain scenes which I have ever before visited.

.   .   .   .

On one side of the road was the immense Roche de St. Julien, which overhung it; through the gateway of the castle we saw the snowy mountains of La Valais, clothed in clouds, and, on the other side, was the willowy plain of the Rhone, in a character of striking contrast with the rest of the scene, bounded by the dark mountains that overhang Clarens, Vevay, and the lake that rolls between. In the midst of the plain rises a little isolated hill, on which the white spire of a church peeps from among the tufted chestnut woods. We returned to St. Gingoux before sunset, and I passed the evening in reading " Julie."

As my companion rises late, I had time before breakfast, on the ensuing morning, to hunt the waterfalls of the river that fall into the lake of St. Gingoux. The stream is, indeed, from the declivity over which it falls, only a succession of waterfalls, which roar over the rocks with a perpetual sound, and suspend their unceasing spray on the leaves and flowers that overhang and adorn its savage banks. The path that conducted along this river sometimes avoided the precipices of its shores, by leading through meadows;

sometimes threaded the base of the perpendicular and caverned rocks. I gathered in these meadows a nosegay of such flowers as I never saw in England, and which I thought more beautiful for that rarity.

On my return, after breakfast, we sailed for Clarens, determining first to see the three mouths of the Rhone, and then the Castle of Chillon; the day was fine, and the water calm. We passed from the blue waters of the lake over the stream of the Rhone, which is rapid even at a great distance from its confluence with the lake; the turbid waters mixed with those of the lake. but mixed with them unwillingly. (See Nouvelle Héloise, Lettre 17, Part. 4.) I read " Julie " all day, — an overflowing, as it now seems, surrounded by the scenes which it has so wonderfully peopled, of sublimest genius, and more than human sensibility. Meillerie, the castle of Chillon, Clarens, the mountains of La Valais and Savoy, present themselves to the imagination as monuments of things that were once familiar, and of beings that were once dear to it. They were created indeed by one mind, but a mind so powerfully bright as to cast a shade of falsehood on the records that are called reality.

We passed on to the castle of Chillon, and visited its dungeons and towers. These prisons are excavated below the lake; the principal dungeon is supported by seven columns, whose branching capitals support the roof. Close to the very walls, the lake is eight hundred feet deep; iron rings are fastened to these columns, and on them were engraven a multitude of names, partly those of visitors, and partly doubtless of the prisoners, of whom now no memory remains, and who thus beguiled a solitude which they have long ceased to feel. One date was as ancient as 1670. At the commencement of the Reformation, and indeed long after that period, this dungeon was the receptacle of those who shook, or who denied the system of idolatry, from the effects of which mankind is even now slowly emerging.

Close to this long and lofty dungeon was a narrow cell, and beyond it one larger and far more lofty and dark, supported upon two unornamented arches. Across one of these arches was a beam, now black and rotten, on which prisoners were hung in secret. I never saw a monument more terrible of that cold and inhuman tyranny, which it had been the delight of man to exercise over man. It was indeed one of those many tremendous fulfilments which render the " pernicies humani generis " of the great Tacitus so solemn and irrefragable a prophecy. The gendarme who conducted us over this castle told us that there was an opening to the lake, by means of a secret spring, connected with which the whole dungeon might be filled with water before the prisoners could possibly escape !

We proceeded with a contrary wind to Clarens, against a heavy swell. I never felt more strongly than on landing at Clarens, that the spirit of old times had deserted its once cherished habitation. A thousand times, thought I, have Julie and St. Preux walked on this terraced road, looking towards these mountains which I now behold ; nay, treading on the ground where I now tread. From the window of our lodging our landlady pointed out " le bosquet de

Julie." At least the inhabitants of this village are impressed with an idea, that the persons of that romance had actual existence. In the evening we walked thither. It is, indeed, Julie's wood. The hay was making under the trees; the trees themselves were aged, but vigorous, and interspersed with younger ones, which are destined to be their successors, and in future years, when we are dead, to afford a shade to future worshippers of nature, who love the memory of that tenderness and peace of which this was the imaginary abode. We walked forward among the vineyards, whose narrow terraces overlook this affecting scene. Why did the cold maxims of the world compel me at this moment to repress the tears of melancholy transport which it would have been so sweet to indulge, immeasurably, even until the darkness of night had swallowed up the objects which excited them?

I forgot to remark, what indeed my companion remarked to me, that our danger from the storm took place precisely in the spot where Julie and her lover were nearly overset, and where St. Preux was tempted to plunge with her into the lake.

On the following day we went to see the castle of Clarens, a square strong house, with very few windows, surrounded by a double terrace that overlooks the valley, or rather the plain of Clarens. The road which conducted to it wound up the steep ascent through woods of walnut and chestnut. We gathered roses on the terrace, in the feeling that they might be the posterity of some planted by Julie's hand. We sent their dead and withered leaves to the absent.

We went again to "the bosquet de Julie," and found that the precise spot was now utterly obliterated, and a heap of stones marked the place where the little chapel had once stood. Whilst we were execrating the author of this brutal folly, our guide informed us that the land belonged to the convent of St. Bernard, and that this outrage had been committed by their orders. I knew before, that, if avarice could harden the hearts of men, a system of prescriptive religion has an influence far more inimical to natural sensibility. I know that an isolated man is sometimes restrained by shame from outraging the venerable feelings arising out of the memory of genius, which once made nature even lovelier than itself; but associated man holds it as the very sacrament of his union to forswear all delicacy, all benevolence, all remorse; all that is true, or tender, or sublime.

We sailed from Clarens to Vevay. Vevay is a town more beautiful in its simplicity than any I have ever seen. Its market-place, a spacious square interspersed with trees, looks directly upon the mountains of Savoy and La Valais, the lake, and the valley of the Rhone. It was at Vevay that Rousseau conceived the design of "Julie."

From Vevay we came to Ouchy, a village near Lausanne. The coasts of the Pays de Vaud, though full of villages and vineyards, present an aspect of tranquillity and peculiar beauty which well compensates for the solitude which I am accustomed to admire. The hills are very high and rocky, crowned and interspersed with woods. Waterfalls echo from the cliffs, and shine afar. In one place we saw the traces of two rocks of immense size, which had fallen from the mountain behind. One of these lodged in a room where a young woman was sleeping, without injuring her. The vineyards were utterly destroyed in its path, and the earth torn up.

The rain detained us two days at Ouchy. We, however, visited Lausanne and saw Gibbon's house. We were shown the decayed summer-house where he finished his History, and the old acacias on the terrace, from which he saw Mont Blanc, after having written the last sentence. There is something grand and even touching in the regret which he expresses at the completion of his task. It was conceived amid the ruins of the Capitol. The sudden departure of his cherished and accustomed toil must have left him, like the death of a dear friend, sad and solitary.

My companion gathered some acacia leaves to preserve in remembrance of him. I refrained from doing so, fearing to outrage the greater and more sacred name of Rousseau, the contemplation of whose imperishable creations had left no vacancy in my heart for mortal things. Gibbon had a cold and unimpassioned spirit. I never felt more inclination to rail at the prejudices which cling to such a thing, than now that Julie and Clarens, Lausanne and the Roman Empire, compelled me to a contrast between Rousseau and Gibbon.

When we returned, in the only interval of sunshine during the day, I walked on the pier which the lake was lashing with its waves. A rainbow spanned the lake, or rather rested one extremity of its arch upon the water, and the other at the foot of the mountains of Savoy. Some white houses, I know not if they were those of Meillerie, shone through the yellow fire.

On Saturday, the 30th of June, we quitted Ouchy, and after two days of pleasant sailing arrived on Sunday evening at Montalegre.

XVII.

TO THOMAS LOVE PEACOCK.

GENEVA, *July* 17, 1816.

MY opinion of turning to one spot of earth and calling it our home, and of the excellences and usefulness of the sentiments arising out of this attachment, has at length produced in me the resolution of acquiring this possession.

You are the only man who has sufficient regard for me to take an interest in the fulfilment of this design, and whose tastes conform sufficiently to mine to engage me to confide the execution of it to your discretion.

I do not trouble you with apologies for giving you this commission. I require only rural exertion, walks, and circuitous wanderings, some slight negotiations about the letting of a house, the superintendence of a disorderly garden, some palings to be mended, some books to be removed and set up.

. . . .

When you have possessed yourself of all my affairs, I wish you to look out for a home for me and Mary

and William, and the kitten, who is now *en pension.*
I wish you to get an unfurnished house, with as good
a garden as may be, near Windsor Forest, and take a
lease of it for fourteen or twenty-one years. The
house must not be too small. I wish the situation to
resemble as nearly as possible that of Bishopgate, and
should think that Sunning Hill, or Winkfield Plain,
or the neighborhood of Virginia Water, would afford
some possibilities.

.　　.　　.　　.　　.　　.　　.

My present intention is to return to England, and
to make that most excellent of nations my perpetual
resting-place. I think it is extremely probable that
we shall return next spring, — perhaps before, perhaps after, — but certainly we shall return.

On the motives and on the consequences of this
journey, I reserve much explanation for some future
winter walk or summer expedition. This much alone
is certain, that before we return we shall have seen,
and felt, and heard, a multiplicity of things which will
haunt our talk, and make us a little better worth knowing than we were before our departure.

If possible we think of descending the Danube in
a boat, of visiting Constantinople and Athens, then
Rome and the Tuscan cities, and returning by the
south of France, always following great rivers, — the
Danube, the Po, the Rhone, and the Garonne. Rivers are not like roads, the work of the hands of man ;
they imitate mind, which wanders at will over pathless deserts, and flows through nature's loveliest recesses, which are inaccessible to anything besides.
They have the viler advantage also of affording a
cheaper mode of conveyance.

This eastern scheme is one which has just seized on our imaginations. I fear that the detail of execution will destroy it, as all other wild and beautiful visions; but at all events you will hear from us wherever we are, and to whatever adventures destiny enforces us.

Tell me in return all English news. What has become of my poem?[1] I hope it has already sheltered itself in the bosom of its mother, Oblivion, from whose embraces no one could have been so barbarous as to tear it except me.

Tell me of the political state of England, — its literature, of which when I speak Coleridge is in my thoughts, — yourself; lastly, your own employments, your historical labors.

I had written thus far when your letter to Mary dated the 8th arrived. What you say of Bishopsgate of course modifies that part of this letter which relates to it. I confess I did not learn the destined ruin without some pain, but it is well for me, perhaps, that a situation requiring so large an expense should be placed beyond our hopes.

You must shelter my roofless Penates, dedicate some new temple to them, and perform the functions of a priest in my absence. They are innocent deities, and their worship neither sanguinary nor absurd.

Leave Mammon and Jehovah to those who delight in wickedness and slavery. — their altars are stained with blood, or polluted with gold, the price of blood. But the shrines of the Penates are good wood fires, or window frames intertwined with creeping plants; their hymns are the purring of kittens, the hissing of

---

[1] "Alastor."

kettles ; the long talks over the past and dead, the laugh of children, the warm wind of summer filling the quiet house, and the pelting storm of winter struggling in vain for entrance. In talking of the Penates, will you not liken me to Julius Cæsar dedicating a temple to Liberty? As I have said in the former part of my letter, I trust entirely to your discretion on the subject of a house. Certainly the Forest engages my preference, because of the sylvan nature of the place and the beasts with which it is filled. But I am not insensible to the beauties of the Thames, and any extraordinary eligibility of situation you mention in your letter would overwhelm our habitual affection for the neighborhood of Bishopsgate.

Its proximity to the spot you have chosen is an argument with us in favor of the Thames. Recollect, however, we are now choosing a fixed, settled, eternal home, and as such its internal qualities will affect us more constantly than those which consist in the surrounding scenery, which, whatever it may be at first, will shortly be no more than the colors with which our own habits shall invest it.

I am glad that circumstances do not permit the choice to be my own. I shall abide by yours, as others abide by the necessity of their birth.

.   .   .   .

XVIII.

TO THOMAS L. PEACOCK.[1]

HÔTEL DE LONDRES, CHAMOUNI, *July* 22, 1816.

WHILST you, my friend, are engaged in securing a home for us, we are wandering in search of recollections to embellish it. I do not err in conceiving that you are interested in details of all that is majestic or beautiful in nature; but how shall I describe to you the scenes by which I am now surrounded? To exhaust the epithets which express the astonishment and the admiration, — the very excess of satisfied astonishment, — where expectation scarcely acknowledged any boundary, is this to impress upon your mind the images which fill mine now, even till it overflow? I too have read the raptures of travellers; I will be warned by their example; I will simply detail to you all that I can relate, or all that, if related, would enable you to conceive, what we have done or seen since the morning of the 20th, when we left Geneva.

We commenced our intended journey to Chamouni at half past eight in the morning. We passed through the champagne country, which extends from Mont Saléve to the base of the higher Alps. The country is sufficiently fertile, covered with corn-fields and orchards, and intersected by sudden acclivities with flat summits. The day was cloudless and excessively

---

[1] Compare this letter with his poem, "Mont Blanc," written July 23, 1816.

hot, the Alps were perpetually in sight, and, as we
advanced, the mountains, which form their outskirts,
closed in around us. We passed a bridge over a
stream, which discharges itself into the Arve. The
Arve itself, much swollen by the rains, flows constantly to the right of the road.

.   .   .   .

From Bonneville to Cluses the road conducts
through a spacious and fertile plain, surrounded on
all sides by mountains, covered like those of Meillerie with forests of intermingled pine and chestnut.
At Cluses the road turns suddenly to the right, following the Arve along the chasm, which it seems to
have hollowed for itself among the perpendicular
mountains. The scene assumes here a more savage
and colossal character; the valley becomes narrow,
affording no more space than is sufficient for the
river and the road. The pines descend to the banks,
imitating, with their irregular spires, the pyramidal
crags, which lift themselves far above the regions of
forest into the deep azure of the sky and among the
white dazzling clouds. The scene, at the distance
of half a mile from Cluses, differs from that of Matlock in little else than in the immensity of its proportions, and in its untamable inaccessible solitude,
inhabited only by the goats which we saw browsing
on the rocks.

Near Maglans, within a league of each other, we
saw two waterfalls. They were no more than mountain rivulets, but the height from which they fell, at
least of *twelve* hundred feet, made them assume a
character inconsistent with the smallness of their

stream. The first fell from the overhanging brow of a black precipice on an enormous rock, precisely resembling some colossal Egyptian statue of a female deity. It struck the head of the visionary image, and, gracefully dividing there, fell from it in folds of foam more like to cloud than water, imitating a veil of the most exquisite woof. It then united, concealing the lower part of the statue, and, hiding itself in a winding of its channel, burst into a deeper fall, and crossed our route in its path towards the Arve.

The other waterfall was more continuous and larger. The violence with which it fell made it look more like some shape which an exhalation had assumed than like water, for it streamed beyond the mountain, which appeared dark behind it, as it might have appeared behind an evanescent cloud.

. . . .

The following morning we proceeded from St. Martin, on mules, to Chamouni, accompanied by two guides. We proceeded, as we had done the preceding day, along the valley of the Arve, — a valley surrounded on all sides by immense mountains, whose rugged precipices are intermixed on high with dazzling snow. Their bases were still covered with the eternal forests, which perpetually grew darker and more profound as we approached the inner regions of the mountains.

On arriving at a small village at the distance of a league from St. Martin, we dismounted from our mules, and were conducted by our guides to view a cascade. We beheld an immense body of water fall two hundred and fifty feet, dashing from rock to rock, and casting a spray which formed a mist around it, in the midst of which hung a multitude of sunbows, which faded or became unspeakably vivid as the inconstant sun shone through the clouds. When we approached near to it, the rain of the spray reached us, and our clothes were wetted by the quick-falling but minute particles of water. The cataract fell from above into a deep craggy chasm at our feet, where, changing its character to that of a mountain stream, it pursued its course towards the Arve, roaring over the rocks that impeded its progress.

·   ·   ·   ·   ·   ·   ·

From Servos three leagues remain to Chamouni. Mont Blanc was before us; the Alps, with their innumerable glaciers on high all around, closing in the complicated windings of the single vale; forests inexpressibly beautiful, but majestic in their beauty, intermingled beech and pine and oak, overshadowed our road, or receded, whilst lawns of such verdure as I have never seen before occupied these openings, and gradually became darker in their recesses. Mont Blanc was before us, but it was covered with cloud; its base, furrowed with dreadful gaps, was seen above. Pinnacles of snow intolerably bright, part of the chain connected with Mont Blanc, shone through the clouds at intervals on high. I never knew — I never imagined — what mountains were before. The immensity of these aerial summits excited, when they suddenly burst upon the sight, a sentiment of ecstatic wonder, not unallied to madness. And remember this was all one scene, it all pressed home to our regard and our imagination. Though it embraced a vast extent of space, the snowy pyramids which shot into the bright blue sky seemed to overhang our path; the ravine, clothed with gigantic pines, and black with its depth below, so deep that the very roaring of the untamable Arve, which rolled through it, could not be heard above;—all was as much our own as if we had been the creators of such impressions in the minds of others as now occupied our own. Nature was the poet, whose harmony held our spirits more breathless than that of the divinest.

As we entered the valley of Chamouni, (which, in fact, may be considered as a continuation of those which we have followed from Bonneville and Cluses,) clouds hung upon the mountains at the distance perhaps of 6,000 feet from the earth, but so as effectually to conceal, not only Mont Blanc, but the other *aiguilles*, as they call them here, attached and subordinate to it. We were travelling along the valley, when suddenly we heard a sound as of the burst of smothered thunder rolling above; yet there was something in the sound that told us it could not be thunder. Our guide hastily pointed out to us a part of the mountain opposite, from whence the sound came. It was an avalanche. We saw the smoke. of its path among the rocks, and continued to hear at intervals the bursting of its fall. It fell on the bed of a torrent, which it displaced, and presently we saw its tawny-colored waters also spread themselves over the ravine, which was their couch.

We did not, as we intended, visit the Glacier des Bossons to-day, although it descends within a few minutes' walk of the road, wishing to survey it at

least when unfatigued. We saw this glacier, which
comes close to the fertile plain, as we passed. Its
surface was broken into a thousand unaccountable
figures; conical and pyramidical crystallizations, more
than fifty feet in height, rise from its surface, and
precipices of ice, of dazzling splendor, overhang
the woods and meadows of the vale. This glacier
winds upwards from the valley, until it joins the
masses of frost from which it was produced above,
winding through its own ravine like a bright belt
flung over the black region of pines. There is more
in all these scenes than mere magnitude of proportion : there is a majesty of outline ; there is an awful
grace in the very colors which invest these wonderful
shapes, — a charm which is peculiar to them, quite
distinct even from the reality of their unutterable
greatness.

July 24.

Yesterday morning we went to the source of the
Arveiron.   It is about a league from this village ; the
river rolls forth impetuously from an arch of ice, and
spreads itself in many streams over a vast space of
the valley, ravaged and laid bare by its inundations.
The glacier by which its waters are nourished overhangs this cavern and the plain, and the forests of
pine which surround it, with terrible precipices of
solid ice. On the other side rises the immense glacier
of Montanvert, fifty miles in extent, occupying a
chasm among mountains of inconceivable height,
and of forms so pointed and abrupt that they seem
to pierce the sky. From this glacier we saw, as we
sat on a rock close to one of the streams of the

Arveiron, masses of ice detach themselves from on high, and rush with a loud dull noise into the vale. The violence of their fall turned them into powder, which flowed over the rocks in imitation of waterfalls, whose ravines they usurped and filled.

In the evening, I went with Ducrée, my guide, the only tolerable person I have seen in this country, to visit the glacier of Bossons. This glacier, like that of Montanvert, comes close to the vale, overhanging the green meadows and the dark woods with the dazzling whiteness of its precipices and pinnacles, which are like spires of radiant crystal, covered with a network of frosted silver. These glaciers flow perpetually into the valley, ravaging in their slow but irresistible progress the pastures and the forests which surround them, performing a work of desolation in ages which a river of lava might accomplish in an hour, but far more irretrievably; for where the ice has once descended, the hardiest plant refuses to grow; if even, as in some extraordinary instances, it should recede after its progress has once commenced.

.   .   .   .

The verge of a glacier like that of Bossons presents the most vivid image of desolation that it is possible to conceive. No one dares to approach it; for the enormous pinnacles of ice which perpetually fall are perpetually reproduced. The pines of the forest, which bound it at one extremity, are overthrown and shattered, to a wide extent, at its base. There is something inexpressibly dreadful in the aspect of the few branchless trunks, which, nearest to

the ice rifts, still stand in the uprooted soil. The
meadows perish, overwhelmed with sand and stones.

.   .   .   .

I will not pursue Buffon's sublime but gloomy
theory, — that this globe which we inhabit will, at
some future period, be changed into a mass of frost
by the encroachments of the polar ice, and of that
produced on the most elevated points of the earth.
Do you, who assert the supremacy of Ahriman,
imagine him throned among these desolating snows,
among these palaces of death and frost, so sculptured
in this their terrible magnificence by the adamantine
hand of necessity, and that he casts around him, as
the first essays of his final usurpation, avalanches,
torrents, rocks, and thunders, and, above all, these
deadly glaciers, at once the proof and symbols of
his reign? Add to this, the degradation of the
human species, who, in these regions, are half deformed or idiotic, and most of whom are deprived of
anything that can excite interest or admiration. This
is part of the subject more mournful and less sublime;
but such as neither the poet nor the philosopher
should disdain to regard.

This morning we departed, on the promise of a
fine day, to visit the glacier of Montanvert. In that
part where it fills a slanting valley, it is called the Sea
of Ice. This valley is 950 toises, or 7,600 feet, above
the level of the sea. We had not proceded far before
the rain began to fall, but we persisted until we had
accomplished more than half of our journey, when
we returned, wet through.

CHAMOUNI, *July* 25.

We have returned from visiting the glacier of Montanvert, or, as it is called, the Sea of Ice, a scene in truth of dizzying wonder. The path that winds to it along the side of a mountain, now clothed with pines, now intersected with snowy hollows, is wide and steep. The cabin of Montanvert is three leagues from Chamouni, half of which distance is performed on mules, not so sure-footed but that on the first day the one which I rode fell in what the guides call a *mauvais pas*, so that I narrowly escaped being precipitated down the mountain. We passed over a hollow covered with snow, down which vast stones are accustomed to roll. One had fallen the preceding day, a little time after we had returned; our guides desired us to pass quickly, for it is said that sometimes the least sound will accelerate their descent. We arrived at Montanvert, however, safe.

On all sides precipitous mountains, the abodes of unrelenting frost, surround this vale : their sides are banked up with ice and snow, broken, heaped high, and exhibiting terrific chasms. The summits are sharp and naked pinnacles, whose overhanging steepness will not even permit snow to rest upon them. Lines of dazzling ice occupy here and there their perpendicular rifts, and shine through the driving vapors with inexpressible brilliance ; they pierce the clouds, like things not belonging to this earth. The vale itself is filled with a mass of undulating ice, and has an ascent sufficiently gradual even to the remotest abysses of these horrible deserts. It is only half a league (about two miles) in breadth, and seems much less.　It exhibits an appearance as if frost had suddenly bound up the waves and whirlpools of a mighty torrent.　We walked some distance upon its surface. The waves are elevated about twelve or fifteen feet from the surface of the mass, which is intersected by long gaps of unfathomable depth, the ice of whose sides is more beautifully azure than the sky.　In these regions everything changes, and is in motion.　This vast mass of ice has one general progress, which ceases neither day nor night; it breaks and bursts forever: some undulations sink while others rise; it is never the same.　The echo of rocks, or of the ice and snow which fall from their overhanging precipices, or roll from their aerial summits, scarcely ceases for one moment.　One would think that Mont Blanc, like the god of the Stoics, was a vast animal, and that the frozen blood forever circulated through his stony veins.

We dined (M——, C——, and I) on the grass, in the open air, surrounded by this scene.　The air is piercing and clear.　We returned down the mountain, sometimes encompassed by the driving vapors, sometimes cheered by the sunbeams, and arrived at our inn by seven o'clock.

MONTALEGRE, *July* 28.

The next morning we returned through the rain to St. Martin.　The scenery had lost something of its immensity, thick clouds hanging over the highest mountains; but visitings of sunlight intervened between the showers, and the blue sky shone between the accumulated clouds of snowy whiteness which brought them; the dazzling mountains sometimes glittered through a chasm of the clouds above our heads, and all the charm of its grandeur remained. We repassed Pont Pellisier, a wooden bridge over the Arve, and the ravine of the Arve. We repassed the pine forests which overhang the defile, the chateau of St. Michael, — a haunted ruin, built on the edge of a precipice, and shadowed over by the eternal forest. We repassed the vale of Servoz, a vale more beautiful, because more luxuriant, than that of Chamouni. Mont Blanc forms one of the sides of this vale also, and the other is enclosed by an irregular amphitheatre of enormous mountains, one of which is in ruins, and fell fifty years ago into the higher part of the valley; the smoke of its fall was seen in Piedmont, and people went from Turin to investigate whether a volcano had not burst forth among the Alps. It continued falling many days, spreading, with the shock and thunder of its ruin, consternation into the neighboring vales. In the evening we arrived at St. Martin. The next day we wound through the valley, which I have described before, and arrived in the evening at our home.

We have bought some specimens of minerals and plants, and two or three crystal seals, at Mont Blanc, to preserve the remembrance of having approached it. There is a cabinet of *histoire naturelle* at Chamouni, just as at Keswick, Matlock, and Clifton; the proprietor of which is the very vilest specimen of that vile species of quack, that, together with the whole army of aubergistes and guides, and indeed the entire mass of the population, subsist on the

weakness and credulity of travellers, as leeches subsist
on the sick. The most interesting of my purchases
is a large collection of all the seeds of rare alpine
plants, with their names written upon the outside of
the papers that contain them. These I mean to
colonize in my garden in England, and to permit you
to make what choice you please from them. They
are companions which the Celandine — the classic
Celandine — need not despise ; they are as wild and
more daring than he, and will tell him tales of things
even as touching and sublime as the gaze of a vernal
poet.

.   .   .   .

XIX.

TO LEIGH HUNT.

1816.

.   .   .   .

WILL I own the " Hymn to Intellectual Beauty "?
I do not care, — as you like.   And yet the poem was
composed under the influence of feelings which agitated me even to tears, so that I think it deserves a
better fate than being linked with so stigmatized and
unpopular a name (so far as it is known) as mine.
You will say that it is not thus, that I am morbidly
sensitive to what I esteem the injustice of neglect.
But I do not say that I am unjustly neglected.   The
oblivion which overtook my little attempt of " Alastor," I am ready to acknowledge, was sufficiently
merited in itself; but then it was not accorded in

the correct proportion, considering the success of the most contemptible drivellings. I am undeceived in the belief that I have powers deeply to interest, or substantially to improve mankind. How far my conduct and my opinions have rendered the zeal and ardor with which I have engaged in the attempt ineffectual, I know not. Self-love prompts me to assign much weight to a cause which perhaps has none. But thus much I do not seek to conceal from myself, that I am an outcast from human society; my name is execrated by all who understand its entire import, — by those very beings whose happiness I ardently desire. I am an object of compassion to a few more benevolent than the rest; all else abhor and avoid me. With you, and perhaps some others (though in a less degree I fear), my gentleness and sincerity find favor, because they are themselves gentle and sincere; they believe in self-devotion and generosity, because they are themselves generous and self-devoted. Perhaps I should have shrunk from persisting in the task which I had undertaken in early life, of opposing myself, in these evil times and among these evil tongues, to what I esteem misery and vice, if I must have lived in the solitude of the heart. Fortunately my domestic circle encloses that within it which compensates for the loss. But these are subjects for conversation, and I find that, in using the privilege which you have permitted me of friendship, I have indulged in that quantity of self-love which only friendship can excuse or endure.

. . . .

XX.

TO MARY SHELLEY.[1]

LONDON, *December* 15, 1816.

I HAVE spent a day, my beloved, of somewhat agonizing sensations, such as the contemplation of vice and folly and hard-heartedness exceeding all conception must produce.   Leigh Hunt has been with me all day, and his delicate and tender attentions to me, his kind speeches of you, have sustained me against the horror of this event.   The children I have not got.   I have seen Longdill, who recommends proceeding with the utmost caution and resoluteness ; he seems interested.   I told him I was under contract of marriage to you, and he said that in such an event all pretence to detain the children would cease.   Hunt said, very delicately, that this would be soothing intelligence to you.   Yes, my only hope, my darling love, this will be one among the innumerable benefits which you will have bestowed upon me, and which will still be inferior in value to the greatest of benefits, — yourself.

.   .   .   .

How is Claire?   I do not tell her, but I may tell you, how deeply I am interested in her safety.   I need not recommend her to your care.   Give her any kind message from me, and calm her spirits as

[1] This letter was written during the progress of the suit for his children.

well as you can. I do not ask you to calm your own.

I am well in health, though somewhat faint and agitated ; but the affectionate attentions shown me by Hunt have been sustainers and restoratives more than I can tell. Do you, dearest and best, seek happiness — where it ought to reside — in your own pure and perfect bosom ; in the thoughts of how dear and how good you are to me ; how wise and how extensively beneficial you are perhaps now destined to become. Remember my poor babes, Ianthe and Charles. How tender and dear a mother they will find in you ! — darling William, too. My eyes overflow with tears. To-morrow I will write again.

XXI.

TO WILLIAM GODWIN.

[MARLOW,] *March* 9, 1817.

I WISH you knew me better than to be vexed or disappointed at anything I do. Either circumstances of petty difficulty and embarrassment find some peculiar attraction in me, or I have a fainter power of repulsion in regard to them. Certain it is that nothing gives me serener and more pure pleasure than your society, and that if, in breaking an engagement with you, I have forced an exercise of your philosophy upon you, I have in my own person incurred a penalty which mine has not yet taught me

to alleviate. . . . We are immersed in all kind of confusion here. Mary said you meant to come hither
soon enough to see the leaves come out. Which
leaves do you mean, for the wild-briar buds are already unfolded? And what of " Mandeville," [1] and
how will he bear to be transplanted here? All my
people, little Willy not excepted, desire their kindest
love to you. I beg to unite in kind remembrances
to Mrs. Godwin, whose health is, I hope, improved.

XXII.

TO WILLIAM GODWIN.

MARLOW, *March* 22, 1817.

.   .   .   .   .   .

IT was spring when I wrote to you, and winter
when your answer arrived. But the frost is very transitory ; every bud is ready to burst into leaf. It is a
wise distinction you make between the development
and the complete expansion of the leaves. The oak
and the chestnut, the latest and earliest parents of
foliage, would afford you a still subtler subdivision,
which would enable you to defer the visit from which
we expect so much delight for six weeks. I hope we
shall really see you before that time, and that you
will allow the chestnut, or any other impartial tree, as
he stands in the foreground, to be considered as a
virtual representation of the rest. Will is quite well

---

[1] Godwin's novel.

and very beautiful. Mary unites with me in presenting her kind remembrances to Mrs. Godwin, and begs her most affectionate love to you.

. . . .

XXIII.

TO MR. AND MRS. LEIGH HUNT.

GREAT MARLOW, *June* 29, 1817.

MY DEAR FRIENDS, — I performed my promise, and arrived here the night after I set off. Everybody up to this minute has been and continues well. I ought to have written yesterday, for to-day, I know not how, I have so constant a pain in my side, and such a depression of strength and spirits, as to make my holding the pen whilst I write to you an almost intolerable exertion. This, you know, with me is transitory. Do not mention that I am unwell to your nephew; for the advocate of a new system of diet is held bound to be invulnerable by disease, in the same manner as the sectaries of a new system of religion are held to be more moral than other people, or as a reformed Parliament must at least be assumed as the remedy of all political evils. No one will change the diet, adopt the religion, or reform the Parliament else.

Well, I am very anxious to hear how you get on, and I entreat Marianne to excite Hunt not to delay a minute in writing the necessary letters, and in informing me of the result. Kings are only to be approached through their ministers; who, indeed, as Marianne shall know to her cost, if she don't take care, are responsible not only for all their commissions, but, a more dreadful responsibility, for all their *omissions*. And I know not who has a right to the title of king, if not, according to the Stoics, he to whom the King of kings had delegated the prerogative of lord of the creation.

Let me know how Henry gets on, and make my best respects to your brother and Mrs. Hunt. Adieu.

XXIV.

TO A PUBLISHER.[1]

13 LISSON GROVE NORTH, *October* 13, 1817.

I SEND you the first four sheets of my poem entitled "Laon and Cyntha, or the Revolution of the Golden City." I believe this commencement affords a sufficient specimen of the work. I am conscious, indeed, that some of the concluding cantos, when "the plot thickens," and human passions are brought into more critical situations of development, are written with more energy and clearness; and that to see a work of which unity is one of the qualifications aimed at by the author in a disjointed state is, in a certain degree, unfavorable to the general impression. If, however, you submit it to Mr. Moore's judgment, he will make due allowance for these circumstances.

---

[1] Probably Longman & Co.

The whole poem, with the exception of the first canto and part of the last, is a mere human story, without the smallest intermixture of supernatural interference. The first canto is indeed in some measure a distinct poem, though very necessary to the wholeness of the work. I say this because, if it were all written in the manner of the first canto, I could not expect that it would be interesting to any great number of people. I have attempted in the progress of my work to speak to the common elementary emotions of the human heart, so that, though it is the story of violence and revolution, it is relieved by milder pictures of friendship and love and natural affection. The scene is supposed to be laid in Constantinople and Modern Greece, but without much attempt at minute delineation of Mahometan manners. It is, in fact, a tale illustrative of such a revolution as might be supposed to take place in a European nation, acted upon by the opinions of what has been called the modern philosophy, and contending with ancient notions, and the supposed advantage derived from them to those who support them. It is a revolution of this kind that is the beau ideal, as it were, of the French Revolution, but produced by the influence of individual genius, and out of general knowledge. The authors of it are supposed to be my hero and heroine, whose names appear in the title. My private friends have expressed to me a very high, and therefore, I do not doubt, a very erroneous, judgment of my work. However, of this I can determine neither way. I have resolved to give it a fair chance, and my wish therefore is,

first, to know whether you would purchase my interest
in the copyright, — an arrangement which, if there be
any truth in the opinions of my friends Lord Byron
and Mr. Leigh Hunt of my powers, cannot be dis-
advantageous to you ; and, in the second place, how
far you are willing to be the publisher of it on my
own account, if such an arrangement, which I should
infinitely prefer, cannot be made.   I rely, however,
on your having the goodness at least to send the
sheets to Mr. Moore, and ask his opinion of their
merits.

XXV.

TO WILLIAM GODWIN.

MARLOW, *December* 7, 1817.

.   .   .   .

My health has been materially worse.   My feelings
at intervals are of a deadly and torpid kind, or
awakened to a state of such unnatural and keen excitement, that, only to instance the organ of sight, I
find the very blades of grass and the boughs of distant trees present themselves to me with microscop-
ical distinctness.   Towards evening, I sink into a
state of lethargy and inanimation, and often remain
for hours on the sofa, between sleep and waking, a
prey to the most painful irritability of thought.   Such,
with little intermission, is my condition.   The hours
devoted to study are selected with vigilant caution
from among these periods of endurance.   It is not for
this that I think of travelling to Italy, even if I knew

that Italy would relieve me.   But I have experienced
a decisive pulmonary attack ; and, although at present it has passed away without any very considerable
vestige of its existence, yet this symptom sufficiently
shows the true nature of my disease to be consumption.   It is to my advantage that this malady is in its
nature slow, and, if one is sufficiently alive to its ad-
vances, is susceptible of cure from a warm climate.
In the event of its assuming any decided shape, it
would be my *duty* to go to Italy without delay ; and
it is only when that measure becomes an indispensable duty that, contrary to both Mary's feelings and
to mine, as they regard you, I shall go to Italy.   I
need not remind you (besides the mere pain endured
by the survivors) of the train of evil consequences
which my death would cause to ensue.   I am thus
circumstantial and explicit, because you seem to have
misunderstood me.   It is not health, but life, that I
should seek in Italy ; and that not for my own sake,
— I feel that I am capable of trampling on all such
weaknesses, — but for the sake of those to whom my
life may be a source of happiness, utility, security,
and honor, and to some of whom my death might be
all that is the reverse.

I ought to say I cannot persevere in the meat diet.
What you say of Malthus fills me, as far as my intellect is concerned, with life and strength.   I believe
that I have a most anxious desire that the time should
quickly come that, even so far as you are personally
concerned, you should be tranquil and independent.
But when I consider the intellectual lustre with which
you clothe this world, and how much the last genera-

tion of mankind may be benefited by that light flowing forth without the intervention of one shadow, I am elevated above all thoughts which tend to you or myself as an individual, and become, by sympathy, part of those distant and innumerable minds to whom your writings must be present.

I meant to have written to you about "Mandeville"[1] solely; but I was so irritable and weak that I could not write, although I thought I had much to say. I have read Mandeville, but I must read it again soon, for the interest is of that irresistible and overwhelming kind, that the mind in its influence is like a cloud borne on by an impetuous wind, — like one breathlessly carried forward, who has no time to pause or observe the causes of his career. I think the power of Mandeville is inferior to nothing you have done; and, were it not for the character of Falkland,[2] no instance in which you have exerted that power of *creation* which you possess beyond all contemporary writers might compare with it. Falkland is still alone; power is, in Falkland, not, as in Mandeville, tumult hurried onward by the tempest, but tranquillity standing unshaken amid its fiercest rage. But "Caleb Williams" never shakes the deepest soul like Mandeville. It must be said of the latter, you rule with a rod of iron. The picture is never bright; and we wonder whence you drew the darkness with which its shades are deepened, until the epithet of tenfold might almost cease to be a metaphor. The *noun smorfia* touches some cord within us, with such a

---

[1] Godwin's novel.

[2] In "Caleb Williams," by Godwin.

cold and jarring power, that I started, and for some time could scarce believe but that I was Mandeville, and that this hideous grin was stamped upon my own face. In style and strength of expression, Mandeville is wonderfully great, and the energy and the sweetness of the sentiments scarcely to be equalled. Clifford's character, as mere beauty, is a divine and soothing contrast ; and I do not think — if, perhaps, I except (and I know not if I ought to do so) the speech of Agathon in the "Symposium" of Plato — that there ever was produced a moral discourse more characteristic of all that is admirable and lovely in human nature, more lovely and admirable in itself, than that of Henrietta to Mandeville, as he is recovering from madness. Shall I say that, when I discovered that she was pleading all this time sweetly for her lover, and when at last she weakly abandoned poor Mandeville, I felt an involuntary, and perhaps an unreasonable pang? Adieu !

XXVI.

TO WILLIAM GODWIN.

MARLOW, *December* 11, 1817.

I HAVE read and considered all that you say about my general powers, and the particular instance of the poem in which I have attempted to develop them. Nothing can be more satisfactory to me than the interest which your admonitions express. But I think you are mistaken in some points with regard to the peculiar nature of my powers, whatever be their amount. I listened with deference and self-suspicion to your censures of " Laon and Cythna "; but the productions of mine which you commend hold a very low place in my own esteem, and this reassured me, in some degree at least. The poem was produced by a series of thoughts which filled my mind with unbounded and sustained enthusiasm. I felt the precariousness of my life, and I resolved in this book to leave some records of myself. Much of what the volume contains was written with the same feeling, as real, though not so prophetic, as the communications of a dying man. I never presumed, indeed, to consider it anything approaching to faultless; but when I considered contemporary productions of the same apparent pretensions, I will own that I was filled with confidence. I felt that it was in many respects a genuine picture of my own mind. I felt that the sentiments were true, not assumed; and in this have I long believed, — that my power consists in sympathy, and that part of imagination which relates to sentiment and contemplation. I am formed, if for anything not in common with the herd of mankind, to apprehend minute and remote distinctions of feeling, whether relative to external nature or the living beings which surround us, and to communicate the conceptions which result from considering either the moral or the material universe as a whole. . . . Yet, after all, I cannot but be conscious, in much of what I write, of an absence of that tranquillity which is the attribute and accompaniment of power. This feeling alone would make your most kind and wise admonitions on the subject of the economy of intellectual force valuable to me. And if I live, or if I see any trust in coming years, doubt not but that I shall do something, whatever it might be, which a serious and earnest estimate of my powers will suggest to me, and which will be in every respect accommodated to their utmost limits.

.   .   .   .

XXVII.

TO CHARLES OLLIER.

MARLOW, *December* 11, 1817.

DEAR SIR, — It is to be regretted that you did not consult your own safety and advantage (if you consider it connected with the non-publication of my book[1]) before your declining the publication, after having accepted it, would have operated to so extensive and serious an injury to my views as now. The instances of abuse and menace which you cite were such as you expected, and were, as I conceived, prepared for. If not, it would have been just to me to have given them their due weight and consideration before. You foresaw, you foreknew, all that these people would say. You do your best to condemn my book before it is given forth, because you publish it, and then withdraw; so that no other

---

[1] "Laon and Cythna." Ollier feared the effect it would have on account of its radical character. Shelley afterwards revised it, and it was published as "The Revolt of Islam."

bookseller will publish it, because one has already rejected it. You must be aware of the great injury which you prepare for me. If I had never consulted your advantage, my book would have had a fair hearing. But now it is first published, and then the publisher — as if the author had deceived him as to the contents of the work, and as if the inevitable consequence of its publication would be ignominy and punishment, and as if none should dare to touch it or look at it — retracts, at a period when nothing but the most extraordinary and unforeseen circumstances can justify his retraction.

I beseech you to reconsider the matter, for your sake no less than for my own. Assume the high and secure ground of courage. The people who visit your shop, and the wretched bigot who gave his worthless custom to some other bookseller, are not the public. The public respect talent; and a large portion of them are already undeceived with regard to the prejudices which my book attacks. You would lose some customers, but you would gain others. Your trade would be diverted into a channel more consistent with your own principles. Not to say that a publisher is in no wise pledged to all the opinions of his publications, or to any; and that he may enter his protest, with each copy sold, either against the truth or the discretion of the principles of the books he sells. But there is a much more important consideration in the case. You are, and have been to a certain extent, the publisher. I don't believe that, if the book was quietly and regularly published, the Government would touch anything of a character so refined, and so remote from the conceptions of the vulgar. They would hesitate before they invaded a member of the higher circles of the republic of letters. But if they see us tremble, they will make no distinctions; they will feel their strength. You might bring the arm of the law down upon us by flinching now. Directly these scoundrels see that people are afraid of them, they seize upon them and hold them up to mankind as criminals already convicted by their own fears. You lay yourself prostrate, and they trample on you. How glad they would be to seize on any connection of Hunt's by this most powerful of all their arms, — the terrors and self-condemnation of their victim. Read all the *ex officio* cases, and see what reward booksellers and printers have received for their submission.

If, contrary to common sense and justice, you resolve to give me up, you shall receive no detriment from a connection with me in small matters, though you determine to inflict so serious a one on me in great. You shall not be at a farthing's expense. I shall still, so far as my powers extend, do my best to promote your interest. On the contrary supposition, even admitting you derive no benefit from the book itself, — and it should be my care that you shall do so, — I hold myself ready to make ample indemnity for any loss you may sustain.

There is one compromise you might make, though that would be still injurious to me. Sherwood and Neely wished to be the principal publishers. Call on them, and say that it was through a mistake that you undertook the principal direction of the book, as it was *my wish* that it should be theirs, and that I have written to you to that effect. This, if it would be advantageous to you, would be detrimental to, but not utterly destructive of, my views. To withdraw your name entirely would be to inflict on me a bitter and undeserved injury.

Let me hear from you by return of post. I hope that you will be influenced to fulfil your engagement with me, and proceed with the publication, as justice to me, and, indeed, a well understood estimate of your own interest and character, demand. I do hope that you will have too much regard to the well chosen motto of your seal[1] to permit the murmurs of a few bigots to outweigh the serious and permanent considerations presented in this letter. To their remonstrances you have only to reply, " I did not write the book; I am not responsible; here is the author's address, — state your objections to him. I do no more than sell it to those who inquire for it; and, if they are not pleased with their bargain, the author empowers me to receive the book and to return the money." As to the interference of Government, nothing is more improbable than that in any case it would be attempted; but if it should, it would be owing entirely to your perseverance in the groundless apprehensions which dictated your communication received this day, and conscious terror would be perverted into an argument of guilt.

I have just received a most kind and encouraging letter from Mr. Moore on the subject of my poem.

---

1 " In omnibus libertas."

I have the fairest chance of the public approaching my work with unbiased and unperverted feeling : the fruit of reputation (and you know for *what purposes* I value it) is within my reach. It is for you, now you have been once named as publisher, and have me in your power, to blast all this, and to hold up my literary character in the eye of mankind as that of a proscribed and rejected outcast. And for no evil that I have ever done you, but in return for a preference which, although you falsely now esteem injurious to you, was solicited by Hunt, and conferred by me, as a source and a proof of nothing but kind intentions.

Dear Sir, I remain your sincere well-wisher.

XXVIII.

TO LEIGH HUNT.

LYONS, *March* 22, 1818.

MY DEAR FRIEND, — Why did you not wake me that night before we left England, you and Marianne? I take this as rather an unkind piece of kindness in you ; but which, in consideration of the six hundred miles between us, I forgive.

We have journeyed towards the spring, that has been hastening to meet us from the south ; and though our weather was at first abominable, we have now warm sunny days, and soft winds, and a sky of deep azure, the most serene I ever saw. The heat in this city to-day is like that of London in the midst of summer. My spirits and health sympathize in the change. Indeed, before I left London, my spirits were as feeble as my health, and I had demands on them which I found it difficult to supply. I have read "Foliage"; with most of the poems I am already familiar. What a delightful poem the "Nymphs" is! It is truly *poetical*, in the intense and emphatic sense of the word. If six hundred miles were not between us, I should say what pity that *glib* was not omitted, and that the poem is not as faultless as it is beautiful. But for fear I should *spoil* your next poem, I will not let slip a word upon the subject.

Give my love to Marianne and her sister, and tell Marianne she defrauded me of a kiss by not waking me when she went away, and that, as I have no better mode of conveying it, I must take the best, and ask you to pay the debt. When shall I see you again? Oh that it might be in Italy! I confess that the thought of how long we may be divided makes me very melancholy. Adieu, my dear friends. Write soon.

XXIX.

TO T. L. PEACOCK.

MY DEAR P., — Behold us arrived at the end of our journey, — that is, within a few miles of it, — because we design to spend the summer on the shore of the Lake of Como. Our journey was somewhat painful from the cold, and in no other manner interesting until we passed the Alps : of course I except the Alps themselves ; but no sooner had we arrived at Italy than the loveliness of the earth and the serenity of the sky made the greatest difference in my sensations. I depend on these things for life ; for in the smoke of cities, and the tumult of human kind, and the chilling fogs and rain of our own country, I can hardly be said to live. With what delight did I hear the woman, who conducted us to see the triumphal arch of Augustus at Susa, speak the clear and complete language of Italy, though half unintelligible to me, after that nasal and abbreviated cacophony of the French ! A ruined arch of magnificent proportions in the Greek taste, standing in a kind of road of green lawn, overgrown with violets and primroses, and in the midst of stupendous mountains, and a *blonde* woman, of light and graceful manners, something in the style of Fuseli's Eve, were the first things we met in Italy.

This city is very agreeable. We went to the opera last night, — which is a most splendid exhibition. The opera itself was not a favorite, and the singers very inferior to our own. But the ballet, or rather a kind of melodrame or pantomimic drama, was the most splendid spectacle I ever saw. We have no Miss Melanie here, — in every other respect Milan is unquestionably superior. The manner in which language is translated into gesture, the complete and full effect of the whole as illustrating the history in question, the unaffected self-possession of each of the actors, even to the children, made this choral drama more impressive than I could have conceived possible. The story is " Othello," and, strange to say, it left no disagreeable impression.

I write, but I am not in the humor to write, and you must expect longer, if not more entertaining, letters soon ; — that is, in a week or so, when I am a little recovered from my journey. Pray tell us all the news with regard to our own offspring, whom we left at nurse in England, as well as those of our friends. Mention Cobbett and politics too, — and Hunt, to whom Mary is now writing, — and particularly your own plans and yourself. You shall hear more of me and my plans soon. My health is improved already, and my spirits something ; and I have many literary schemes, and one in particular, which I thirst to be settled that I may begin. I have ordered Ollier to send you some sheets, etc., for revision. Adieu.

XXX.

TO T. L. PEACOCK.

MILAN, *April* 20, 1818.

MY DEAR P., — I had no conception that the distance between us, measured by time in respect of letters, was so great. I have but just received yours dated the 2d, — and when you will receive mine, written from this city somewhat later than the same date, I cannot know. I am sorry to hear that you have been obliged to remain at Marlow, a certain degree of society being almost a necessity of life, particularly as we are not to see you this summer in Italy. But this, I suppose, must be as it is. I often revisit Marlow in thought. The curse of this life is, that whatever is once known can never be unknown. You inhabit a spot which before you inhabit it is as indifferent to you as any other spot upon earth, and when, persuaded by some necessity, you think to leave it, you leave it not; it clings to you, and with memories of things which, in your experience of them, gave no such promise, revenges your desertion. Time flows on, places are changed; friends who were with us are no longer with us; yet what has been seems yet to be, but barren and stripped of life. See, I have sent you a study for " Nightmare Abbey." [1]

Since I last wrote to you we have been to Como, looking for a house. This lake exceeds anything I ever beheld in beauty, with the exception of the ar- butus islands of Killarney. It is long and narrow, and has the appearance of a mighty river winding among the mountains and the forests. We sailed from the town of Como to a tract of country called the Tremezina, and saw the various aspects presented by that part of the lake. The mountains between Como and that village, or rather cluster of villages, are covered on high with chestnut forests (the eating chestnuts, on which the inhabitants of the country subsist in time of scarcity), which sometimes descend to the very verge of the lake, overhanging it with their hoary branches. But usually the immediate

---

[1] Peacock's novel, in course of preparation at this time.

border of this shore is composed of laurel trees, and bay, and myrtle, and wild fig trees, and olives which grow in the crevices of the rocks, and overhang the caverns, and shadow the deep glens, which are filled with the flashing light of the waterfalls. Other flowering shrubs, which I cannot name, grow there also. On high, the towers of village churches are seen white among the dark forests. Beyond, on the opposite shore, which faces the south, the mountains descend less precipitously to the lake, and although they are much higher, and some covered with perpetual snow, there intervenes between them and the lake a range of lower hills, which have glens and rifts opening to the other, such as I should fancy the *abysses* of Ida or Parnassus. Here are plantations of olive, and orange, and lemon trees, — which are now so loaded with fruit that there is more fruit than leaves, — and vineyards. This shore of the lake is one continued village, and the Milanese nobility have their villas here. The union of culture and the untamable profusion and loveliness of nature is here so close, that the line where they are divided can hardly be discovered. But the finest scenery is that of the Villa Pliniana ; so called from a fountain which ebbs and flows every three hours, described by the younger Pliny, which is in the courtyard. This house, which was once a magnificent palace, and is now half in ruins, we are endeavoring to procure. It is built upon terraces *raised from* the bottom of the lake, together with its garden, at the foot of a semicircular precipice, overshadowed by profound forests of chestnut. The scene from the colonnade is the most extraordinary at once and the most lovely that eye ever beheld. On one side is the mountain, and immediately over you are clusters of cypress trees of an astonishing height, which seem to pierce the sky. Above you, from among the clouds, as it were, descends a waterfall of immense size, broken by the woody rocks into a thousand channels to the lake. On the other side is seen the blue extent of the lake and the mountains, speckled with sails and spires. The apartments of the Pliniana are immensely large, but ill furnished and antique. The terraces, which overlook the lake, and conduct under the shade of such immense laurel trees as deserve the epithet of Pythian, are most delightful. We stayed at Como two days, and have now returned to Milan, waiting the issue of our negotiation about a house. Como is only six leagues from Milan, and its mountains are seen from the cathedral.

This cathedral is a most astonishing work of art. It is built of white marble, and cut into pinnacles of immense height and the utmost delicacy of workmanship, and loaded with sculpture. The effect of it, piercing the solid blue with those groups of dazzling spires, relieved by the serene depth of this Italian heaven, or by moonlight, when the stars seem gathered among those clustered shapes, is beyond anything I had imagined architecture capable of producing. The interior, though very sublime, is of a more earthly character, and with its stained glass and massy granite columns overloaded with antique figures, and the silver lamps, that burn forever under the canopy of black cloth beside the brazen altar and the marble fretwork of the dome, give it the aspect of some gorgeous sepulchre. There is one solitary spot among those aisles, behind the altar, where the light of day is dim and yellow under the storied window, which I have chosen to visit, and read Dante there.

I have devoted this summer, and indeed the next year, to the composition of a tragedy on the subject of Tasso's madness, which I find upon inspection is, if properly treated, admirably dramatic and poetical. But, you will say, I have no dramatic talent; very true, in a certain sense ; but I have taken the resolution to see what kind of a tragedy a person without dramatic talent could write. It shall be better morality than " Fazio," and better poetry than " Bertram," at least. You tell me nothing of " Rhododaphne," a book from which, I confess, I expected extraordinary success.[1]

Who lives in my house at Marlow now, or what is to be done with it? I am seriously persuaded that the situation was injurious to my health, or I should be tempted to feel a very absurd interest in who is to be its next possessor. The expense of our journey here has been very considerable ; but we are now living at the hotel here, in a kind of Pension, which is very reasonable in respect of price, and when we get into a menage of our own, we have every reason to expect that we shall experience something of the boasted cheapness of Italy. The finest bread, made of a sifted flour, the whitest and the best I ever tasted, is only one English penny a pound. All

---

[1] Peacock had just published this book, which, however, did not meet with the success Shelley anticipated.

the necessaries of life bear a proportional relation to this. But then the luxuries, tea, etc., are very dear; and the English, as usual, are cheated in a way that is quite ridiculous, if they have not their wits about them. We do not know a single human being, and the opera, until last night, has been always the same. Lord Byron, we hear, has taken a house for three years, at Venice; whether we shall see him or not, I do not know. The number of English who pass through this town is very great. They ought to be in their own country in the present crisis. Their conduct is wholly inexcusable. The people here, though inoffensive enough, seem both in body and soul a miserable race. The men are hardly men; they look like a tribe of stupid and shrivelled slaves, and I do not think that I have seen a gleam of intelligence in the countenance of man since I passed the Alps. The women in enslaved countries are always better than the men; but they have tight-laced figures, and figures and mien which express (Oh how unlike the French!) a mixture of the coquette and prude, which reminds me of the worst characteristics of the English. Everything but humanity is in much greater perfection here than in France. The cleanliness and comfort of the inns is something quite English. The country is beautifully cultivated; and altogether, if you can, as one ought always to do, find your happiness in yourself, it is a most delightful and commodious place to live in. Adieu.

XXXI.

TO HORACE SMITH.[1]

MILAN, *April* 30, 1818.

I RECEIVED your note a few hours before I left England, and have designed to write to you from every town on the route; but the difficulty, not so much of knowing what to say as how to say it, prevented me till this moment. I was sorry that I did not see you again before my departure. On my return, which will not perhaps take place so soon as I at first expected, we shall meet again; meanwhile my letters to Hunt and Peacock are, as it were, common property, of which, if you feel any curiosity about me which I neglect to satisfy myself, you are at liberty to avail yourself of. To-morrow we leave this city for Pisa, where, or in its neighborhood, we shall remain during the summer.

.   .   .   .

We have been to the Lake of Como, and indeed had some thought of taking our residence there for the summer. The scenery is very beautiful, abounding among other things with those green banks for the sake of which you represented me as wandering over the world. You are more interested in the human part of the experience of travelling; a thing of which I see little and understand less, and which,

[1] There is some doubt as to whom this letter was addressed. Professor Dowden gives it as his opinion that it was Horace Smith.

if I saw and understood more, I fear I should be little able to describe. I am just reading a novel of Wieland's called "Aristippus," which I think you would like. It is very Greek, although perhaps not religious enough for a true pagan. If you can get it otherwise do not read it in the French translation, as the impudent translator has omitted much of the original, to accommodate it, as he says, to the "fastidious taste and powerful understanding of his countrymen."

I have read some Greek, but not much, on my journey, — two or three plays of Euripides, and among them the "Ion," which you praised, and which I think is exquisitely beautiful. But I have now made some Italian book my companion from my [wish] to learn the language, so as to speak it. I have been studying the history of Tasso's life, with some idea of making a drama of his adventures and misfortunes.

.   .   .   .

XXXII.

TO T. L. PEACOCK.

LIVORNO, *June* 5, 1818.

MY DEAR P., — We have not heard from you since the middle of April; that is, we have received only *one* letter from you since our departure from England. It necessarily follows that some accident has intercepted them. Address, in future, to the care of Mr. Gisborne, Livorno, and I shall receive them, though sometimes somewhat circuitously, yet always securely.

We left Milan on the 1st of May, and travelled across the Apennines to Pisa. This part of the Apennines is far less beautiful than the Alps; the mountains are wide and wild, and the whole scenery broad and undetermined, — the imagination cannot find a home in it. The Plain of the Milanese, and that of Parma, is exquisitely beautiful, — it is like one garden, or rather cultivated wilderness; because the corn and the meadow-grass grow under high and thick trees, festooned to one another by regular festoons of vines. On the seventh day we arrived at Pisa, where we remained three or four days. A large disagreeable city, almost without inhabitants. We then proceeded to this great trading town, where we have remained a month, and which in a few days we leave for the Bagni di Lucca, a kind of watering-place situated in the depth of the Apennines; the scenery surrounding this village is very fine.

We have made some acquaintance with a very amiable and accomplished lady, Mrs. Gisborne, who is the sole attraction in this most unattractive of cities. We had no idea of spending a month here, but she has made it even agreeable. We shall see something of Italian society at the Bagni di Lucca, where the most fashionable people resort.

.   .   .   .

I write as if writing where perhaps my letter may never arrive.

With every good wish from all of us, believe me most sincerely yours.

XXXIII.

TO MR. AND MRS. GISBORNE.

BAGNI DI LUCCA, *July* 10, 1818.

.   .   .   .

YOU cannot know, as some friends in England do, to whom my silence is still more inexcusable, that this silence is no proof of forgetfulness or neglect.

I have, in truth, nothing to say, but that I shall be happy to see you again, and renew our delightful walks, until the desire or the duty of seeing new things hurries us away. We have spent a month here in our accustomed solitude, with the exception of one night at the Casino; and the choice society of all ages, which I took care to pack up in a large trunk before we left England, have revisited us here. I am employed just now, having little better to do, in translating into my faint and inefficient periods the divine eloquence of Plato's "Symposium"; only as an exercise, or, perhaps, to give Mary some idea of the manners and feelings of the Athenians, — so different on many subjects from that of any other community that ever existed.

We have almost finished Ariosto, — who is entertaining and graceful, and *sometimes* a poet. Forgive me, worshippers of a more equal and tolerant divinity in poetry, if Ariosto pleases me less than you. Where is the gentle seriousness, the delicate sensibility, the calm and sustained energy, without which true greatness cannot be? He is so cruel, too, in his descriptions ; his most prized virtues are vices almost without disguise. He constantly vindicates and embellishes revenge in its grossest form, — the most deadly superstition that ever infested the world. How different from the tender and solemn enthusiasm of Petrarch, — or even the delicate moral sensibility of Tasso, though somewhat obscured by an assumed and artificial style.

We read a good deal here, — and we read little in Livorno. We have ridden, Mary and I, once only, to a place called Prato Fiorito, on the top of the mountains: the road, winding through forests, and over torrents, and on the verge of green ravines, affords scenery magnificently fine. I cannot describe it to you, but bid you, though vainly, come and see. I take great delight in watching the changes of the atmosphere here, and the growth of the thunder showers with which the noon is often overshadowed, and which break and fade away towards evening into flocks of delicate clouds. Our fire-flies are fading away fast ; but there is the planet Jupiter, who rises majestically over the rift in the forest-covered mountains to the south, and the pale summer lightning which is spread out every night, at intervals, over the sky. No doubt Providence has contrived these things, that, when the fire-flies go out, the low-flying owl may see her way home.

Remember me kindly to the Machinista.

With the sentiment of impatience until we see you again in the autumn, I am yours most sincerely.

XXXIV.

TO WILLIAM GODWIN

BAGNI DI LUCCA, *July* 25, 1818.

MY DEAR GODWIN, — We have, as yet, seen nothing of Italy which marks it to us as the habitation of departed greatness. The serene sky, the magnificent scenery, the delightful productions of the climate, are known to us, indeed, as the same with those which the ancients enjoyed. But Rome and Naples — even Florence — are yet to see ; and if we were to write you at present a history of our impressions, it would give you no idea that we lived in Italy.

I am exceedingly delighted with the plan you propose of a book illustrating the character of our calumniated republicans. It is precisely the subject for Mary; and I imagine that, but for the fear of being excited to refer to books not within her reach, she would attempt to begin it here, and order the works you notice. I am unfortunately little skilled in English history, and the interest which it excites in me is so feeble that I find it a duty to attain merely to that general knowledge of it which is indispensable.

Mary has just finished Ariosto with me, and, indeed, has attained a very competent knowledge of Italian. She is now reading Livy. I have been constantly occupied in literature, but have written little, — except some translations from Plato, in which I exercised myself, in the despair of producing anything original. The " Symposium " of Plato seems to me one of the most valuable pieces of all antiquity, whether we consider the intrinsic merit of the composition, or the light which it throws on the inmost state of manners and opinions among the ancient Greeks. I have occupied myself in translating this, and it has excited me to attempt an essay upon the cause of some differences in sentiment between the Ancients and Moderns, with respect to the subject of the dialogue.

Two things give us pleasure in your last letters. The resumption of [your answer to] Malthus,[1] and the favorable turn of the general election. If Ministers do not find some means, totally inconceivable to me, of plunging the nation in war, do you imagine that they can subsist? Peace is all that a country, in the present state of England, seems to require, to afford it tranquillity and leisure for attempting some remedy, not to the universal evils of all constituted society, but to the peculiar system of misrule under which those evils have been exasperated now. I wish that I had health or spirits that would enable me to enter into public affairs, or that I could find words to express all that I feel and know.

The modern Italians seem a miserable people, without sensibility, or imagination, or understanding. Their outside is polished, and an intercourse with them seems to proceed with much facility, though it ends in nothing, and produces nothing. The women are particularly empty, and, though possessed of the same kind of superficial grace, are devoid of every cultivation and refinement. They have a ball at the

1 See Kegan Paul's Life of Godwin.

Casino here every Sunday, which we attend, — but neither Mary nor C—— dance. I do not know whether they refrain from philosophy or protestantism.

I hear that poor Mary's book[1] is attacked most violently in the Quarterly Review. We have heard some praise of it, and, among others, an article of Walter Scott's in Blackwood's Magazine.

If you should have anything to send us, — and, I assure you, anything relating to England is interesting to us, — commit it to the care of Ollier, the bookseller, or P——; they send me a parcel every quarter.

My health is, I think, better, and I imagine continues to improve, but I still have busy thoughts and dispiriting cares, which I would shake off, — and it is now summer. — A thousand good wishes to yourself and your undertakings.

XXXV.

TO T. L. PEACOCK.

BAGNI DI LUCCA, *July* 25, 1818.

MY DEAR PEACOCK, — I received on the same day your letters marked 5 and 6, the one directed to Pisa and the other to Livorno, and I can assure you that they are most welcome visitors.

Our life here is as unvaried by any external events

---

[1] "Frankenstein."

as if we were at Marlow, where a sail up the river or
a journey to London makes an epoch. Since I last
wrote to you, I have ridden over to Lucca, once
with C., and once alone; and we have been over
to the Casino, where I cannot say there is anything
remarkable, the women being far removed from
anything which the most liberal annotator would
interpret into beauty or grace, and apparently pos-
sessing no intellectual excellences to compensate the
deficiency. I assure you it is well that it is so, for
the dances, especially the waltz, are so exquisitely
beautiful that it would be a little dangerous to the
newly unfrozen senses and imaginations of us migra-
tors from the neighborhood of the pole. As it is, —
except in the dark, — there can be no peril. The
atmosphere here, unlike that of the rest of Italy, is
diversified with clouds, which grow in the middle of
the day, and sometimes bring thunder and lightning,
and hail about the size of a pigeon's egg, and de-
crease towards the evening, leaving only those finely
woven webs of vapor which we see in English skies,
and flocks of fleecy and slowly moving clouds, which
all vanish before sunset; and the nights are forever
serene, and we see a star in the east at sunset, — I
think it is Jupiter, — almost as fine as Venus was
last summer; but it wants a certain silver and aerial
radiance, and soft yet piercing splendor, which belongs, I suppose, to the latter planet by virtue of its
at once divine and female nature. I have forgotten
to ask the ladies if Jupiter produces on them the
same effect. I take great delight in watching the
changes of the atmosphere. In the evening, Mary

and I often take a ride, for horses are cheap in this country. In the middle of the day I bathe in a pool or fountain, formed in the middle of the forests by a torrent. It is surrounded on all sides by precipitous rocks, and the waterfall of the stream which forms it falls into it on one side with perpetual dashing. Close to it, on the top of the rocks, are alders, and above the great chestnut trees, whose long and pointed leaves pierce the deep blue sky in strong relief. The water of this pool, which, to venture an unrhythmical paraphrase, is " sixteen feet long and ten feet wide," is as transparent as the air, so that the stones and sand at the bottom seem, as it were, trembling in the light of noonday. It is exceedingly cold also. My custom is to undress, and sit on the rocks, reading Herodotus until the perspiration has subsided, and then to leap from the edge of the rock into this fountain, — a practice in the hot weather excessively refreshing. This torrent is composed, as it were, of a succession of pools and waterfalls, up which I sometimes amuse myself by climbing when I bathe, and receiving the spray over all my body, whilst I clamber up the moist crags with difficulty.

I have lately found myself totally incapable of original composition. I employed my mornings, therefore, in translating the " Symposium," which I accomplished in ten days. Mary is now transcribing it, and I am writing a prefatory essay. I have been reading scarcely anything but Greek, and a little Italian poetry with Mary. We have finished Ariosto together, — a thing I could not have done again alone.

"Frankenstein" seems to have been well received; for although the unfriendly criticism of the Quarterly is an evil for it, yet it proves that it is read in some considerable degree, and it would be difficult for them, with any appearance of fairness, to deny it merit altogether. Their notice of me, and their exposure of their true motives for not noticing my book, shows how well understood an hostility must subsist between me and them.

The news of the result of the elections, especially that of the metropolis, is highly inspiriting. I received a letter, of two days' later date, with yours, which announced the unfortunate termination of that of Westmoreland. I wish you had sent me some of the overflowing villany of those apostates. What a pitiful wretch that Wordsworth! That such a man should be such a poet! I can compare him with no one but Simonides, that flatterer of the Sicilian tyrants, and at the same time the most natural and tender of lyric poets.

What pleasure would it have given me if the wings of imagination could have divided the space which divides us, and I could have been of your party. I have seen nothing so beautiful as Virginia Water in its kind. And my thoughts forever cling to Windsor Forest, and the copses of Marlow, like the clouds which hang upon the woods of the mountains, low trailing, and, though they pass away, leave their best dew when they themselves have faded. You tell me that you have finished "Nightmare Abbey." I hope that you have given the enemy no quarter. Remember, it is a sacred war. We have found an excellent quotation in Ben Jonson's " Every Man in his Humor." I will transcribe it, as I do not think you have these plays at Marlow : —

" MATTHEW. O, it's only your fine humor, sir. Your true melancholy breeds your fine wit, sir. I am melancholy myself divers times, sir ; and then do I no more but take pen and paper presently, and overflow you half a score or a dozen of sonnets at a sitting.

" ED. KNOWELL. Sure, he utters them by the gross.

" STEPHEN. Truly, sir ; and I love such things out of measure.

" ED. KNOWELL. I' faith, better than in measure, I 'll undertake.

" MATTHEW. Why, I pray you, sir, make use of my study ; it 's at your service.

" STEPHEN. I thank you, sir ; I shall be bold, I warrant you. *Have you a stool there to be melancholy upon ?* " — Act III. Scene 1.

The last expression would not make a bad motto.[1]

XXXVI.

TO T. L. PEACOCK.

BAGNI DI LUCCA, *August* 16, 1818.

MY DEAR PEACOCK, — No new event has been added to my life since I wrote last : at least none which might not have taken place as well on the banks of the Thames as on those of the Serchio. I project soon a short excursion, of a week or so, to

---

[1] Peacock adopted this suggestion, omitting Knowell's interlocutions.

some of the neighboring cities; and on the 10th of
September we leave this place for Florence, when I
shall at least be able to tell you of some things which
you cannot see from your windows.

I have finished — by taking advantage of a few
days of inspiration, which the Camenæ have been
lately very backward in conceding — the little poem
I began sending to the press in London.[1] Ollier
will send you the proofs. Its structure is slight and
airy, its subject ideal. The metre corresponds with
the spirit of the poem, and varies with the flow of
the feeling. I have translated, and Mary has transcribed the "Symposium," as well as my poem; and
I am proceeding to employ myself on a discourse,
upon the subject of which the Symposium treats,
considering the subject with reference to the difference of sentiments respecting it existing between
the Greeks and modern nations; a subject to be
handled with that delicate caution which either I
cannot or I will not practise in other matters, but
which here I acknowledge to be necessary. Not
that I have any serious thought of publishing either
this discourse or the Symposium, at least till I
return to England, when we may discuss the pro-
priety of it.

"Nightmare Abbey" finished. Well, what is in
it? What is it? You are as secret as if the priest
of Ceres had dictated its sacred pages. However, I
suppose I shall see in time, when my second parcel

---

[1] "Rosalind and Helen." Shelley began this poem at
Marlow, and on his departure for Italy left what he had
written with Ollier. He finished it at Bagni di Lucca.

arrives. My first is yet absent. By what conveyance did you send it?

Pray, are you yet cured of your Nympholepsy? 'T is a sweet disease : but one as obstinate and dangerous as any, — even when the Nymph is a Poliad. Whether such be the case or not, I hope your nympholeptic tale is not abandoned. The subject, if treated with a due spice of Bacchic fury, and interwoven with the manners and feelings of those divine people who, in their very errors, are the mirrors, as it were, in which all that is delicate and graceful contemplates itself, is perhaps equal to any. What a wonderful passage there is in " Phædrus," — the beginning, I think, of one of the speeches of Socrates,[1] — in praise of poetic madness, and in definition of what poetry is, and how a man becomes a poet. Every man who lives in this age and desires to write poetry ought, as a preservative against the false and narrow systems of criticism which every poetical empiric vents, to impress himself with this sentence, if he would be numbered among those to

---

[1] The passage alluded to is this. " There are several kinds," says Socrates, " of divine madness. That which proceeds from the Muses taking possession of a tender and unoccupied soul, awakening and bacchically inspiring it towards songs and other poetry, adorning myriads of ancient deeds, instructs succeeding generations, but he who, without this madness from the Muses, approaches the poetical gates, having persuaded himself that by art alone he may become sufficiently a poet, will find in the end his own imperfection, and see the poetry of his cold prudence vanish into nothingness before the light of that which has sprung from divine insanity." — *Platonis Phædrus*, p. 245 a. — T. L. P.

whom may apply this proud, though sublime, expression of Tasso : " Non c' è in mondo chi merita nome di creatore, che Dio ed il Poeta."

The weather has been brilliantly fine ; and now, among these mountains, the autumnal air is becoming less hot, especially in the mornings and evenings. The chestnut woods are now inexpressibly beautiful, for the chestnuts have become large, and add a new richness to the full foliage. We see here Jupiter in the east ; and Venus, I believe, as the evening star, directly after sunset.

More and better in my next. M. and C. desire their kind remembrances.

XXXVII.

TO MARY SHELLEY.

(Bagni di Lucca.)

FIORENCE, Thursday, 11 o'clock,
August 20, 1818.

DEAREST MARY, — We have been delayed in this city four hours, for the Austrian Minister's passport, but are now on the point of setting out with a vetturino, who engages to take us on the third day to Padua ; that is, we shall only sleep three nights on the road. Yesterday's journey, performed in a one-horse cabriolet, almost without springs, over a rough road, was excessively fatiguing. C——[1] suffered most

---

[1] Claire Clairmont, Mary's half-sister, was Shelley's companion on this journey.

from it ; for, as to myself, there are occasions in
which fatigue seems a useful medicine, as I have
felt no pain in my side — a most delightful respite —
since I left you. The country was various and exceedingly beautiful. Sometimes there were those
low cultivated lands, with their vine festoons, and
large bunches of grapes just becoming purple ; at
others we passed between high mountains, crowned
with some of the most majestic Gothic ruins I ever
saw, which frowned from the bare precipices, or were
half seen among the olive copses. As we approached
Florence, the country became cultivated to a very
high degree, the plain was filled with the most beautiful villas, and, as far as the eye could reach, the
mountains were covered with them ; for the plains
are bounded on all sides by blue and misty mountains. The vines are here trailed on low trellises of
reeds interwoven into crosses to support them, and
the grapes, now almost ripe, are exceedingly abun-
dant. You everywhere meet those teams of beautiful white oxen, which are now laboring the little
vine-divided fields with their Virgilian ploughs and
carts.

Florence itself, that is the Lung' Arno (for I have
seen no more), I think is the most beautiful city I
have yet seen. It is surrounded with cultivated hills,
and from the bridge which crosses the broad channel of the Arno the view is the most animated and
elegant I ever saw. You see three or four bridges,
one apparently supported by Corinthian pillars, and
the white sails of the boats, relieved by the deep
green of the forest, which comes to the water's edge,

and the sloping hills covered with bright villas on every side. Domes and steeples rise on all sides, and the cleanliness is remarkably great. On the other side there are the foldings of the Vale of Arno above; first the hills of olive and vine, then the chestnut woods, and then the blue and misty pine forests which invest the aerial Apennines, that fade in the distance. I have seldom seen a city so lovely at first sight as Florence.

We shall travel hence within a few hours, with the speed of the post, since the distance is one hundred and ninety miles, and we are to do it in three days, besides the half day, which is somewhat more than sixty miles a day. We have now got a comfortable carriage and two mules, and, thanks to Paolo, have made a very decent bargain, comprising everything, to Padua. I should say we had delightful fruit for breakfast, — figs, very fine, — and peaches, unfortunately gathered before they were ripe, whose smell was like what one fancies of the wakening of Paradise flowers.

Well, my dearest Mary, are you very lonely? Tell me truth, my sweetest, do you ever cry? I shall hear from you once at Venice, and once on my return here. If you love me you will keep up your spirits, — and, at all events, tell me truth about it; for, I assure you, I am not of a disposition to be flattered by your sorrow, though I should be by your cheerfulness; and, above all, by seeing such fruits of my absence as were produced when we were at Geneva.[1] What acquaintances have you made? I

---

[1] Referring to " Frankenstein."

might have travelled to Padua with a German, who had just come from Rome, and had scarce recovered from a malarial fever, caught in the Pontine Marshes, a week or two since; and I conceded to C——'s entreaties, and to *your* absent suggestions, and omitted the opportunity, although I have no great faith in such species of contagion. It is not very hot, — not at all too much so for my sensations; and the only thing that incommodes me are the gnats at night, who roar like so many humming-tops in one's ear, — and I do not always find *zanzariere.* How is Willmouse and little Clara? They must be kissed for me, — and you must particularly remember to speak my name to William, and see that he does not quite forget me before I return. Adieu, my dearest girl, I think that we shall soon meet. I shall write again from Venice. Adieu, dear Mary!

I have been reading the "Noble Kinsmen," in which, with the exception of that lovely scene, to which you added so much grace in reading to me, I have been disappointed. The Jailer's Daughter is a poor imitation, and deformed. The whole story wants moral discrimination and modesty. I do not believe that Shakespeare wrote a word of it.

XXXVIII.

TO MARY SHELLEY.
(Bagni di Lucca.)

VENICE, Sunday Morning.

MY DEAREST MARY, — We arrived here last night at twelve o'clock, and it is now before breakfast the next morning. I can, of course, tell you nothing of the future ; and though I shall not close this letter till post time, yet I do not know exactly when that is. Yet, if you are very impatient, look along the letter and you will see another date, when I may have something to relate.

I came from Padua hither in a gondola, and the gondoliere, among other things, without any hint on my part, began talking of Lord Byron. He said he was a *giovinotto Inglese*, with a *nome stravagante*, who lived very luxuriously, and spent great sums of money. This man, it seems, was one of Lord B.'s gondolieri. No sooner had we arrived at the inn than the waiter began talking about him, — said that he frequented Mrs. H.'s *conversazioni* very much.

Our journey from Florence to Padua contained nothing which may not be related another time. At Padua, as I said, we took a gondola — and left it at three o'clock. These gondolas are the most beautiful and convenient boats in the world. They are finely carpeted and furnished with black, and painted black. The couches on which you lean are extraordinarily soft, and are so disposed as to be the most comfortable to those who lean or sit. The windows have at will either Venetian plate-glass flowered, or Venetian blinds, or blinds of black cloth to shut out the light. The weather here is extremely cold, — indeed, sometimes very painfully so, and yesterday it began to rain. We passed the laguna in the middle of the night in a most violent storm of wind, rain, and lightning. It was very curious to observe the elements above in a state of such tremendous convulsion, and the surface of the water almost calm; for these lagunas, though five miles broad, a space enough in a storm to sink a gondola, are so shallow that the boatmen drive the boat along with a pole. The sea-water, furiously agitated by the wind, shone with sparkles like stars. Venice, now hidden and now disclosed by the driving rain, shone dimly with its lights. We were all this while safe and comfortable. Well, adieu, dearest: I shall, as Miss Byron says, resume the pen in the evening.

Sunday Night, 5 o'clock in the Morning.

Well, I will try to relate everything in its order.

.   .   .   .

At three o'clock I called on Lord Byron: he was delighted to see me.

He took me in his gondola across the laguna to a long sandy island, which defends Venice from the Adriatic. When we disembarked, we found his horses waiting for us, and we rode along the sands of the sea, talking. Our conversation consisted in histories of his wounded feelings, and questions as to my affairs, and great professions of friendship and regard for me. He said, that if he had been in England at the time of the Chancery affair, he would have moved heaven and earth to have prevented such a decision. We talked of literary matters, his Fourth Canto, which, he says, is very good, and indeed repeated some stanzas of great energy to me.

.   .   .   .

The Hoppners are the most amiable people I ever knew. They are much attached to each other, and have a nice little boy, seven months old. Mr. H. paints beautifully, and this excursion, which he has just put off, was an expedition to the Julian Alps, in this neighborhood, for the sake of sketching, to procure winter employment. He has only a fortnight's leisure, and he has sacrificed two days of it to strangers whom he never saw before. Mrs. H. has hazel eyes and sweet looks.

.   .   .   .

Well, but the time presses ; I am now going to the banker's to send you money for the journey, which I shall address to you at Florence, Post-office. Pray come instantly to Este, where I shall be waiting in the utmost anxiety for your arrival. You can pack up directly you get this letter, and employ the next day on that. The day after, get up at four o'clock, and go post to Lucca, where you will arrive at six. Then take a vetturino for Florence to arrive the same evening. From Florence to Este is three days' vetturino journey, — and you could not, I think, do it quicker by the post. Make Paolo take you to good inns, as we found very bad ones; and pray avoid the Tre Mori at Bologna, *perche vi sono cose inespressibili nei letti.* I do not think you can, but *try* to get from Florence to Bologna in one day. Do not take the post, for it is not much faster and very expensive. I have been obliged to decide on all these things without you: I have done for the best. And, my own beloved Mary, you must soon come and scold me if I have done wrong, and kiss me if I have done right, — for, I am sure, I do not know which, — and it is only the event that can show. We shall at least be saved the trouble of introduction, and have formed acquaintance with a lady who is so good, so beautiful, so angelically mild, that, were she as wise too, she would be quite a ——. Her eyes are like a reflection of yours. Her manners are like yours when you know and like a person.

Do you know, dearest, how this letter was written? By scraps and patches, and interrupted every minute. The gondola is now come to take me to the banker's. Este is a little place, and the house found without difficulty. I shall count four days for this letter: one day for packing, four for coming here, — and on the ninth or tenth day we shall meet.

.   .   .   .

Dearest love, be well, be happy, come to me, — confide in your own constant and affectionate

P. B. S.

Kiss the blue-eyed darlings for me, and do not let William forget me. Clara cannot recollect me.

XXXIX.

TO MARY SHELLEY.

(I Cappuccini, Este.)

PADUA, Mezzogiorno.

MY BEST MARY, — I found at Mont Selice a favorable opportunity for going to Venice, where I shall try to make some arrangement for you and little Ca. to come for some days, and shall meet you, if I do not write anything in the mean time, at Padua, on Thursday morning. C. says she is obliged to come to see the Medico, whom we missed this morning, and who has appointed as the only hour at which he can be at leisure half-past eight in the morning. You must, therefore, arrange matters so that you should come to the Stella d' Oro a little before that hour, — a thing to be accomplished only by setting out at half-past three in the morning. You will by this means arrive at Venice very early in the day, and avoid the heat, which might be bad for the babe, and take the time when she would at least sleep great part of the time. C. will return with the return carriage, and I shall meet you, or send to you at Padua.

Meanwhile remember Charles the First, — and do you be prepared to bring at least *some* of " Myrra " translated ; bring the book also with you, and the sheets of " Prometheus Unbound," which you will find numbered from one to twenty-six on the table of the pavilion. My poor little Clara, how is she to-day?

Indeed, I am somewhat uneasy about her, and though I feel secure that there is no danger, it would be very comfortable to have some reasonable person's opinion about her. The Medico at Padua is certainly a man in great practice, but I confess he does not satisfy me.

Am I not like a wild swan to be gone so suddenly? But, in fact, to set off alone to Venice required an exertion. I felt myself capable of making it, and I knew that you desired it. What will not be — if so it is destined — the lonely journey through that wide, cold France? But we shall see.

Adieu, my dearest love, — remember Charles I. and Myrra. I have been already imagining how you will conduct some scenes. The second volume of St. Leon begins with this proud and true sentiment: "There is nothing which the human mind can conceive which it may not execute." Shakespeare was only a human being.

Adieu till Thursday.

XL.

TO T. L. PEACOCK.

ESTE, *October* 8, 1818.

MY DEAR P., — I have not written to you, I think, for six weeks. But I have been on the point of writing many times, and have often felt that I had many things to say. But I have not been without events to disturb and distract me, amongst which is the death of my little girl. She died of a disorder peculiar to the climate. We have all had bad spirits enough, and I, in addition, bad health. I *intend* to be better soon : there is no malady, bodily or mental, which does not either kill or is killed.

We left the Baths of Lucca, I think, the day after I wrote to you — on a visit to Venice — partly for the sake of seeng the city. We made a very delightful acquaintance there with a Mr. and Mrs. Hoppner, the gentleman an Englishman, and the lady a Swiss-esse, mild and beautiful, and unprejudiced, in the best sense of the word. The kind attentions of these people made our short stay at Venice very pleasant. I saw Lord Byron, and really hardly knew him again ; he is changed into the liveliest and happiest-looking man I ever met. He read me the first canto of his " Don Juan," — a thing in the style of " Beppo," but infinitely better, and dedicated to Southey, in ten or a dozen stanzas, more like a mixture of wormwood and verdigris than satire. Venice is a wonderfully fine city. The approach to it over the laguna, with its domes and turrets glittering in a long line over the blue waves, is one of the finest architectural delusions in the world. It seems to have — and literally it has — its foundations in the sea. The silent streets are paved with water, and you hear nothing but the dashing of the oars, and the occasional cries of the gon-dolieri. I heard nothing of Tasso. The gondolas themselves are things of a most romantic and pic-turesque appearance ; I can only compare them to moths of which a coffin might have been the chrysalis. They are hung with black, and painted black, and car-peted with gray ; they curl at the prow and stern, and

at the former there is a nondescript beak of shining
steel, which glitters at the end of its long black mass.

The Doge's palace, with its library, is a fine monument of aristocratic power. I saw the dungeons
where these scoundrels used to torment their victims.
They are of three kinds, — one adjoining the place of
trial, where the prisoners destined to immediate execution were kept. I could not descend into them,
because the day on which I visited it was festa. Another under the leads of the palace, where the suf-
ferers were roasted to death or madness by the
ardors of an Italian sun ; and others called the Pozzi,
or wells, deep underneath, and communicating with
those on the roof by secret passages — where the
prisoners were confined sometimes half up to their
middles in stinking water. When the French came
here, they found only one old man in the dungeons,
and he could not speak. But Venice, which was once
a tyrant, is now the next worst thing, a slave ; for in
fact it ceased to be free or worth our regret as a
nation from the moment that the oligarchy usurped
the rights of the people. Yet I do not imagine that
it was ever so degraded as it has been since the
French, and especially the Austrian yoke. The Austrians take sixty per cent in taxes, and impose free
quarters on the inhabitants. A horde of German
soldiers, as vicious and more disgusting than the
Venetians themselves, insult these miserable people.
I had no conception of the excess to which avarice,
cowardice, superstition, ignorance, passionless lust,
and all the inexpressible brutalities which degrade
human nature, could be carried, until I had passed a
few days at Venice.

We have been living this last month near the little town from which I date this letter, in a very pleasant villa which has been lent to us, and we are now on the point of proceeding to Florence, Rome, and Naples, — at which last city we shall spend the winter, and return northwards in the spring. Behind us here are the Euganean hills, not so beautiful as those of the Bagni di Lucca, with Arqua, where Petrarch's house and tomb are religiously preserved and visited. At the end of our garden is an extensive Gothic castle, now the habitation of owls and bats, where the Medici family resided before they came to Florence. We see before us the wide flat plains of Lombardy, in which we see the sun and moon rise and set, and the evening star, and all the golden magnificence of autumnal clouds. But I reserve wonder for Naples.

I have been writing; and indeed have just finished the first act of a lyric and classical drama, to be called " Prometheus Unbound." Will you tell me what there is in Cicero about a drama supposed to have been written by Æschylus under this title.

I ought to say that I have just read Malthus in a French translation. Malthus is a very clever man, and the world would be a great gainer if it would seriously take his lessons into consideration, if it were capable of attending seriously to anything but mischief. But what on earth does he mean by some of his inferences?

.   .   .   .

I will write again from Rome and Florence, — in better spirits and to more agreeable purpose, I hope.

You saw those beautiful stanzas in the fourth canto about the Nymph Egeria. Well, I did not whisper a word about nympholepsy: I hope you acquit me, — and I hope you will not carry delicacy so far as to let this suppress anything nympholeptic.

XLI.

TO T. L. PEACOCK.

[FERRARA,] *November* 9 [1818].

WE have had heavy rain and thunder all night; and the former still continuing, we went in the carriage about the town. We went first to look at the cathedral, but the beggars very soon made us sound a retreat; so, whether, as it is said, there is a copy of a picture of Michael Angelo there or no, I cannot tell. At the public library we were more successful. This is, indeed, a magnificent establishment, containing, as they say, 100,000 volumes. We saw some illuminated manuscripts of church music, with verses of the Psalms interlined between the square notes, each of which consisted of the most delicate tracery, in colors inconceivably vivid. They belonged to the neighboring convent of Certosa, and are three or four hundred years old; but their hues are as fresh as if they had been executed yesterday. The tomb of Ariosto occupies one end of the largest saloon of which the library is composed; it is formed of various marbles, surmounted by an expressive bust of the poet, and subscribed with a few Latin verses, in a less miserable taste than those usually employed for similar purposes. But the most interesting exhibitions here are the writings, etc., of Ariosto and Tasso, which are preserved, and were concealed from the undistinguishing depredations of the French with pious care. There is the arm-chair of Ariosto, an old plain wooden piece of furniture, the hard seat of which was once occupied by, but has now survived, its cushion, as it has its master. I could fancy Ariosto sitting in it; and the satires in his own handwriting which they unfold beside it, and the old bronze inkstand, loaded with figures, which belonged also to him, assist the willing delusion. This inkstand has an antique, rather than an ancient appearance. Three Nymphs lean forth from the circumference, and on the top of the lid stands a Cupid winged and looking up, with a torch in one hand, his bow in the other, and his quiver beside him. A medal was bound round the skeleton of Ariosto, with his likeness impressed upon it. I cannot say I think it had much native expression; but perhaps the artist was in fault. On the reverse is a hand, cutting with a pair of scissors the tongue from a serpent, upraised from the grass, with this legend: " Pro bono malum." What this reverse of the boasted Christian maxim means, or how it applies to Ariosto, either as a satirist or a serious writer, I cannot exactly tell. The cicerone attempted to explain, and it is to his commentary that my bewildering is probably due, — if, indeed, the meaning be very plain, as is possibly the case.

There is here a manuscript of the entire " Gerusalemme Liberata," written by Tasso's own hand; a manuscript of some poems, written in prison, to the Duke Alfonso; and the satires of Ariosto, written also by his own hand; and the " Pastor Fido " of Guarini. The Gerusalemme, though it had evidently been copied and recopied, is interlined, particularly towards the end, with numerous corrections. The handwriting of Ariosto is a small, firm, and pointed character, expressing, as I should say, a strong and keen, but circumscribed energy of mind; that of Tasso is large, free, and flowing, except that there is a checked expression in the midst of its flow, which brings the letters into a smaller compass than one expected from the beginning of the word. It is the symbol of an intense and earnest mind, exceeding at times its own depth, and admonished to return by the chillness of the waters of oblivion striking upon its adventurous feet. You know I always seek in what I see the manifestation of something beyond the present and tangible object; and as we do not agree in physiognomy, so we may not agree now. But my business is to relate my own sensations, and not to attempt to inspire others with them. Some of the MSS. of Tasso were sonnets to his persecutor, which contain a great deal of what is called flattery. If Alfonso's ghost were asked how he felt those praises now, I wonder what he would say. But to me there is much more to pity than to condemn in these entreaties and praises of Tasso. It is as a bigot prays to and praises his god, whom he knows to be the most remorseless, capricious, and inflexible of tyrants, but whom he knows also to be omnipotent. Tasso's situation was widely different from that of any persecuted being of the present day; for from the depth of dungeons, public opinion might now at length be awakened to an echo that would startle the oppressor. But then there was no hope. There is something irresistibly pathetic to me in the sight of Tasso's own handwriting, moulding expressions of adulation and entreaty to a deaf and stupid tyrant, in an age when the most heroic virtue would have exposed its possessor to hopeless persecution, and — such is the alliance between virtue and genius — which unoffending genius could not escape.

We went afterwards to see his prison in the hospital of Sant' Anna, and I enclose you a piece of the wood of the very door, which for seven years and three months divided this glorious being from the air and the light which had nourished in him those influences which he has communicated, through his poetry, to thousands. The dungeon is low and dark, and when I say that it is really a very decent dungeon, I speak as one who has seen the prisons in the Doges' palace of Venice. But it is a horrible abode for the coarsest and meanest thing that ever wore the shape of man, much more for one of delicate susceptibilities and elevated fancies. It is low, and has a grated window, and, being sunk some feet below the level of the earth, is full of unwholesome damps. In the darkest corner is a mark in the wall where the chains were riveted, which bound him hand and foot. After some time, at the instance of some cardinal, his friend, the Duke allowed his victim a fireplace; the mark where it was walled up yet remains.

At the entrance of the Liceo, where the library is,

we were met by a penitent; his form was completely enveloped in a ghost-like drapery of white flannel; his bare feet were sandalled; and there was a kind of network visor drawn over his eyes, so as entirely to conceal his face. I imagine that this man had been adjudged to suffer this penance for some crime known only to himself and his confessor, and this kind of exhibition is a striking instance of the power of the Catholic superstition over the human mind. He passed, rattling his wooden box for charity.

Adieu. — You will hear from me again before I arrive at Naples.

XLII.

TO T. L. PEACOCK.

BOLOGNA, Monday, *November* 9, 1818.

MY DEAR P., — I have seen a quantity of things here, — churches, palaces, statues, fountains, and pictures; and my brain is at this moment like a portfolio of an architect, or a print-shop, or a commonplace-book. I will try to recollect something of what I have seen; for indeed it requires, if it will obey, an act of volition. First, we went to the cathedral, which contains nothing remarkable, except a kind of shrine, or rather a marble canopy, loaded with sculptures, and supported on four marble columns. We went then to a palace, — I am sure I forget the name of it, — where we saw a large gallery of pictures. Of course, in a picture gallery you see three hundred pictures you forget for one you remember. I remember, however, an interesting picture by Guido, of the Rape of Proserpine, in which Proserpine casts back her languid and half-unwilling eyes, as it were, to the flowers she had left ungathered in the fields of Enna. There was an exquisitely executed piece of Correggio, about four saints, one of whom seemed to have a pet dragon in a leash. I was told that it was the Devil who was bound in that style. But who can make anything of four saints? For what can they be supposed to be about? There was one painting, indeed, by this master, Christ beatified, inexpressibly fine. It is a half figure, seated on a mass of clouds, tinged with an ethereal, rose-like lustre; the arms are expanded; the whole frame seems dilated with expression; the countenance is heavy, as it were, with the weight of the rapture of the spirit; the lips parted, but scarcely parted, with the breath of intense but regulated passion; the eyes are calm and benignant; the whole features harmonized in majesty and sweetness. The hair is parted on the forehead, and falls in heavy locks on each side. It is motionless, but seems as if the faintest breath would move it. The coloring, I suppose, must be very good, if I could remark and understand it. The sky is of a pale aerial orange, like the tints of latest sunset; it does not seem painted around and beyond the figure, but everything seems to have absorbed, and to have been penetrated by its hues. I do not think we saw any other of Correggio, but this specimen gives me a very exalted idea of his powers.

We went to see Heaven knows how many more

palaces, — Ranuzzi, Marriscalchi, Aldobrandi. If you want Italian names for any purpose, here they are ; I should be glad of them if I were writing a novel. I saw many more of Guido. One, a Samson drinking water out of an ass's jaw-bone in the midst of the slaughtered Philistines. Why he is supposed to do this, God, who gave him this jaw-bone, alone knows, — but certain it is that the painting is a very fine one. The figure of Samson stands in strong relief in the foreground, colored, as it were, in the hues of human life, and full of strength and elegance. Round him lie the Philistines in all the attitudes of death. One prone, with the slight convulsion of pain just passing from his forehead, whilst on his lips and chin death lies as heavy as sleep. Another leaning on his arm, with his hand, white and motionless, hanging out beyond. In the distance, more dead bodies ; and, still further beyond, the blue sea and the blue mountains, and one white and tranquil sail.

There is a Murder of the Innocents, also by Guido, finely colored, with much fine expression, — but the subject is very horrible, and it seemed deficient in strength, — at least, you require the highest ideal energy, the most poetical and exalted conception of the subject, to reconcile you to such a contemplation. There was a Jesus Christ crucified, by the same, very fine. One gets tired, indeed, whatever may be the conception and execution of it, of seeing that monotonous and agonized form forever exhibited in one prescriptive attitude of torture. But the Magdalen, clinging to the cross with the look of passive and gentle despair beaming from beneath her bright flaxen hair; and the figure of St. John, with his looks uplifted in passionate compassion, his hands clasped, and his fingers twisting themselves together, as it were, with involuntary anguish, his feet almost writhing up from the ground with the same sympathy, and the whole of this arrayed in colors of a diviner nature, yet most like nature's self; — of the contemplation of this one would never weary.

There was a " Fortune," too, of Guido; a piece of mere beauty. There was the figure of Fortune on a globe, eagerly proceeding onwards, and Love was trying to catch her back by the hair, and her face was half turned towards him; her long chestnut hair was floating in the stream of the wind, and threw its shadow over her fair forehead. Her hazel eyes were fixed on her pursuer, with a meaning look of playfulness, and a light smile was hovering on her lips. The colors which arrayed her delicate limbs were ethereal and warm.

But perhaps the most interesting of all the pictures of Guido which I saw was a Madonna Lattante. She is leaning over her child, and the maternal feelings with which she is pervaded are shadowed forth on her soft and gentle countenance, and in her simple and affectionate gestures there is what an unfeeling observer would call a dulness in the expression of her face; her eyes are almost closed; her lip depressed; there is a serious, and even a heavy relaxation, as it were, of all the muscles which are called into action by ordinary emotions : but it is

only as if the spirit of love, almost insupportable
from its intensity, were brooding over and weighing
down the soul, or whatever it is, without which the
material frame is inanimate and inexpressive.

There is another painter here, called Franceschini,
a Bolognese, who, though certainly very inferior to
Guido, is yet a person of excellent powers. One entire church, that of Santa Catarina, is covered by his
works. I do not know whether any of his pictures
have ever been seen in England. His coloring is
less warm than that of Guido, but nothing can be
more clear and delicate; it is as if he could have
dipped his pencil in the hues of some serenest and
star-shining twilight. His forms have the same delicacy and aerial loveliness; their eyes are all bright
with innocence and love; their lips scarce divided
by some gentle and sweet emotion. His winged children are the loveliest ideal beings ever created by the
human mind. These are generally, whether in the
capacity of Cherubim or Cupid, accessories to the rest
of the picture; and the underplot of their lovely and
infantine play is something almost pathetic, from the
excess of its unpretending beauty. One of the best
of his pieces is an Annunciation of the Virgin: the
Angel is beaming in beauty; the Virgin, soft, retiring,
and simple.

We saw, besides, one picture of Raphael, — St.
Cecilia. This is in another and higher style; you
forget that it is a picture as you look at it, and yet it
is most unlike any of those things which we call reality. It is of the inspired and ideal kind, and seems
to have been conceived and executed in a similar

state of feeling to that which produced among the ancients those perfect specimens of poetry and sculpture which are the baffling models of succeeding generations. There is a unity and a perfection in it of an incommunicable kind. The central figure, St. Cecilia, seems rapt in such inspiration as produced her image in the painter's mind: her deep, dark, eloquent eyes lifted up; her chestnut hair flung back from her forehead; she holds an organ in her hands; her countenance, as it were, calmed by the depth of its passion and rapture, and penetrated throughout with the warm and radiant light of life. She is listening to the music of heaven, and, as I imagine, has just ceased to sing, for the four figures that surround her evidently point, by their attitudes, towards her; particularly St. John, who, with a tender yet impassioned gesture, bends his countenance towards her, languid with the depth of his emotion. At her feet lie various instruments of music, broken and unstrung. Of the coloring I do not speak; it eclipses Nature, yet it has all her truth and softness.

We saw some pictures of Domenichino, Caracci, Albano, Guercino, Elizabetta Sirani. The two former — remember, I do not pretend to taste — I cannot admire. Of the latter there are some beautiful Madonnas. There are several of Guercino, which they said were very fine. I dare say they were, for the strength and complication of his figures made my head turn round. One, indeed, was certainly powerful. It was the representation of the founder of the Carthusians exercising his austerities in the desert, with a youth as his attendant, kneeling beside him at an altar ; on another altar stood a skull and a crucifix ; and around were the rocks and the trees of the wilderness. I never saw such a figure as this fellow. His face was wrinkled like a dried snake's skin, and drawn in long hard lines ; his very hands were wrinkled. He looked like an animated mummy. He was clothed in a loose dress of death-colored flannel, such as you might fancy a shroud might be after it had wrapped a corpse a month or two. It had a yellow, putrified, ghastly hue, which it cast on all the objects around, so that the hands and face of the Carthusian and his companion were jaundiced by this sepulchral glimmer. Why write books against religion, when we may hang up such pictures? But the world either will not or cannot see. The gloomy effect of this was softened, and, at the same time, its sublimity diminished, by the figure of the Virgin and Child in the sky, looking down with admiration on the monk, and a beautiful flying figure of an angel.

Enough of pictures. I saw the place where Guido and his mistress, Elizabetta Sirani, were buried. This lady was poisoned at the age of twenty-six, by another lover, a rejected one of course. Our guide said she was very ugly, and that we might see her portrait to-morrow.

Well, good night, for the present. "To-morrow to fresh fields and pastures new."

November 16.

To-day we first went to see those divine pictures of Raffaelle and Guido again, and then rode up the mountains behind this city, to visit a chapel dedi-

cated to the Madonna. It made me melancholy to
see that they had been varnishing and restoring some
of these pictures, and that even some had been
pierced by the French bayonets. These are symptoms of the mortality of man, and perhaps few
of his works are more evanescent than paintings.
Sculpture retains its freshness for twenty centuries,
— the Apollo and the Venus are as they were. But
books are perhaps the only productions of man
coeval with the human race. Sophocles and Shakespeare can be produced and reproduced forever.
But how evanescent are paintings ! and must necessarily be.   Those of Zeuxis and Apelles are no more ;
and perhaps they bore the same relation to Homer
and Æschylus that those of Guido and Raffaelle
bear to Dante and Petrarch.   There is one refuge
from the despondency of this contemplation.   The
material part, indeed, of their works must perish, but
they survive in the mind of man, and the remembrances connected with them are transmitted from
generation to generation.   The poet embodies them
in his creations ; the systems of philosophers are
modelled to gentleness by their contemplation ;
opinion, that legislator, is infected with their influence ; men become better and wiser ; and the
unseen seeds are perhaps thus sown, which shall
produce a plant more excellent even than that from
which they fell.   But all this might as well be said
or thought at Marlow as Bologna.

The chapel of the Madonna is a very pretty Corinthian building, very beautiful indeed.   It commands
a fine view of these fertile plains, the many-folded

Apennines, and the city. I have just returned from a moonlight walk through Bologna. It is a city of colonnades, and the effect of moonlight is strikingly picturesque. There are two towers here, — one four hundred feet high, — ugly things, built of brick, which lean both different ways; and with the delusion of moonlight shadows, you might almost fancy that the city is rocked by an earthquake. They say they were built so on purpose; but I observe in all the plain of Lombardy the church towers lean.

Adieu. — God grant you patience to read this long letter, and courage to support the expectation of the next. Pray part them from the Cobbetts on your breakfast table, — they may fight it out in your mind.

XLIII.

TO T. L. PEACOCK.

ROME, *November* 20, 1818.

MY DEAR P., — Behold me in the capital of the vanished world! But I have seen nothing except St. Peter's and the Vatican, overlooking the city in the mist of distance, and the Dogana, where they took us to have our luggage examined, which is built between the ruins of a temple to Antoninus Pius. The Corinthian columns rise over the dwindled palaces of the modern town, and the wrought cornice is changed on one side, as it were, to masses of wave-worn precipices, which overhang you, far, far on high.

I take advantage of this rainy evening, and before
Rome has effaced all other recollections, to endeavor
to recall the vanished scenes through which we have
passed.   We left Bologna, I forget on what day,
and passing by Rimini, Fano, and Foligno, along
the Via Flaminia and Terni, have arrived at Rome
after ten days' somewhat tedious, but most interesting journey.   The most remarkable things we saw
were the Roman excavations in the rock, and the
great waterfall of Terni.

.   .   .   .

From Fano we left the coast of the Adriatic, and
entered the Apennines, following the course of the
Metaurus, the banks of which were the scene of the
defeat of Asdrubal : and it is said (you can refer to
the book) that Livy has given a very exact and
animated description of it.   I forget all about it, but
shall look as soon as our boxes are opened.   Following the river, the vale contracts, the banks of the
river become steep and rocky, the forests of oak and
ilex which overhang its emerald-colored stream cling
to their abrupt precipices.   About four miles from
Fossombrone, the river forces for itself a passage
between the walls and toppling precipices of the
loftiest Apennines, which are here rifted to their
base, and undermined by the narrow and tumultuous
torrent.   It was a cloudy morning, and we had no
conception of the scene that awaited us.   Suddenly
the low clouds were struck by the clear north wind,
and, like curtains of the finest gauze removed one
by one, were drawn from before the mountain, whose
heaven-cleaving pinnacles and black crags overhang-

ing one another stood at length defined in the light of day. The road runs parallel to the river, at a considerable height, and is carried through the mountain by a vaulted cavern. The marks of the chisel of the legionaries of the Roman Consul are yet evident.

We passed on day after day, until we came to Spoleto, I think the most romantic city I ever saw. There is here an aqueduct of astonishing elevation, which unites two rocky mountains: there is the path of a torrent below, whitening the green dell with its broad and barren track of stones, and above there is a castle, apparently of great strength and of tremendous magnitude, which overhangs the city, and whose marble bastions are perpendicular with the precipice. I never saw a more impressive picture, in which the shapes of nature are of the grandest order, but over which the creations of man, sublime from their antiquity and greatness, seem to predominate. The castle was built by Belisarius or Narses, I forget which, but was of that epoch.

From Spoleto we went to Terni, and saw the cataract of the Velino. The glaciers of Montanvert and the source of the Arveiron is the grandest spectacle I ever saw. This is the second. Imagine a river sixty feet in breadth, with a vast volume of waters, the outlet of a great lake among the higher mountains, falling three hundred feet into a sightless gulf of snow-white vapor, which bursts up forever and forever from a circle of black crags, and thence, leaping downwards, make five or six other cataracts, each fifty or a hundred feet high, which exhibit, on a smaller scale, and with beautiful and sublime variety, the same appearances. But words (and far less could painting) will not express it. Stand upon the brink of the platform of cliff, which is directly opposite. You see the ever-moving water stream down. It comes in thick and tawny folds, flaking off like solid snow gliding down a mountain. It does not seem hollow within, but without it is unequal, like the folding of linen thrown carelessly down; your eye follows it, and it is lost below; not in the black rocks which gird it around, but in its own foam and spray, in the cloud-like vapor boiling up from below, which is not like rain, nor mist, nor spray, nor foam, but water, in a shape wholly unlike anything I ever saw before. It is as white as snow, but thick and impenetrable to the eye. The very imagination is bewildered in it. A thunder comes up from the abyss wonderful to hear, for, though it ever sounds, it is never the same, but, modulated by the changing motion, rises and falls intermittingly; we passed half an hour in one spot looking at it, and thought but a few minutes had gone by. The surrounding scenery is, in its kind, the loveliest and most sublime that can be conceived. In our first walk we passed through some olive groves, of large and ancient trees, whose hoary and twisted trunks leaned in all directions. We then crossed a path of orange trees by the river side, laden with their golden fruit, and came to a forest of ilex of a large size, whose evergreen and acorn-bearing boughs were intertwined over our winding path. Around, hemming in the narrow vale, were pinnacles of lofty mountains of pyramidical rock clothed with all evergreen plants and trees; the vast pine, whose feathery foliage trembled in the blue air, the ilex, that ancestral inhabitant of these mountains, the arbutus with its crimson-colored fruit and glittering leaves. After an hour's walk, we came beneath the cataract of Terni, within the distance of half a mile; nearer you cannot approach, for the Nar, which has here its confluence with the Velino, bars the passage. We then crossed the river formed by this confluence, over a narrow natural bridge of rock, and saw the cataract from the platform I first mentioned. We think of spending some time next year near this waterfall. The inn is very bad, or we should have stayed there longer.

We came from Terni last night to a place called Nepi, and to-day arrived at Rome across the much-belied Campagna di Roma, a place I confess infinitely to my taste. It is a flattering picture of Bagshot Heath. But then there are the Apennines on one side, and Rome and St. Peter's on the other, and it is intersected by perpetual dells clothed with arbutus and ilex. Adieu.

XLIV.

TO T. L. PEACOCK.

Naples, *December* 22, 1818.

My dear P., — I have received a letter from you here, dated November 1st; you see the reciprocation of letters from the term of our travels is more slow.

I entirely agree with what you say about "Childe Harold." The spirit in which it is written is, if insane, the most wicked and mischievous insanity that ever was given forth. It is a kind of obstinate and self-willed folly, in which he hardens himself. I remonstrated with him in vain on the tone of mind from which such a view of things alone arises. For its real root is very different from its apparent one. Nothing can be less sublime than the true source of these expressions of contempt and desperation. The fact is, that, first, the Italian women with whom he associates are perhaps the most contemptible of all who exist under the moon, — the most ignorant, the most disgusting, the most bigoted ; countesses [who] smell so strongly of garlic that an ordinary Englishman cannot approach them. Well, L. B. is familiar with the lowest sort of these women, the people his gondolieri pick up in the streets. He associates with wretches who seem almost to have lost the gait and physiognomy of man, and who do not scruple to avow practices which are not only not named, but I believe seldom even conceived in England. He says he disapproves, but he endures. He is heartily and deeply discontented with himself; and contemplating in the distorted mirror of his own thoughts the nature and the destiny of man, what can he behold but objects of contempt and despair? But that he is a great poet, I think the address to Ocean proves. And he has a certain degree of candor while you talk to him, but unfortunately it does not outlast your departure. No, I do not doubt, and, for his sake, I ought to hope, that his present career must end soon in some violent circumstance.

Since I last wrote to you, I have seen the ruins of
Rome, the Vatican, St. Peter's, and all the miracles
of ancient and modern art contained in that majestic
city. The impression of it exceeds anything I have
ever experienced in my travels. We stayed there
only a week, intending to return at the end of February, and devote two or three months to its mines of
inexhaustible contemplation, to which period I refer
you for a minute account of it. We visited the Forum
and the ruins of the Coliseum every day. The Coliseum is unlike any work of human hands I ever saw
before. It is of enormous height and circuit, and the
arches built of massy stones are piled on one another,
and jut into the blue air, shattered into the forms of
overhanging rocks. It has been changed by time
into the image of an amphitheatre of rocky hills
overgrown by the wild olive, the myrtle, and the fig
tree, and threaded by little paths, which wind among
its ruined stairs and immeasurable galleries : the
copsewood overshadows you as you wander through
its labyrinths, and the wild weeds of this climate of
flowers bloom under your feet. The arena is covered
with grass, and pierces, like the skirts of a natural
plain, the chasms of the broken arches around.[1] But
a small part of the exterior circumference remains.
It is exquisitely light and beautiful ; and the effect of
the perfection of its architecture, adorned with ranges
of Corinthian pilasters, supporting a bold cornice,
is such as to diminish the effect of its greatness.

[1] A friend who has recently visited Rome tells me that this
exquisite mass of foliage has been torn away, leaving the ruin
perfectly bare.

The interior is all ruin. I can scarcely believe that when incrusted with Dorian marble and ornamented by columns of Egyptian granite its effect could have been so sublime and so impressive as in its present state. It is open to the sky, and it was the clear and sunny weather of the end of November in this climate when we visited it, day after day.

Near it is the arch of Constantine, or rather the arch of Trajan ; for the servile and avaricious Senate of degraded Rome ordered that the monument of his predecessor should be demolished in order to dedicate one to the Christian reptile who had crept among the blood of his murdered family to the supreme power. It is exquisitely beautiful and perfect. The Forum is a plain in the midst of Rome, a kind of desert, full of heaps of stones and pits, and, though so near the habitations of men, is the most desolate place you can conceive. The ruins of temples stand in and around it, shattered columns and ranges of others complete, supporting cornices of exquisite workmanship, and vast vaults of shattered domes distinct with regular compartments, once filled with sculptures of ivory or brass. The temples of Jupiter, and Concord, and Peace, and the Sun, and the Moon, and Vesta, are all within a short distance of this spot. Behold the wrecks of what a great nation once dedicated to the abstractions of the mind ! Rome is a city, as it were, of the dead, or rather of those who cannot die, and who survive the puny generations which inhabit and pass over the spot which they have made sacred to eternity. In Rome, at least in the first enthusiasm of your recognition of ancient time, you see nothing of the Italians. The nature of the city assists the delusion, for its vast and antique walls describe a circumference of sixteen miles, and thus the population is thinly scattered over this space, nearly as great as London. Wide wild fields are enclosed within it, and there are grassy lanes and copses winding among the ruins, and a great green hill, lonely and bare, which overhangs the Tiber. The gardens of the modern palaces are like wild woods of cedar, and cypress, and pine, and the neglected walks are overgrown with weeds. The English burying-place is a green slope near the walls, under the pyramidal tomb of Cestius, and is, I think, the most beautiful and solemn cemetery I ever beheld. To see the sun shining on its bright grass, fresh, when we first visited it, with the autumnal dews, and hear the whispering of the wind among the leaves of the trees which have overgrown the tomb of Cestius, and the soil which is stirring in the sun-warm earth, and to mark the tombs, mostly of women and young people who were buried there, one might, if one were to die, desire the sleep they seem to sleep. Such is the human mind, and so it peoples with its wishes vacancy and oblivion.[1]

---

[1] In " Adonais " Shelley gives an exquisite description of this " most beautiful and solemn cemetery," where Keats lay buried, and where his own dust reposed but a few years later. The following lines sound almost like an extract from this letter changed into musical verse : —

" Go thou to Rome, — at once the paradise,
   The grave, the city, and the wilderness ;
And where its wrecks like shattered mountains rise,

I have told you little about Rome ; but I reserve the Pantheon, and St. Peter's, and the Vatican, and Raffaelle, for my return. About a fortnight ago I left Rome, and Mary and C—— followed in three days, for it was necessary to procure lodgings here without alighting at an inn. From my peculiar mode of travelling I saw little of the country, but could just observe that the wild beauty of the scenery and the barbarous ferocity of the inhabitants progressively increased. On entering Naples, the first circumstance that engaged my attention was an assassination. A youth ran out of a shop, pursued by a woman with a bludgeon, and a man armed with a knife. The man overtook him, and with one blow in the neck laid him dead in the road. On my expressing the emotions of horror and indignation which I felt, a Calabrian priest, who travelled with me, laughed heartily, and attempted to quiz me, as what the

>   And flowering weeds, and fragrant copses dress
>   The bones of desolation's nakedness,
>   Pass, till the Spirit of the spot shall lead
>   Thy footsteps to a slope of green access,
>   Where, like an infant's smile over the dead
>   A light of laughing flowers along the grass is spread.
>
> "And gray walls moulder round, on which dull time
>   Feeds, like slow fire upon a hoary brand ;
>   And one keen pyramid with wedge sublime,
>   Pavilioning the dust of him who planned
>   This refuge for his memory, doth stand
>   Like flame transformed to marble ; and beneath
>   A field is spread, on which a newer band
>   Have pitched in heaven's smile their camp of death,
>   Welcoming him we lose with scarce extinguished breath."

English call a flat. I never felt such an inclination to beat any one. Heaven knows I have little power, but he saw that I looked extremely displeased, and was silent. This same man, a fellow of gigantic strength and stature, had expressed the most frantic terror of robbers on the road; he cried at the sight of my pistol, and it had been with great difficulty that the joint exertions of myself and the vetturino had quieted his hysterics.

But external nature in these delightful regions contrasts with and compensates for the deformity and degradation of humanity. We have a lodging divided from the sea by the royal gardens, and from our windows we see perpetually the blue waters of the bay, forever changing, yet forever the same, and encompassed by the mountainous island of Ca-preæ, the lofty peaks which overhang Salerno, and the woody hill of Posilippo, whose promontories hide from us Misenum and the lofty isle Inarime, which, with its divided summit, forms the opposite horn of the bay. From the pleasant walks of the garden we see Vesuvius; a smoke by day and a fire by night is seen upon its summit, and the glassy sea often reflects its light or shadow. The climate is delicious. We sit without a fire, with the windows open, and have almost all the productions of an English summer. The weather is usually like what Wordsworth calls "the first fine day of March"; sometimes very much warmer, though perhaps it wants that "each minute sweeter than before," which gives an intoxicating sweetness to the awaken-ing of the earth from its winter's sleep in England.

We have made two excursions, one to Baiæ and one
to Vesuvius and we propose to visit, successively,
the islands, Pæstum, Pompeii, and Beneventum.

We set off an hour after sunrise one radiant morning in a little boat; there was not a cloud in the sky,
nor a wave upon the sea, which was so translucent
that you could see the hollow caverns clothed with
the glaucous sea-moss, and the leaves and branches
of those delicate weeds that pave the unequal bottom
of the water.[1] As noon approached, the heat, and
especially the light, became intense. We passed
Posilippo, and came first to the eastern point of the
bay of Pozzuoli, which is within the great bay of
Naples, and which again encloses that of Baiæ. Here
are lofty rocks and craggy islets, with arches and
portals of precipice standing in the sea, and enormous caverns, which echoed faintly with the murmur
of the languid tide. This is called La Scuola di
Virgilio. We then went directly across to the promontory of Misenum, leaving the precipitous island
of Nesida on the right. Here we were conducted
to see the Mare Morto, and the Elysian Fields; the
spot on which Virgil places the scenery of the Sixth
Æneid. Though extremely beautiful, as a lake, and
woody hills, and this divine sky must make it, I
confess my disappointment. The guide showed us
an antique cemetery, where the niches used for plac-
ing the cinerary urns of the dead yet remain. We
then coasted the bay of Baiæ to the left, in which

[1] Compare this description with his note to the "Ode to
the West Wind," and with the third stanza of that poem,
which was written shortly after this letter.

we saw many picturesque and interesting ruins ; but
I have to remark that we never disembarked but we
were disappointed, while from the boat the effect
of the scenery was inexpressibly delightful. The
colors of the water and the air breathe over all
things here the radiance of their own beauty. After
passing the bay of Baiæ, and observing the ruins of
its antique grandeur standing like rocks in the transparent sea under our boat, we landed to visit Lake
Avernus. We passed through the cavern of the Sibyl
(not Virgil's Sibyl), which pierces one of the hills
which circumscribe the lake, and came to a calm
and lovely basin of water, surrounded by dark woody
hills, and profoundly solitary. Some vast ruins of
the temple of Pluto stand on a lawny hill on one side
of it, and are reflected in its windless mirror. It is
far more beautiful than the Elysian Fields ; but there
are all the materials for beauty in the latter, and the
Avernus was once a chasm of deadly and pestilential
vapors. About half a mile from Avernus, a high
hill, called Monte Novo, was thrown up by volcanic
fire.

Passing onward we came to Pozzuoli, the ancient
Dicæarchea, where there are the columns remaining
of a temple to Serapis, and the wreck of an enormous amphitheatre, changed, like the Coliseum, into
a natural hill of the overteeming vegetation. Here
also is the Solfatara, of which there is a poetical
description in the Civil War of Petronius, beginning,
" Est locus," and in which the verses of the poet
are infinitely finer than what he describes, for it is
not a very curious place. After seeing these things,

we returned by moonlight to Naples in our boat. What colors there were in the sky, what radiance in the evening star, and how the moon was encompassed by a light unknown to our regions !

Our next excursion was to Vesuvius. We went to Resina in a carriage, where Mary and I mounted mules, and C—— was carried in a chair on the shoulders of four men, much like a member of Parliament after he has gained his election, and looking, with less reason, quite as frightened. So we arrived at the hermitage of San Salvador, where an old hermit, belted with rope, set forth the plates for our refreshment.

Vesuvius is, after the glaciers, the most impressive exhibition of the energies of nature I ever saw. It has not the immeasurable greatness, the overpowering magnificence, nor, above all, the radiant beauty of the glaciers ; but it has all their character of tremendous and irresistible strength. From Resina to the hermitage you wind up the mountain, and cross a vast stream of hardened lava, which is an actual image of the waves of the sea, changed into hard black stone by enchantment. The lines of the boiling flood seem to hang in the air, and it is difficult to believe that the billows which seem hurrying down upon you are not actually in motion. This plain was once a sea of liquid fire. From the hermitage we crossed another vast stream of lava, and then went on foot up the cone. This is the only part of the ascent in which there is any difficulty, and that difficulty has been much exaggerated. It is composed of rocks of lava, and declivities of ashes ; by ascending the former and descending the latter, there is very little fatigue. On the summit is a kind of irregular plain, the most horrible chaos that can be imagined ; riven into ghastly chasms, and heaped up with tumuli of great stones and cinders, and enormous rocks blackened and calcined, which had been thrown from the volcano upon one another in terrible confusion. In the midst stands the conical hill from which volumes of smoke and the fountains of liquid fire are rolled forth forever. The mountain is at present in a slight state of eruption, and a thick, heavy, white smoke is perpetually rolled out, interrupted by enormous columns of an impenetrable black, bituminous vapor, which is hurled up, fold after fold, into the sky, with a deep, hollow sound, and fiery stones are rained down from its darkness, and a black shower of ashes fell even where we sat. The lava, like the glacier, creeps on perpetually, with a crackling sound as of suppressed fire. There are several springs of lava ; and in one place it rushes precipitously over a high crag, rolling down the half-molten rocks and its own overhanging waves, a cataract of quivering fire. We approached the extremity of one of the rivers of lava ; it is about twenty feet in breadth and ten in height, and as the inclined plane was not rapid, its motion was very slow. We saw the masses of its dark exterior surface detach themselves as it moved, and betray the depth of the liquid flame. In the day the fire is but slightly seen ; you only observe a tremulous motion in the air, and streams and fountains of white sulphurous smoke.

At length we saw the sun sink between Capreæ

and Inarime, and, as the darkness increased, the effect of the fire became more beautiful. We were, as it were, surrounded by streams and cataracts of the red and radiant fire ; and in the midst, from the column of bituminous smoke shot up into the air, fell the vast masses of rock, white with the light of their intense heat, leaving behind them through the dark vapor trains of splendor. We descended by torchlight, and I should have enjoyed the scenery on my return, but they conducted me, I know not how, to the hermitage in a state of intense bodily suffering, the worst effect of which was spoiling the pleasure of Mary and C——. Our guides on the occasion were complete savages. You have no idea of the horrible cries which they suddenly utter, no one knows why ; the clamor, the vociferation, the tumult. C—— in her palanquin suffered most from it ; and when I had gone on before, they threatened to leave her in the middle of the road, which they would have done had not my Italian servant promised them a beating, after which they became quiet. Nothing, however, can be more picturesque than the gestures and the physiognomies of these savage people. And when, in the darkness of night, they unexpectedly begin to sing in chorus some fragments of their wild but sweet national music, the effect is exceedingly fine.

Since I wrote this, I have seen the museum of this city. Such statues ! There is a Venus, an ideal shape of the most winning loveliness. A Bacchus, more sublime than any living being. A Satyr, making love to a youth, in which the expressed life of the sculpture and the inconceivable beauty of the form of the youth overcome one's repugnance to the subject. There are multitudes of wonderfully fine statues found in Herculaneum and Pompeii. We are going to see Pompeii the first day that the sea is waveless. Herculaneum is almost filled up ; no more excavations are made ; the King bought the ground, and built a palace upon it.

You don't see much of Hunt. I wish you could contrive to see him when you go to town, and ask him what he means to answer to Lord Byron's invitation. He has now an opportunity, if he likes, of seeing Italy. What do you think of joining his party, and paying us a visit next year, — I mean as soon as the reign of winter is dissolved? Write to me your thoughts upon this. I cannot express to you the pleasure it would give me to welcome such a party.

I have depression enough of spirits and not good health, though I believe the warm air of Naples does me good. We see absolutely no one here.

Adieu, my dear P——.

XLV.

TO T. L. PEACOCK.

NAPLES, *January* 26, 1819.

MY DEAR P., — Your two letters arrived within a few days of each other, one being directed to Naples, and the other to Livorno. They are more welcome visitors to me than mine can be to you,— I writing as from sepulchres, you from the habitations of men yet unburied; though the sexton, Castlereagh, after having dug their grave, stands with his spade in his hand, evidently doubting whether he will not be forced to occupy it himself. Your news about the bank-note trials is excellent good. Do I not recognize in it the influence of Cobbett? You don't tell me what occupies Parliament. I know you will laugh at my demand, and assure me that it is indifferent. Your pamphlet I want exceedingly to see. Your calculations in the letter are clear, but require much oral explanation. You know I am an infernal arithmetician. If none but me had contemplated "lucentemque globum lunæ, Titaniaque astra," the world would yet have doubted whether they were many hundred feet higher than the mountain tops.

In my accounts of pictures and things, I am more pleased to interest you than the many; and this is fortunate, because, in the first place, I have no idea of attempting the latter, and if I did attempt it I should assuredly fail. A perception of the beautiful characterizes those who differ from ordinary men, and those who can perceive it would not buy enough to pay the printer. Besides, I keep no journal, and the only records of my voyage will be the letters I send you. The bodily fatigue of standing for hours in galleries exhausts me ; I believe that I don't see half that I ought, on that account. And then we know nobody ; and the common Italians are so sullen and stupid, it's impossible to get information from them. At Rome, where the people seem superior to any in Italy, I cannot fail to stumble on something more.

Oh, if I had health, and strength, and equal spirits, what boundless intellectual improvement might I not gather in this wonderful country! At present I write little else but poetry, and little of that. My first act of " Prometheus " is complete, and I think you would like it. I consider poetry very subordinate to moral and political science, and if I were well, certainly I would aspire to the latter; for I can conceive a great work, embodying the discoveries of all ages, and harmonizing the contending creeds by which mankind have been ruled. Far from me is such an attempt, and I shall be content, by exercising my fancy, to amuse myself, and perhaps some others, and cast what weight I can into the scale of that balance, which the Giant of Arthegall holds.

Since you last heard from me, we have been to see Pompeii, and are waiting now for the return of spring weather, to visit, first Pæstum, and then the islands; after which we shall return to Rome. I was astonished at the remains of this city; I had no conception of anything so perfect yet remaining.

.   .   .   .

We entered the town from the side towards the sea, and first saw two theatres; one more magnificent than the other, strewn with the ruins of the white marble which formed their seats and cornices, wrought with deep, bold sculpture. In the front, between the stage and the seats, is the circular space occasionally occupied by the chorus. The stage is very narrow, but long, and divided from this space by a narrow enclosure parallel to it, I suppose for the orchestra. On each side are the Consuls' boxes, and below, in the theatre at Herculaneum, were found two equestrian statues of admirable workmanship, occupying the same place as the great bronze lamps did at Drury Lane. The smallest of the theatres is said to have been comic, though I should doubt. From both you see, as you sit on the seats, a prospect of the most wonderful beauty.

You then pass through the ancient streets; they are very narrow, and the houses rather small, but all constructed on an admirable plan, especially for this climate. The rooms are built round a court, or sometimes two, according to the extent of the house. In the midst is a fountain, sometimes surrounded with a portico, supported on fluted columns of white stucco; the floor is paved with mosaic, sometimes wrought in imitation of vine leaves, sometimes in quaint figures, and more or less beautiful, according to the rank of the inhabitant. There were paintings on all, but most of them have been removed to decorate the royal museums. Little winged figures, and small ornaments of exquisite elegance, yet remain. There is an ideal life in the forms of these paintings of an incomparable loveliness, though most are evidently the work of very inferior artists. It seems as if, from the atmosphere of mental beauty which surrounded them, every human being caught a splendor not his own. In one house you see how the bedrooms were managed. A small sofa was built up, where the cushions were placed; two pictures, one representing Diana and Endymion, the other Venus and Mars, decorate the chamber; and a little niche, which contains the statue of a domestic god. The floor is composed of a rich mosaic of the rarest marbles, agate, jasper, and porphyry; it looks to the marble fountain and the snow-white columns, whose entablatures strew the floor of the portico they supported. The houses have only one story, and the apartments, though not large, are very lofty. A great advantage results from this, wholly unknown in our cities. The public buildings, whose ruins are now forests, as it were, of white fluted columns, and which then supported entablatures, loaded with sculptures, were seen on all sides over the roofs of the houses. This was the excellence of the ancients. Their private expenses were comparatively moderate; the dwelling of one of the chief senators of Pompeii is elegant indeed, and adorned with most beautiful specimens of art, but small. But their public buildings are everywhere marked by the bold and grand designs of an unsparing magnificence. In the little town of Pompeii, (it contained about twenty thousand inhabitants,) it is wonderful to see the number and the grandeur of their public buildings. Another advantage, too, is, that in the present case the glorious scenery around is not shut out, and that, unlike the inhabitants of the Cimmerian ravines of modern cities, the ancient Pompeians could contemplate the clouds and the lamps of heaven, — could see the moon rise high behind Vesuvius, and the sun set in the sea, tremulous with an atmosphere of golden vapor, between Inarime and Misenum.

We next saw the temples. Of the temple of Æsculapius little remains but an altar of black stone, adorned with a cornice imitating the scales of a serpent. His statue, in terra-cotta, was found in the cell. The temple of Isis is more perfect. It is surrounded by a portico of fluted columns, and in the area around it are two altars, and many *ceppi* for statues; and a little chapel of white stucco, as hard as stone, of the most exquisite proportion; its panels are adorned with figures in bas-relief, slightly indicated, but of a workmanship the most delicate and perfect that can be conceived. They are Egyptian subjects, executed by a Greek artist, who has harmonized all the unnatural extravagances of the original conception into the supernatural loveliness of his country's genius. They scarcely touch the ground with their feet, and their wind-uplifted robes seem in the place of wings. The temple in the midst, raised on a high platform and approached by steps, was decorated with exquisite paintings, some of which we saw in the museum at Portici. It is small, of the same materials as the chapel, with a pavement of mosaic, and fluted Ionic columns of white stucco, so white that it dazzles you to look at it.

Thence through other porticos and labyrinths of walls and columns (for I cannot hope to detail everything to you), we came to the Forum.

  . . . .

Here was a magnificent spectacle. Above and between the multitudinous shafts of the sun-shining columns was seen the sea, reflecting the purple heaven of noon above it, and supporting, as it were, on its line the dark lofty mountains of Sorrento, of a blue inexpressibly deep, and tinged towards their summits with streaks of new-fallen snow. Between was one small green island. To the right was Capreæ, Inarime, Prochyta, and Misenum. Behind was the single summit of Vesuvius, rolling forth volumes of thick, white smoke, whose foam-like column was sometimes darted into the clear, dark sky, and fell in little streaks along the wind. Between Vesuvius and the nearer mountains, as through a chasm, was seen the main line of the loftiest Apennines, to the east. The day was radiant and warm. Every now and then we heard the subterranean thunder of Vesuvius; its distant deep peals seemed to shake the very air and light of day, which interpenetrated our frames with the sullen and tremendous sound. This sound was what the Greeks beheld (Pompeii, you know, was a Greek city). They lived in harmony with nature; and the interstices of their incomparable columns were portals, as it were, to admit the spirit of beauty which animates this glorious universe to visit those whom it inspired. If such is Pompeii, what was Athens? What scene was exhibited from the Acropolis, the Parthenon, and the temples of Hercules, and Theseus, and the Winds? the islands and the Ægean Sea, the mountains of Argolis, and the peaks of Pindus and Olympus, and the darkness of the Bœotian forests interspersed?

. . . .

Returning hence, and following the consular road, we came to the eastern gate of the city. The walls are of enormous strength, and enclose a space of three miles. On each side of the road beyond the gate are built the tombs. How unlike ours! They seem not so much hiding-places for that which must decay, as voluptuous chambers for immortal spirits. They are of marble, radiantly white ; and two, especially beautiful, are loaded with exquisite bas-reliefs. On the stucco wall that encloses them are little emblematic figures, of a relief exceedingly low, of dead and dying animals, and little winged genii, and female forms bending in groups in some funereal office. The higher reliefs represent, one a nautical subject, and the other a Bacchanalian one. Within the cell stand the cinerary urns, sometimes one, sometimes more. It is said that paintings were found within, which are now, as has been everything movable in Pompeii, removed, and scattered about in royal museums. These tombs were the most impressive things of all. The wild woods surround them on either side, and along the broad stones of the paved road which divides them, you hear the late leaves of autumn shiver and rustle in the stream of the inconstant wind, as it were like the step of ghosts. The radiance and magnificence of these dwellings of the dead, the white freshness of the scarcely finished marble, the impassioned or imaginative life of the figures which adorn them, contrast strangely with the simplicity of the houses of those who were living when Vesuvius overwhelmed them.

I have forgotten the amphitheatre, which is of great magnitude, though much inferior to the Coliseum. I now understand why the Greeks were such great poets ; and, above all, I can account, it seems to me, for the harmony, the unity, the perfection, the uniform excellence, of all their works of art. They lived in a perpetual commerce with external nature, and nourished themselves upon the spirit of its forms. Their theatres were all open to the mountains and the sky. Their columns, the ideal types of a sacred forest, with its roof of interwoven tracery, admitted the light and wind; the odor and the freshness of the country penetrated the cities. Their temples were mostly upaithric; and the flying clouds, the stars, or the deep sky, were seen above. Oh, but for that series of wretched wars which terminated in the Roman conquest of the world, . . . but for those changes that conducted Athens to its ruin, to what an eminence might not humanity have arrived!

In a short time I hope to tell you something of the museum of this city.

You see how ill I follow the maxim of Horace, at least in its literal sense, " Nil admirari," — which I should say, " properes est una," — to prevent there ever being anything admirable in the world. Fortunately Plato is of my opinion; and I had rather err with Plato than be right with Horace.

At this moment I received your letter, indicating that you are removing to London. I am very much interested in the subject of this change, and beg you would write me all the particulars of it. You will be able now to give me perhaps a closer insight into the politics of the times than was permitted you at Marlow. Of H—— I have a very slight opinion. There are rumors here of a revolution in Spain. A ship came in twelve days from Catalonia, and brought a report that the King was massacred; that eighteen thousand insurgents surrounded Madrid ; but that before the popular party gained head enough, seven thousand were murdered by the Inquisition.   Perhaps you know all by this time.   The old King of Spain is dead here.   Corbett is a fine ὑμνοποιός, — does his influence increase or diminish?   What a pity that so powerful a genius should be combined with the most odious moral qualities.

We have reports here of a change in the English ministry.   To what does it amount? for, besides my national interest in it, I am on the watch to vindicate my most sacred rights, invaded by the chancery court.

I suppose now we shall not see you in Italy this spring, whether Hunt comes or not.   It 's probable I shall hear nothing from him for some months, particularly if he does not come.   Give me *ses nouvelles*.

.   .   .   .

I have scarcely been out since I wrote last. Adieu.   Yours most faithfully.

XLVI.

TO T. L. PEACOCK.

NAPLES, *February* 25, 1819.

MY DEAR PEACOCK, — I am much interested to hear your progress in the object of your removal to London.   There is no person in the world who would more sincerely rejoice in any good that might befall you than I should.

We are on the point of quitting Naples for Rome. The scenery which surrounds this city is more delightful than any within the immediate reach of civilized man. I do not think I have mentioned to you the Lago d' Agnano and the Caccia d' Ischieri, and I have since seen what obscures those lovely forms in my memory. They are both the craters of extinguished volcanoes, and nature has thrown forth forests of oak and ilex, and spread mossy lawns and clear lakes over the dead or sleeping fire. The first is a scene of a wider and milder character, with soft sloping wooded hills, and grassy declivities declining to the lake, and cultivated plains of vines woven upon poplar trees, bounded by the theatre of hills. Innumerable wild water birds, quite tame, inhabit this place. The other is a royal chase, is surrounded by steep and lofty hills, and only accessible through a wide gate of massy oak, from the vestibule of which the spectacle of precipitous hills, hemming in a narrow and circular vale, is suddenly disclosed. The hills are covered with thick woods of ilex, myrtle, and laurustinus; the polished leaves of the ilex, as they wave in their multitudes under the partial blasts which rush through the chasms of the vale, glitter above the dark masses of foliage below, like the white foam of waves upon a deep blue sea. The plain so surrounded is at most three miles in circumference. It is occupied partly by a lake, with bold shores wooded by evergreens, and interrupted by a sylvan promontory of the wild forest, whose mossy boughs

overhang its expanse, of a silent and purple darkness,
like an Italian midnight ; and partly by the forest
itself, of all gigantic trees, but the oak especially,
whose jagged boughs, now leafless, are hoary with
thick lichens, and loaded with the massy and deep
foliage of the ivy. The effect of the dark eminences
that surround this plain, seen through the boughs,
is of an enchanting solemnity. (There we saw in
one instance wild boars and a deer, and in another —
a spectacle little suited to the antique and Latonian
nature of the place — King Ferdinand in a winter
enclosure, watching to shoot wild boars.) The underwood was principally evergreen, all lovely kinds of
fern and furze ; the cytisus, a delicate kind of furze
with a pretty yellow blossom, the myrtle, and the
myrica. The willow trees had just begun to put
forth their green and golden buds, and gleamed like
points of lambent fire among the wintry forest. The
Grotta del Cane, too, we saw, because other people
see it ; but would not allow the dogs to be exhibited
in torture for our curiosity. The poor little animals
stood moving their tails in a slow and dismal manner,
as if perfectly resigned to their condition, — a cur-
like emblem of voluntary servitude. The effect of
the vapor, which extinguishes a torch, is to cause
suffocation at last, through a process which makes
the lungs feel as if they were torn by sharp points
within. So a surgeon told us, who tried the experi-
ment on himself.

There was a Greek city, sixty miles to the south
of Naples, called Posidonia, now Pesto, where there
still subsist three temples of Etruscan architecture,

one almost perfect. From this city we have just returned. The weather was most unfavorable for our expedition. After two months of cloudless serenity, it began raining cats and dogs. The first night we slept at Salerno, a large city situate in the recess of a deep bay, surrounded with stupendous mountains of the same name. A few miles from Torre del Greco we entered on the pass of the mountains, which is a line dividing the isthmus of those enormous piles of rock which compose the southern boundary of the bay of Naples, and the northern one of that of Salerno. On one side is a lofty conical hill, crowned with the turrets of a ruined castle, and cut into platforms for cultivation, — at least every ravine and glen whose precipitous sides admitted of other vegetation but that of the rock-rooted ilex ; on the other, the ethereal snowy crags of an immense mountain, whose terrible lineaments were at intervals concealed or disclosed by volumes of dense clouds, rolling under the tempest. Half a mile from this spot, between orange and lemon groves of a lovely village, suspended as it were on an amphitheatral precipice, whose golden globes contrasted with the white walls and dark green leaves which they almost outnumbered, shone the sea. A burst of the declining sunlight illumined it. The road led along the brink of the precipice towards Salerno. Nothing could be more glorious than the scene. The immense mountains covered with the rare and divine vegetation of this climate, with many-folding vales, and deep dark recesses, which the fancy scarcely could penetrate, descended from their snowy summits precipitously to the sea.   Before us was Salerno, built into a declining plain, between the mountains and the sea.   Beyond, the other shore of sky-cleaving mountains, then dim with the mist of tempest. Underneath, from the base of the precipice where the road conducted, rocky promontories jutted into the sea, covered with olive and ilex woods, or with the ruined battlements of some Norman or Saracen fortress.   We slept at Salerno, and the next morning before daybreak proceeded to Posidonia.   The night had been tempestuous, and our way lay by the sea sand.   It was utterly dark, except when the long line of wave burst, with a sound like thunder, beneath the starless sky, and cast up a kind of mist of cold white lustre.   When morning came, we found ourselves travelling in a wide desert plain, perpetually interrupted by wild irregular glens, and bounded on all sides by the Apennines and the sea.   Sometimes it was covered with forest, sometimes dotted with underwood, or mere tufts of fern and furze, and the wintry dry tendrils of creeping plants.   I have never, but in the Alps, seen an amphitheatre of mountains so magnificent.   After travelling fifteen miles we came to a river, the bridge of which had been broken, and which was so swollen that the ferry would not take the carriage across.   We had, therefore, to walk seven miles of a muddy road which led to the ancient city across the desolate Maremma. The air was scented with the sweet smell of violets of an extraordinary size and beauty.   At length we saw the sublime and massy colonnades, skirting the horizon of the wilderness.   We entered by the ancient gate, which is now no more than a chasm in the rock-like wall. Deeply sunk in the ground beside it, were the ruins of a sepulchre, which the ancients were in the custom of building beside the public way. The first temple, which is the smallest, consists of an outer range of columns, quite perfect, and supporting a perfect architrave and two shattered frontispieces. The proportions are extremely massy, and the architecture entirely unornamented and simple. These columns do not seem more than forty feet high, but the perfect proportions diminish the apprehension of their magnitude; it seems as if inequality and irregularity of form were requisite to force on us the relative idea of greatness. The scene from between the columns of the temple consists, on one side, of the sea, to which the gentle hill on which it is built slopes, and on the other, of the grand amphitheatre of the loftiest Apennines, dark purple mountains, crowned with snow and intercepted there by long bars of hard and leaden-colored cloud. The effect of the jagged outline of mountains, through groups of enormous columns on one side, and on the other the level horizon of the sea, is inexpressibly grand. The second temple .is much larger, and also more perfect. Beside the outer range of columns, it contains an interior range of column above column, and the ruins of a wall, which was the screen of the penetralia. With little diversity of ornament, the order of architecture is similar to that of the first temple.

.　.　.　.　.　.　.

We only contemplated these sublime monuments

for two hours, and of course could only bring away so imperfect a conception of them as is the shadow of some half-remembered dream.

The royal collection of paintings in this city is sufficiently miserable. Perhaps the most remarkable is the original studio by Michael Angelo of the "Day of Judgment," which is painted in *fresco* on the Sixtine Chapel of the Vatican. It is there so defaced as to be wholly indistinguishable. I cannot but think the genius of this artist highly overrated. He has not only no temperance, no modesty, no feeling for the just boundaries of art, (and in these respects an admirable genius may err,) but he has no sense of beauty, and to want this is to want the sense of the creative power of mind. What is terror without a contrast with, and a connection with, loveliness. How well Dante understood this secret,— Dante, with whom this artist has been so presumptuously compared ! What a thing his "Moses" is; how distorted from all that is natural and majestic. . . . In the picture to which I allude, God is leaning out of heaven. The Holy Ghost, in the shape of a dove, is under him. Under the Holy Ghost stands Jesus Christ, in an attitude of haranguing the assembly. This figure, which his subject, or rather the view which it became him to take of it, ought to have modelled of a calm, severe, awe-inspiring majesty, is in the attitude of commonplace resentment. On one side of this figure are the elect ; on the other, the host of heaven ; they ought to have been what the Christians call *glorified bodies*, floating onward, and radiant with that everlasting light (I speak in the spirit of their faith) which had consumed their mortal veil. They are in fact very ordinary people. Below is the ideal purgatory, I imagine, in mid air, in the shapes of spirits, some of whom demons are dragging down, others falling as it were by their own weight, others half suspended in that Mahomet-coffin kind of attitude which most moderate Christians, I believe, expect to assume. Every step towards hell approximates to the region of the artist's exclusive power. There is great imagination in many of the situations of these unfortunate spirits. But hell and death are his real sphere. The bottom of the picture is divided by a lofty rock, in which there is a cavern whose entrance is thronged by devils, some coming in with spirits, some going out for prey. The blood-red light of the fiery abyss glows through their dark forms. On one side are the devils in all hideous forms, struggling with the damned, who have received their sentence, and are chained in all forms of agony by knotted serpents, and writhing on the crags in every variety of torture. On the other are the dead, coming out of their graves, — horrible forms. Such is the famous "Day of Judgment" of Michael Angelo; a kind of "Titus Andronicus" in painting, but the author surely no Shakespeare. The other paintings are one or two of Raffaelle or his pupils, very sweet and lovely. A "Danaë" of Titian, a picture, the softest and most voluptuous form, with languid and uplifted eyes, and warm yet passive limbs. A "Madalena," by Guido, with dark brown hair, and dark brown eyes, and an earnest, soft, melancholy look. And some excellent pictures, in point of execution, by Annibal Caracci. None others worth a second look.   Of the gallery of statues I cannot speak.   They require a volume, not a letter.   Still less what can I do at Rome?

I have just seen the Quarterly for September, not from my own box.   I suppose there is no chance now of the organization of a review!   This is a great pity.   The Quarterly is undoubtedly conducted with talent, great talent, and affords a dreadful preponderance against the cause of improvement.   If a band of stanch reformers, resolute and skilful, were united in so close and constant a league as that in which interest and fanaticism have bound the members of that literary coalition !

Adieu.   Address your next letter to Rome, whence you shall hear from me soon again.   M. and C. unite with me in the very kindest remembrances.

XLVII.

TO T. L. PEACOCK.

ROME, *March* 23, 1819.

MY DEAR P., — I wrote to you the day before our departure from Naples.   We came by slow journeys, with our own horses, to Rome, resting one day at Mola di Gaeta, at the inn called Villa di Cicerone, from being built on the ruins of his villa, whose immense substructions overhang the sea, and are scattered among the orange groves.   Nothing can be lovelier than the scene from the terraces of the inn. On one side precipitous mountains, whose bases slope into an inclined plane of olive and orange copses, the latter forming, as it were, an emerald sky of leaves, starred with innumerable globes of their ripening fruit, whose rich splendor contrasted with the deep green foliage; on the other the sea, bounded on one side by the antique town of Gaeta, on the other by what appears to be an island, the promontory of Circe. From Gaeta to Terracina the whole scenery is of the most sublime character. At Terracina, precipitous conical crags of immense height shoot into the sky and overhang the sea. At Albano, we arrived again in sight of Rome. Arches after arches in unending lines stretching across the uninhabited wilderness, the blue defined line of the mountains seen between them; masses of nameless ruin standing like rocks out of the plain; and the plain itself, with its billowy and unequal surface, announced the neighborhood of Rome. And what shall I say to you of Rome? If I speak of the inanimate ruins, the rude stones piled upon stones, which are the sepulchres of the fame of those who once arrayed them with the beauty which has faded, will you believe me insensible to the vital, the almost breathing creations of genius yet subsisting in their perfection? What has become, you will ask, of the Apollo, the Gladiator, the Venus of the Capitol? What of the Apollo di Belvedere, the Laocoön? What of Raffaelle and Guido? These things are best spoken of when the mind has drunk in the spirit of their forms; and little indeed can I, who must devote no more than a few months to the contemplation of them, hope to know or feel of their profound beauty.

I think I told you of the Coliseum, and its impressions on me on my first visit to this city. The next most considerable relic of antiquity, considered as a ruin, is the Thermæ of Caracalla. These consist of six enormous chambers, above two hundred feet in height, and each enclosing a vast space like that of a field. There are, in addition, a number of towers and labyrinthine recesses, hidden and woven over by the wild growth of weeds and ivy. Never was any desolation more sublime and lovely. The perpendicular wall of ruin is cloven into steep ravines filled up with flowering shrubs, whose thick twisted roots are knotted in the rifts of the stones. At every step the aerial pinnacles of shattered stone group into new combinations of effect, and tower above the lofty yet level walls, as the distant mountains change their aspect to one travelling rapidly along the plain. The perpendicular walls resemble nothing more than that cliff of Bisham wood, that is overgrown with wood, and yet is stony and precipitous, — you know the one I mean ; not the chalk-pit, but the spot that has the pretty copse of fir trees and privet bushes at its base, and where H—— and I scrambled up, and you, to my infinite discontent, would go home. These walls surround green and level spaces of lawn, on which some elms have grown, and which are interspersed towards their skirts by masses of the fallen ruin, overtwined with the broad leaves of the creeping weeds. The blue sky canopies it, and is as the everlasting roof of these enormous halls.

But the most interesting effect remains. In one

of the buttresses, that supports an immense and lofty arch, " which bridges the very winds of heaven," are the crumbling remains of an antique winding staircase, whose sides are open in many places to the precipice. This you ascend, and arrive on the summit of these piles. There grow on every side thick entangled wildernesses of myrtle, and the myrletus, and bay, and the flowering laurestinus, whose white blossoms are just developed, the white fig, and a thousand nameless plants sown by the wandering winds. These woods are intersected on every side by paths, like sheep-tracks through the copsewood of steep mountains, which wind to every part of the immense labyrinth. From the midst rise those pinnacles and masses, themselves like mountains, which have been seen from below. In one place you wind along a narrow strip of weed-grown ruin : on one side is the immensity of earth and sky, on the other a narrow chasm, which is bounded by an arch of enormous size, fringed by the many-colored foliage and blossoms, and supporting a lofty and irregular pyramid, overgrown like itself with the all-prevailing vegetation. Around rise other crags and other peaks, all arrayed, and the deformity of their vast desolation softened down, by the undecaying investiture of nature. Come to Rome. It is a scene by which expression is overpowered, — which words cannot convey. Still further, winding up one half of the shattered pyramids, by the path through the blooming copsewood, you come to a little mossy lawn, surrounded by the wild shrubs ; it is overgrown with anemones, wall-flowers, and violets, whose stalks pierce the starry moss, and with radiant blue flowers, whose names I know not, and which scatter through the air the divinest odor, which, as you recline under the shade of the ruin, produces sensations of voluptuous faintness, like the combinations of sweet music. The paths still wind on, threading the perplexed windings, other labyrinths, other lawns, and deep dells of wood, and lofty rocks, and terrific chasms. When I tell you that these ruins cover several acres, and that the paths above penetrate at least half their extent, your imagination will fill up all that I am unable to express of this astonishing scene.

I speak of these things, not in the order in which I visited them, but in that of the impression which they made on me, or perhaps chance directs. The ruins of the ancient Forum are so far fortunate that they have not been walled up in the modern city. They stand in an open, lonesome place, bounded on one side by the modern city, and the other by the Palatine Mount, covered with shapeless masses of ruin. The tourists tell you all about these things, and I am afraid of stumbling on their language when I enumerate what is so well known. There remain eight granite columns of the Ionic order, with their entablature, of the temple of Concord, founded by Camillus. I fear that the immense expanse demanded by these columns forbids us to hope that they are the remains of any edifice dedicated by that most perfect and virtuous of men. It is supposed to have been repaired under the Eastern Emperors; alas, what a contrast of recollections! Near them stand those Corinthian fluted columns, which supported the

angle of a temple; the architrave and entablature
are worked with delicate sculpture. Beyond, to the
south, is another solitary column; and still more
distant, three more, supporting the wreck of an
entablature. Descending from the Capitol to the
Forum, is the triumphal arch of Septimius Severus,
less perfect than that of Constantine, though from
its proportions and magnitude a most impressive
monument. That of Constantine, or rather of Titus,
(for the relief and sculpture, and even the colossal
images of Dacian captives, were torn by a decree of
the Senate from an arch dedicated to the latter, to
adorn that of this stupid and wicked monster, Constantine, one of whose chief merits consists in estab-
lishing a religion the destroyer of those arts which
would have rendered so base a spoliation unnecessary,)
is the most perfect. It is an admirable work of art.
It is built of the finest marble, and the outline of the
reliefs is in many parts as perfect as if just finished.
Four Corinthian fluted columns support, on each
side, a bold entablature, whose bases are loaded
with reliefs of captives in every attitude of humiliation and slavery. The compartments above express,
in bolder relief, the enjoyment of success, — the conqueror on his throne, or in his chariot, or nodding
over the crushed multitudes, who writhe under his
horses' hoofs; as those below express the torture and
abjectness of defeat. There are three arches, whose
roofs are panelled with fretwork, and their sides
adorned with similar reliefs. The keystone of these
arches is supported each by two winged figures of
Victory, whose hair floats on the wind of their own

speed, and whose arms are outstretched, bearing trophies, as if impatient to meet. They look, as it were, borne from the subject extremities of the earth, on the breath which is the exhalation of that battle and desolation which it is their mission to commemorate. Never were monuments so completely fitted to the purpose for which they were designed, of expressing that mixture of energy and error which is called a triumph.

I walk forth in the purple and golden light of an Italian evening, and return by star or moonlight, through this scene. The elms are just budding, and the warm spring winds bring unknown odors, all sweet from the country. I see the radiant Orion through the mighty columns of the temple of Concord, and the mellow fading light softens down the modern buildings of the Capitol, the only ones that interfere with the sublime desolation of the scene. On the steps of the Capitol itself stand two colossal statues of Castor and Pollux, each with his horse, finely executed, though far inferior to those of Monte Cavallo, the cast of one of which you know we saw together in London. This walk is close to our lodging, and this is my evening walk.

What shall I say of the modern city? Rome is yet the capital of the world. It is a city of palaces and temples, more glorious than those which any other city contains, and of ruins more glorious than they. Seen from any of the eminences that surround it, it exhibits domes beyond domes, and palaces, and colonnades, interminably, even to the horizon; interspersed with patches of desert, and mighty ruins which stand girt by their own desolation, in the midst of the fanes of living religions and the habitations of living men, in sublime loneliness.

.   .   .   .   .   .

The effect of the Pantheon is totally the reverse of that of St. Peter's. Though not a fourth part of the size, it is, as it were, the visible image of the universe ; in the perfection of its proportions, as when you regard the unmeasured dome of heaven, the idea of magnitude is swallowed up and lost. It is open to the sky, and its wide dome is lighted by the ever-changing illumination of the air. The clouds of noon fly over it, and at night the keen stars are seen through the azure darkness, hanging immovably, or driving after the driving moon among the clouds. We visited it by moonlight ; it is supported by sixteen columns, fluted and Corinthian, of a certain rare and beautiful yellow marble, exquisitely polished, called here *giallo antico*. Above these are the niches for the statues of the twelve gods. This is the only defect of this sublime temple ; there ought to have been no interval between the commencement of the dome and the cornice, supported by the columns. Thus there would have been no diversion from the magnificent simplicity of its form. This improvement is alone wanting to have completed the unity of the idea.

The fountains of Rome are, in themselves, magnificent combinations of art, such as alone it were worth coming to see. That in the Piazza Navona, a large square, is composed of enormous fragments of rock, piled on each other, and penetrated as by caverns. This mass supports an Egyptian obelisk of immense height. On the four corners of the rock recline, in different attitudes, colossal figures representing the four divisions of the globe. The water bursts from the crevices beneath them. They are sculptured with great spirit; one impatiently tearing a veil from his eyes; another with his hands stretched upwards. The Fontana di Trevi is the most celebrated, and is rather a waterfall than a fountain, gushing out from masses of rock, with a gigantic figure of Neptune; and below are two river gods, checking two winged horses, struggling up from among the rocks and waters. The whole is not ill conceived nor executed; but you know not how delicate the imagination becomes by dieting with antiquity day after day! The only things that sustain the comparison are Raffaelle, Guido, and Salvator Rosa.

The fountain on the Quirinal, or rather the group formed by the statues, obelisk, and the fountain, is, however, the most admirable of all. From the Piazza Quirinale, or rather Monte Cavallo, you see the boundless ocean of domes, spires, and columns, which is the city, Rome. On a pedestal of white marble rises an obelisk of red granite, piercing the blue sky. Before it is a vast basin of porphyry, in the midst of which rises a column of the purest water, which collects into itself all the overhanging colors of the sky, and breaks them into a thousand prismatic hues and graduated shadows; they fall together with its dashing water-drops into the outer basin. The elevated situation of this fountain produces, I imagine, this effect of color. On each side, on an elevated pedestal, stand the statues of Castor and Pollux, each in the act of taming his horse ; which are said, but I believe wholly without authority, to be the work of Phidias and Praxiteles. These figures combine the irresistible energy with the sublime and perfect loveliness supposed to have belonged to their divine nature. The reins no longer exist, but the position of their hands, and the sustained and calm command of their regard, seem to require no mechanical aid to enforce obedience. The countenances at so great a height are scarcely visible, and I have a better idea of that of which we saw a cast together in London than of the other. But the sublime and living majesty of their limbs and mien, the nervous and fiery animation of the horses they restrain, seen in the blue sky of Italy, and overlooking the city of Rome, surrounded by the light and the music of that crystalline fountain, no cast can communicate.

These figures were found at the Baths of Constantine, but, of course, are of remote antiquity. I do not acquiesce, however, in the practice of attributing to Phidias, or Praxiteles, or Scopas, or some great master, any admirable work that may be found. We find little of what remained, and perhaps the works of these were such as greatly surpassed all that we conceive of most perfect and admirable in what little has escaped the *deluge*. If I am too jealous of the honor of the Greeks, our masters and creators, the gods whom we should worship, pardon me.

. . . .

XLVIII.

TO T. L. PEACOCK.

ROME, *April* 6, 1819.

MY DEAR P., — I sent you yesterday a long letter, all about antique Rome, which you had better keep for some leisure day. I received yours, and one of Hunt's, yesterday. — So you know the B——s? I could not help considering Mrs. B., when I knew her, as the most admirable specimen of a human being I had ever seen. Nothing earthly ever appeared to be more perfect than her character and manners. It is improbable that I shall ever meet again the person whom I so much esteemed, and still admire. I wish, however, that when you see her you would tell her that I have not forgotten her, nor any of the amiable circle once assembled round her; and that I desire such remembrances to her as an exile and a *Pariah* may be permitted to address to an acknowledged member of the community of mankind. I hear they dined at your lodgings. But no mention of A—— and his wife, — where were they? C——, though so young when I saw her, gave indications of her mother's excellences, and, certainly less fascinating, is, I doubt not, equally amiable, and more sincere. It was hardly possible for a person of the extreme subtlety and delicacy of Mrs. B——'s understanding and affections, to be quite sincere and constant.

.   .   .   .

When shall I return to England? The Pythia has ascended the tripod, but she replies not. Our present plans — and I know not what can induce us to alter them — lead us back to Naples in a month or six weeks, where it is almost decided that we should remain until the commencement of 1820. You may imagine, when we receive such letters as yours and Hunt's, what this resolution costs us, but these are not our only communications from England. My health is materially better; my spirits, not the most brilliant in the world; but that we attribute to our solitary situation, and, though happy, how should I be lively? We see something of Italian society indeed. The Romans please me much, especially the women, who, though totally devoid of every kind of information, or culture of the imagination, or affections, or understanding — and in this respect a kind of gentle savages — yet contrive to be interesting. Their extreme innocence and naïveté, the freedom and gentleness of their manners; the total absence of affectation, makes an intercourse with them very like an intercourse with uncorrupted children, whom they resemble in loveliness as well as simplicity. I have seen two women in society here of the highest beauty; their brows and lips, and the moulding of the face, modelled with sculptural exactness, and the dark luxuriance of their hair floating over their fine complexions; and the lips, — you must hear the commonplaces which escape from them before they cease to be dangerous. The only inferior part are the eyes, which, though good and gentle, want the mazy depth of color behind color, with which the intellectual women of England

and Germany entangle the heart in soul-inwoven labyrinths.

This is holy week, and Rome is quite full. The
Emperor of Austria is here, and Maria Louisa is
coming.   On their journey through the other cities of
Italy, she was greeted with loud acclamations, and
vivas of Napoleon. Idiots and slaves ! Like the
frogs in the fable, because they are discontented with
the log, they call upon the stork, who devours them.
Great festas, and magnificent funzioni here,— we cannot get tickets to all.   There are five thousand strangers in Rome, and only room for five hundred at the
celebration of the famous Miserere in the Sixtine
Chapel, the only thing I regret we shall not be present at.   After all, Rome is eternal ; and were all that
is extinguished, that which *has been*, the ruins and
the sculptures, would remain, and Raffaelle and Guido
be alone regretted.

In the Square of St. Peter's there are about three
hundred fettered criminals at work, hoeing out the
weeds that grow between the stones of the pavement.
Their legs are heavily ironed, and some are chained
two by two.   They sit in long rows, hoeing out the
weeds, dressed in parti-colored clothes.   Near them
sit or saunter groups of soldiers, armed with loaded
muskets.   The iron discord of those innumerable
chains clanks up into the sonorous air, and produces,
contrasted with the musical dashing of the fountains,
and the deep azure beauty of the sky, and the magnificence of the architecture around, a conflict of
sensations allied to madness.   It is the emblem of
Italy, — moral degradation contrasted with the glory
of nature and the arts.

We see no English society here ; it is not probable that we would if we desired it, and I am certain that we should find it unsupportable. The manners of the rich English are wholly unsupportable, and they assume pretensions which they would not venture upon in their own country. I am yet ignorant of the event of Hobhouse's election. I saw the last numbers were, Lamb 4,200, and Hobhouse 3,900, 14th day. There is little hope. That mischievous Cobbett has divided and weakened the interests of the popular party, so that the factions that prey upon our country have been able to coalesce to its exclusion. The N——s you have not seen. I am curious to know what kind of a girl Octavia becomes ; she promised well. Tell H—— his Melpomene is in the Vatican, and that her attitude and drapery surpass, if possible, the graces of her countenance.

My "Prometheus Unbound" is just finished, and in a month or two I shall send it. It is a drama, with characters and mechanism of a kind yet unattempted ; and I think the execution is better than any of my former attempts. By the by, have you seen Ollier? I never hear from him, and am ignorant whether some verses I sent him from Naples, entitled, I think, "Lines on the Euganean Hills," have reached him in safety or not. As to the Reviews, I suppose there is nothing but abuse, and this is not hearty or sincere enough to amuse me. As to the poem now printing,[1] I lay no stress on it one way or the other. The concluding lines are natural.

[1] "Rosalind and Helen."

I believe, my dear P., that you wish us to come back to England.   How is it possible?   Health, competence, tranquillity, — all these Italy permits, and England takes away.   I am regarded by all who know or hear of me, except, I think, on the whole, five individuals, as a rare prodigy of crime and pollution, whose look even might infect.   This is a large computation, and I don't think I could mention more than three.   Such is the spirit of the English abroad as well as at home.

Few compensate, indeed, for all the rest, and if I were *alone* I should laugh ; or if I were rich enough to do all things, which I shall never be.   Pity me for my absence from those social enjoyments which England might afford me, and which I know so well how to appreciate.   Still I shall return some fine morning out of pure weakness of heart.

XLIX.

TO MR. AND MRS. GISBORNE.

(Leghorn.)

ROME, *April* 6, 1819.

MY DEAR FRIENDS, — A combination of circumstances, which Mary will explain to you, leads us back to Naples in June, or rather the end of May, where we shall remain until the ensuing winter.   We shall take a house at Portici or Castel a Mare, until late in the autumn.

The object of this letter is to ask you to spend

this period with us. There is no society which we have regretted or desired so much as yours, and in our solitude the benefit of your concession would be greater than I can express. What is a sail to Naples? It is the season of tranquil weather and prosperous winds. If I knew the magic that lay in any given form of words, I would employ them to persuade; but I fear that all I can say is, as you know with truth, we desire that you would come, — we wish to see you. You came to see Mary at Lucca, directly I had departed to Venice. It is not our custom, when we can help it, any more than it is yours, to divide our pleasures.

What shall I say to entice you? We shall have a piano, and some books, and — little else, besides ourselves. But what will be most inviting to you, you will give much, though you may receive but little pleasure.

But whilst I write this with more desire than hope, yet some of that, perhaps the project may fall into your designs. It is intolerable to think of your being buried at Livorno. The success assured by Mr. Reveley's talents requires another scene. You may have decided to take this summer to consider, — and why not with us at Naples, rather than at Livorno?

I could address with respect to Naples, the words of Polypheme in Theocritus, to all the friends I wish to see, and you especially :

'Εξένθοις, Γαλάτεια, καὶ ἐξενθοῖσα λάθοιο,
"Ωσπερ ἐγὼ νῦν ᾧδε καθήμενος, οἴκαδ' ἀπενθεῖν.[1]

[1] Come, O Galatea, and having come, forget, as do I, now sitting here, to return home. — M. S.

L.

TO T. L. PEACOCK.

LIVORNO, *June* 20, 1819.

MY DEAR PEACOCK, — Our melancholy journey finishes at this town, but we retrace our steps to Florence, where, as I imagine, we shall remain some months.[1] O that I could return to England! How heavy a weight when misfortune is added to exile, and solitude, as if the measure were not full, heaped high on both. O that I could return to England! I hear you say, " Desire never fails to generate capacity." Ah! but that ever-present Malthus, Necessity, has convinced Desire that, even though it generated capacity, its offspring must starve. Enough of melancholy! " Nightmare Abbey," though no cure, is a palliative. I have just received the parcel which contained it, and at the same time the Examiners, by the way of Malta. I am delighted with " Nightmare Abbey." I think Scythrop a character admirably conceived and executed; and I know not how to praise sufficiently the lightness, chastity, and strength of the language of the whole.[2] It perhaps

---

[1] On June 7th, Shelley's child, William, died at Rome. He immediately left Rome for Livorno, a change being necessary to his wife's health and spirits. They remained at Livorno four months.

[2] In portraying the character of Scythrop, Peacock seized on several of the traits in Shelley's character. See Mrs. Shelley's notes to Poems of 1817.

exceeds all your works in this. The catastrophe is excellent. I suppose the moral is contained in what Falstaff says, " For God's sake, talk like a man of this world " ; and yet, looking deeper into it, is not the misdirected enthusiasm of Scythrop what J. C. calls the " salt of the earth " ? My friends the Gisbornes here admire and delight in it exceedingly. I think I told you that they (especially the lady) are people of high cultivation. She is a woman of profound accomplishments and the most refined taste.

Cobbett still more and more delights me, with all my horror of the sanguinary commonplaces of his creed. His design to overthrow bank-notes by for-gery is very comic. One of the volumes of Birbeck interested me exceedingly. The letters I think stu-pid, but suppose that they are useful.

I do not, as usual, give you an account of my journey, for I had neither the health nor the spirit to take notes. My health was greatly improving, when watching and anxiety cast me into a relapse. The doctors (I put little faith in the best) tell me I must spend the winter in Africa or Spain. I shall of course prefer the latter, if I choose either.

Are you married, or why do I not hear from you? *That* were a good reason.

. . . .

When shall I see you again?

LI.

TO T. L. PEACOCK.

LIVORNO, *July* 6, 1819.

MY DEAR PEACOCK, — I have lost some letters, and, in all probability, at least one from you, as I can account in no other manner for not having heard from you since March 26th. We have changed our design of going to Florence immediately, and are now established for three months in a little country house in a pretty verdant scene near Livorno.

I have a study here in a tower, something like Scythrop's, where I am just beginning to recover the faculties of reading and writing. My health, whenever no Libecchio blows, improves. From my tower I see the sea, with its islands, Gorgona, Capraja, Elba, and Corsica, on one side, and the Apennines on the other. Milly surprised us the other day by first discovering a comet, on which we have been speculating. She may "make a stir, like a great astronomer."

.   .   .   .

All good wishes, and many hopes that you have already that success on which there will be no congratulations more cordial than those you will receive from me.

LII.

TO T. L. PEACOCK.

LIVORNO, *July*, 1819.

MY DEAR P.,—We still remain, and shall remain nearly two months longer, at Livorno. Our house is a melancholy one, and only cheered by letters from England. I got your note, in which you speak of three letters having been sent to Naples, which I have written for. I have heard also from H——, who confirms the news of your success, an intelligence most grateful to me.

The object of the present letter is to ask a favor of you. I have written a tragedy, on the subject of a story well known in Italy, and, in my conception, eminently dramatic. I have taken some pains to make my play fit for representation, and those who have already seen it judge favorably. It is written without any of the peculiar feelings and opinions which characterize my other compositions; I having attended simply to the impartial development of such characters as it is probable the persons represented really were, together with the greatest degree of popular effect to be produced by such a development. I send you a translation of the Italian manuscript on which my play is founded, the chief subject of which I have touched very delicately; for my principal doubt, as to whether it would succeed as an acting play, hangs entirely on the question as to

whether such a thing as incest in this shape, however treated, would be admitted on the stage. I
think, however, it will form no objection : considering, first, that the facts are matter of history ; and,
secondly, the peculiar delicacy with which I have
treated it.[1]

I am exceedingly interested in the question of
whether this attempt of mine will succeed or no. I
am strongly inclined to the affirmative at present,
founding my hopes on this, that, as a composition, it
is certainly not inferior to any of the modern plays
that have been acted, with the exception of "Remorse"; that the interest of its plot is incredibly
greater and more real; and that there is nothing
beyond what the multitude are contented to believe
that they can understand, either in imagery, opinion,
or sentiment. I wish to preserve a complete incog-
nito, and can trust to you that, whatever else you do,
you will at least favor me on this point. Indeed this
is essential, deeply essential to its success. After it
had been acted, and successfully (could I hope such
a thing), I would own it if I pleased, and use the
celebrity it might acquire to my own purposes.

What I want you to do is to procure for me its
presentation at Covent Garden. The principal character, Beatrice, is precisely fitted for Miss O'Neil,
and it might even seem written for her, (God forbid
that I should ever see her play it, it would tear my

---

[1] The tragedy referred to was " The Cenci," which Shelley
first desired his wife to undertake. The materials for it he
secured at Rome. It was rejected by Harris, the manager of
Covent Garden, the subject being objectionable.

nerves to pieces,) and, in all respects, it is fitted only for Covent Garden. The chief male character, I confess, I should be very unwilling that any one but Kean should play; — that is impossible, and I must be contented with an inferior actor. I think you know some of the people of that theatre, or, at least, some one who knows them; and when you have read the play, you may say enough, perhaps, to induce them not to reject it without consideration; but of this, perhaps, I may judge from the tragedies which they have accepted, there is no danger at any rate.

Write to me as soon as you can on this subject, because it is necessary that I should present it, or, if rejected by the theatre, print it this coming season, lest somebody else should get hold of it, as the story, which now only exists in manuscript, begins to be generally known among the English. The translation which I send you is to be prefixed to the play, together with a print of Beatrice. I have a copy of her picture by Guido, now in the Colonna palace at Rome, — the most beautiful creature you can conceive.

Of course, you will not show the manuscript to any one; and write to me by return of post, at which time the play will be ready to be sent.

I expect soon to write again, and it shall be a less selfish letter. As to Ollier, I don't know what has been published, or what has arrived at his hands. — My " Prometheus," though ready, I do not send till I know more.

LIII.

TO LEIGH HUNT.

LIVORNO, *August* 15, 1819.

MY DEAR FRIEND, — How good of you to write to us so often, and such kind letters! But it is like lending to a beggar. What can I offer in return.

Though surrounded by suffering and disquietude, and, latterly, almost overcome by our strange misfortune,[1] I have not been idle. My " Prometheus " is finished, and I am also on the eve of completing another work,[2] totally different from anything you might consider that I should write; of a more popular kind; and if anything of mine could deserve attention, of higher claims. " Be innocent of the knowledge, dearest chuck, till thou approve the performance."

I send you a little poem[3] to give to Ollier for publication, but *without my name*. P. will correct the proofs. I wrote it with the idea of offering it to the " Examiner," but I find it is too long. It was composed last year at Este; two of the characters you will recognize; and the third is also in some degree a painting from nature, but, with respect to time and place, ideal. You will find the little piece,

[1] The sudden death of William Shelley, then our only child, which happened in Rome, 6th June, 1819. — M. S.

[2] " The Cenci."

[3] " Julian and Maddalo."

I think, in some degree consistent with your own ideas of the manner in which poetry ought to be written. I have employed a certain familiar style of language to express the actual way in which people talk with each other, whom education and a certain refinement of sentiment have placed above the use of vulgar idioms. I use the word *vulgar* in its most extensive sense. The vulgarity of rank and fashion is as gross in its way as that of poverty, and its cant terms equally expressive of bare conceptions, and therefore equally unfit for poetry. Not that the familiar style is to be admitted in the treatment of a subject wholly ideal, or in that part of any subject which relates to common life, where the passion, exceeding a certain limit, touches the boundaries of that which is ideal. Strong passion expresses itself in metaphor, borrowed from objects alike remote or near, and casts over all the shadow of its own greatness. But what am I about? If my grandmother sucks eggs, was it I who taught her?

If *you* would really correct the proof, I need not trouble P., who, I suppose, has enough. Can you take it as a compliment that I prefer to trouble you?

I do not particularly wish this poem to be known as mine ; but, at all events, I would not put my name to it. I leave you to judge whether it is best to throw it into the fire, or to publish it. So much for self, — *self,* that burr that will stick to one. Your kind expressions about my Eclogue gave me great pleasure ; indeed, my great stimulus in writing is to have the approbation of those who feel kindly towards me.

The rest is mere duty. I am also delighted to hear that you think of us and form fancies about us. We cannot yet come home.

LIV.

TO T. L. PEACOCK.

LIVORNO, *August* [probably 22], 1819.

MY DEAR PEACOCK, — I ought first to say, that I have not yet received one of your letters from Naples; but your present letter tells me all that I could desire to hear.

My employments are these: I awaken usually at seven; read half an hour; then get up; breakfast; after breakfast ascend *my tower*, and read or write until two. Then we dine. After dinner I read Dante with Mary, gossip a little, eat grapes and figs, sometimes walk, though seldom, and at half past five pay a visit to Mrs. Gisborne, who reads Spanish with me until near seven. We then come for Mary, and stroll about till supper time. Mrs. Gisborne is a sufficiently amiable and very accomplished woman; she is δημοκρατική and ἀθέη, — how far she may be φιλανθρύπη I don't know, for she is the antipodes of enthusiasm. Her husband, a man with little thin lips, receding forehead, and a prodigious nose, is an [ ] bore. His nose is something quite Slawkenbergian, — it weighs on the imagination to look at it. It is that sort of nose which transforms all the g's its wearer utters into k's. It is a nose once seen never to be forgotten, and which requires the utmost stretch of Christian charity to forgive. I, you know, have a little turn-up nose ; Hogg has a large hook one ; but add them both together, square them, cube them, you will have but a faint idea of the nose to which I refer.

I most devoutly wish I were living near London. I do not think I shall settle so far off as Richmond ; and to inhabit any intermediate spot on the Thames would be to expose myself to the river damps ; not to mention that it is not much to my taste. My inclinations point to Hampstead ; but I do not know whether I should not make up my mind to something more completely suburban. What are mountains, trees, heaths, or even the glorious and ever beautiful sky, with such sunsets as I have seen at Hampstead, to friends? Social enjoyment, in some form or other, is the alpha and the omega of existence. All that I see in Italy — and from my tower window I now see the magnificent peaks of the Apennine half enclosing the plain — is nothing ; it dwindles into smoke in the mind, when I think of some familiar forms of scenery, little perhaps in themselves, over which old remembrances have thrown a delightful color. How we prize what we despised when present ! The ghosts of our dead associations rise and haunt us, in revenge for our having let them starve, and abandoned them to perish.

.   .   .   .

One thing, I own, I am curious about ; and in the chance of the letters not coming from Naples, pray

tell me. What is it you do at the India House?
Hunt writes, and says you have got a *situation* in
the India House ; Hogg, that you have an *honorable
employment;* Godwin writes to Mary that you have
got *so much or so much*, but nothing of what you do.
The devil take these general terms. Not content
with having driven all poetry out of the world, at
length they make war on their own allies ; nay, on
their very parents, dry facts. If it had not been the
age of generalities, any one of these people would
have told me what you did.

I have been much better these last three weeks.
My work on the Cenci, which was done in two
months, was a fine antidote to nervous medicines,
and kept up, I think, the pain in my side, as sticks
do a fire. Since then, I have materially improved.
I do not walk enough. C., who is sometimes my
companion, does not dress in exactly the right time.
I have no stimulus to walk. Now, I go sometimes
to Livorno on business ; and that does me good.

England seems to be in a very disturbed state, if
we may judge from some Paris papers. I suspect it
is rather exaggerated. But the change should com-
mence among the higher orders, or anarchy will only
be the last flash before despotism.

I have been reading Calderon in Spanish. A kind
of Shakespeare is this Calderon ; and I have some
thoughts, if I find that I cannot do anything better,
of translating some of his plays.

The Examiners I receive. Hunt, as a political
writer, pleases me more and more. Adieu. M. and
C. send their best remembrances.

Pray send me some books, and Claire would take it as a great favor if you would send her music books.

LV.

TO LEIGH HUNT.

LIVORNO, *September* 3, 1819.

MY DEAR FRIEND, — At length has arrived Ollier's parcel, and with it the portrait. What a delightful present! It is almost yourself, and we sat talking with it, and of it, all the evening. It is a great pleasure to us to possess it, a pleasure in time of need, coming to us when there are few others. How we wish it were you, and not your picture! How I wish we were with you!

This parcel, you know, and all its letters, are now a year old, — some older. There are all kinds of dates, from March to August, and " your date," to use Shakespeare's expression, " is better in a pie or a pudding than in your letter." — " Virginity," Parolles says, but letters are the same thing in another shape.

With it came, too, Lamb's works. I have looked at none of the other books yet. What a lovely thing is his " Rosamund Gray "! How much knowledge of the sweetest and deepest parts of our nature in it!

When I think of such a mind as Lamb's, — when I see how unnoticed remain things of such exquisite and complete perfection, — what should I hope for myself, if I had not higher objects in view than fame?

I have seen too little of Italy, and of pictures. Perhaps P. has shown you some of my letters to him. But at Rome I was very ill, seldom able to go out without a carriage ; and though I kept horses for two months there, yet there is so much to see ! Perhaps I attended more to sculpture than painting, its forms being more easily intelligible than that of the latter. Yet I saw the famous works of Raffaelle, whom I agree with the whole world in thinking the finest painter. Why, I can tell you another time. With respect to Michael Angelo I dissent, and think with astonishment and indignation of the common notion that he equals, and in some respects exceeds Raffaelle. He seems to me to have no sense of moral dignity and loveliness ; and the energy for which he has been so much praised appears to me to be a certain rude, external, mechanical quality, in comparison with anything possessed by Raffaelle, or even much inferior artists. His famous painting in the Sixtine Chapel seems to me deficient in beauty and majesty, both in the conception and the execution. He has been called the Dante of painting ; but if we find some of the gross and strong outlines which are employed in the most distasteful passages of the " Inferno," where shall we find *your* Francesca, — where the spirit coming over the sea in a boat, like Mars rising from the vapors of the horizon, — where Matilda gathering flowers, and all the exquisite tenderness, and sensibility, and ideal beauty, in which Dante excelled all poets except Shakespeare ?

As to Michael Angelo's Moses, — but you have a cast of that in England. I write these things. Heaven knows why !

I have written something and finished it, different from anything else, and a new attempt for me ; and I mean to dedicate it to you.[1] I should not have done so without your approbation, but I asked your picture last night, and it smiled assent. If I did not think it in some degree worthy of you, I would not make you a public offering of it. I expect to have to write to you soon about it. If Ollier is not turned Jew, Christian, or become infected with the murrain, he will publish it. Don't let him be frightened, for it is nothing which, by any courtesy of language, can be termed either moral or immoral.

Mary has written to Marianne for a parcel, in which I beg you will make Ollier enclose what you know would most interest me, — your " Calendar " (a sweet extract from which I saw in the Examiner), and the other poems belonging to you ; and, for some friends of mine, my Eclogue.

.   .   .   .

LVI.

TO C. OLLIER.

LEGHORN, *September* 6, 1819.

DEAR SIR, — I received your packet with Hunt's picture about a fortnight ago ; and your letter with Nos. 1, 2, and 3 yesterday, but not No. 4, which is

---

[1] " The Cenci."

probably lost or mislaid, through the extreme irregularity of the Italian post.

The ill account you give of the success of my poetical attempts sufficiently accounts for your silence; but I believe that the truth is, I write less for the public than for myself. Considering that perhaps the parcel will be another year on its voyage, I rather wish, if this letter arrives in time, that you would send the Quarterly's article by the post, and the rest of the Review in the parcel. Of course, it gives me a certain degree of pleasure to know that any one likes my writings; but it is objection and enmity alone that rouses my *curiosity*. My "Prometheus," which has been long finished, is now being transcribed, and will soon be forwarded to you for publication. It is, in my judgment, of a higher character than anything I have yet attempted, and is perhaps less an imitation of anything that has gone before it. I shall also send you another work, calculated to produce a very popular effect, and totally in a different style from anything I have yet composed. This will be sent already printed. The " Prometheus " you will be so good as to print as usual. . . .

In the " Rosalind and Helen," I see there are some few errors, which are so much the worse because they are errors in the sense. If there should be any danger of a second edition, I will correct them.

I have read your "Altham," and Keats's poem, and Lamb's works. For the second in this list, much praise is due to me for having read it, the author's intention appearing to be that no person should possibly get to the end of it. Yet it is full of some of the highest and the finest gleams of poetry; indeed, everything seems to be viewed by the mind of a poet which is described in it. I think, if he had printed about fifty pages of fragments from it, I should have been led to admire Keats as a poet more than I ought, of which there is now no danger.[1] In "Altham" you have surprised and delighted me. It is a natural story, most unaffectedly told; and, what is more, told in a strain of very pure and powerful English, which is a very rare merit. You seem to have studied our language to some purpose; but I suppose I ought to have waited for "Inesilla."

The same day that your letter came, came the news of the Manchester work, and the torrent of my indignation has not yet done boiling in my veins. I wait anxiously to hear how the country will express its sense of this bloody, murderous oppression of its destroyers. "Something must be done. What, yet I know not."

In your parcel (which I pray you to send in some safe manner, forwarding to me the bill of lading, etc., in a regular mercantile way, so that my parcel may come in six weeks, not twelve months) send me Jones's Greek Grammar and some sealing-wax.

---

[1] Keats's later poems were very much admired by Shelley, although he had no praise for "Endymion." Elsewhere he says of him: "Keats, I hope, is going to show himself a great poet; like the sun, to burst through the clouds, which, though dyed in the finest colors of the air, obscured his rising."

Whenever I publish, send copies of my books to the following people from me : —

Mr. Hunt,	Mr. Keats,
Mr. Godwin,	Mr. Thomas Moore,
Mr. Hogg,	Mr. Horace Smith,
Mr. Peacock,	Lord Byron (at Murray's).

LVII.

TO T. L. PEACOCK.

LIVORNO, *September* 9, 1819.

MY DEAR PEACOCK, — I send you the tragedy. You will see that the subject has not been treated as you suggested, and why it was not susceptible of such treatment.   In fact, it was then already printing when I received your letter, and it has been treated in such a manner that I do not see how the subject forms an objection.   You know " Œdipus " is performed on the fastidious French stage, a play much more broad than this.   I confess I have some hopes, and some friends here persuade me that they are not unfounded.

Many thanks for your attention in sending the papers which contain the terrible and important news of Manchester.   These are, as it were, the distant thunders of the terrible storm which is approaching. The tyrants here, as in the French Revolution, have first shed blood.   May their execrable lessons not be learnt with equal facility !   Pray let me have the *earliest* political news which you consider of importance at this crisis.

LVIII.

TO T. L. PEACOCK.

LEGHORN, *September* 21, 1819.

MY DEAR PEACOCK, — You will have received a short letter sent with the tragedy, and the tragedy itself by this time. I am, you may believe, anxious to hear what you think of it, and how the manager talks about it. I have printed in Italy two hundred and fifty copies, because it costs, with all duties and freightage, about half what it would cost in London, and these copies will be sent by sea. My other reason was a belief that the seeing it in print would enable the people at the theatre to judge more easily. Since I last wrote to you Mr. Gisborne is gone to England for the purpose of obtaining a situation for Henry Reveley. I have given him a letter to you, and you would oblige me by showing what civilities you can, and by forwarding his views, either by advice or recommendation, as you may find opportunity. Henry is a most amiable person, and has great talents as a mechanic and engineer. Mr. Gisborne is a man who knows I cannot tell how many languages, and has read almost all the books you can think of; but all that they contain seems to be to his mind what water is to a sieve. His liberal opinions are all the reflections of Mrs. G.'s, a very amiable, accomplished, and completely unprejudiced woman.

Charles Clairmont is now with us on his way to Vienna. He has spent a year or more in Spain, where he has learned Spanish, and I make him read Spanish all day long. It is a most powerful and expressive language, and I have already learned sufficient to read with great ease their poet Calderon. I have read about twelve of his plays. Some of them certainly deserve to be ranked among the grandest and most perfect productions of the human mind. He exceeds all modern dramatists, with the exception of Shakespeare, whom he resembles however in the depth of thought and subtlety of imagination of his writings, and in the rare power of interweaving delicate and powerful comic traits with the most tragical situations, without diminishing their interest. I rate him far above Beaumont and Fletcher.

.   .   .   .

I have sent you my " Prometheus," which I do not wish to be sent to Ollier for publication until I write to that effect. Mr. Gisborne will bring it, as also some volumes of Spenser, and the two last of Herodotus, and " Paradise Lost," which may be put up with the others.

If my play should be accepted, don't you think it would excite some interest, and take off the unexpected horror of the story, by showing that the events are real, if it could be made to appear in some paper in some form?

You will hear from me again shortly, as I send you by sea " The Cenci " printed, which you will be good enough to keep. Adieu.

LIX.

TO LEIGH HUNT.

LIVORNO, *September* 27, 1819.

MY DEAR FRIEND, — We are now on the point of leaving this place for Florence, where we have taken pleasant apartments for six months, which brings us to the 1st of April, the season at which new flowers and new thoughts spring forth upon the earth and in the mind. What is then our destination is yet undecided. I have not seen Florence, except as one sees the outside of the streets ; but its *physiognomy* indicates it to be a city which, though the ghost of a republic, yet possesses most amiable qualities. I wish you could meet us there in the spring, and we would try to muster up a " lieta brigata," which, leaving behind them the pestilence of remembered misfortunes, might act over again the pleasures of the interlocutors in Boccaccio. I have been lately reading this most divine writer. He is, in a high sense of the word, a poet, and his language has the rhythm and harmony of verse. I think him not equal certainly to Dante or Petrarch, but far superior to Tasso and Ariosto, the children of a later and of a colder day. I consider the three first as the productions of the vigor of the infancy of a new nation, — as rivulets from the same spring as that which fed the greatness of the republics of Florence and Pisa, and which checked the influence of the German Emperors, and from which, through obscurer channels, Raffaelle and Michael Angelo drew the light and the harmony of their inspiration. When the second-rate poets of Italy wrote, the corrupting blight of tyranny was already hanging on every bud of genius. Energy, and simplicity, and unity of idea, were no more. In vain do we seek in the finest passages of Ariosto and Tasso any expression which at all approaches in this respect to those of Dante and Petrarch. How much do I admire Boccaccio! What descriptions of nature are those in his little introductions to every new day! It is the morning of life stripped of that mist of familiarity which makes it obscure to us. Boccaccio seems to me to have possessed a deep sense of the fair ideal of human life, considered in its social relations. His more serious theories of love agree especially with mine. He often expresses things lightly, too, which have serious meanings of a very beautiful kind. He is a moral casuist, the opposite of the Christian, stoical, ready-made, and worldly system of morals. Do you remember one little remark, or rather maxim of his, which might do some good to the common, narrow-minded conceptions of love, — " Bocca bacciata non perde ventura ; anzi rinnuova, come fa la luna " ?

It would give me much pleasure to know Mr. Lloyd. Do you know, when I was in Cumberland, I got Southey to borrow a copy of Berkeley from him, and I remember observing some pencil notes in it, probably written by Lloyd, which I thought particularly acute. One, especially, struck me as being the assertion of a doctrine of which even then I had long been persuaded, and on which I had founded much of my persuasions as regarded the imagined cause of the universe, — " Mind cannot create, it can only perceive." Ask him if he remembers having written it. Of Lamb you know my opinion, and you can bear witness to the regret which I felt, when I learned that the calumny of an enemy had deprived me of his society whilst in England. Ollier told me that the Quarterly are going to review me. I suppose it will be a pretty   , and as I am acquiring a taste for humor and drollery, I confess I am curious to see it. I have sent my " Prometheus Unbound " to P.; if you ask him for it, he will show it you. I think it will please you.

Whilst I went to Florence, Mary wrote, but I did not see her letter. Well, good by. Next Monday I shall write to you from Florence. Love to all.

LX.

TO MRS. GISBORNE.

FLORENCE, *October* 13 *or* 14, 1819.

MY DEAR FRIEND, — The regret we feel at our absence from you persuades me that it is a state which cannot last, and which, so long as it must last, will be interrupted by some intervals, one of which is destined to be your all coming to visit us here. Poor Oscar ! I feel a kind of remorse to think of the unequal love with which two animated beings regard each other, when I experience no such sensations for him as those which he manifested for us. His importunate regret is, however, a type of ours as regards you. Our memory — if you will accept so humble a metaphor — is forever scratching at the door of your absence.

. . . .

I am anxious to hear of Mr. Gisborne's return, and I anticipate the surprise and pleasure with which he will learn that a resolution has been taken which leaves you nothing to regret in that event. It is with unspeakable satisfaction that I reflect that my entreaties and persuasions overcame your scruples on this point, and that whatever advantage shall accrue from it will belong to you, whilst any reproach due to the imprudence of such an enterprise must rest on me. I shall thus share the pleasure of success, and bear the blame and loss (if such a thing were possible) of a reverse ; and what more can a man, who is a friend to another, desire for himself? Let us believe in a kind of optimism, in which we are our own gods. It is best that Mr. Gisborne should have returned ; it is best that I should have over-persuaded you and Henry ; it is best that you should all live together, without any more solitary attempts ; it is best that this one attempt should have been made, otherwise, perhaps, one thing which is best might not have occurred ; and it is best that we should think all this for the best, even though it is not, because Hope, as Coleridge says, is a solemn duty, which we owe alike to ourselves and to the world, — a worship to the spirit of good within, which requires, before it sends that inspiration forth which impresses its likeness upon all that it creates, devoted and disinterested homage.

A different scene is this from that in which you made the chief character of our changing drama. We see no one, as usual. Madame M—— is quiet, and we only meet her now and then, by chance. Her daughter, not so fair, but I fear as cold, as the snowy Florimel in Spenser, is in and out of love with C—— as the winds happen to blow; and C——, who, at the moment I happen to write, is in a high state of transitory contentment, is setting off to Vienna in a day or two.

.   .   .   .

I have yet seen little of Florence. The gallery I have a design of studying piecemeal; one of my chief objects in Italy being the observing in statuary and painting the degree in which, and the rules according to which, that ideal beauty, of which we have so intense yet so obscure an apprehension, is realized in external forms.

.   .   .   .

I had forgotten to say that I should be very much obliged to you, if you would contrive to send " The Cenci," which are at the printer's, to England, by the next ship. I forgot it in the hurry of departure. — I have just heard from P., saying that he don't think that my tragedy will do, and that he don't much like it. But I ought to say, to blunt the edge of his criticism, that he is a nursling of the exact and superficial school in poetry.

If Mr. G. is returned, send the " Prometheus " with them.

LXI.

TO C. OLLIER.

FLORENCE, *October* 15, 1819.

DEAR SIR, — The droll remarks of the Quarterly, and Hunt's kind defence, arrived as safe as such poison, and safer than such an antidote, usually do.

I am on the point of sending to you two hundred and fifty copies of a work which I have printed in Italy, which you will have to pay four or five pounds duty upon, on my account. Hunt will tell you the *kind of thing* it is, and in the course of the winter I shall send directions for its publication, *until the arrival of which directions I request that you would have the kindness not* to open the box, *or, if by necessity it is opened, to abstain from observing yourself, or permitting others to observe, what it contains.* I trust this confidently to you, it being of consequence. Meanwhile, assure yourself that this work has no reference, direct or indirect, to politics, or religion, or personal satire, and that this precaution is merely literary.

The "Prometheus," a poem in my best style, whatever that may amount to, will arrive with it, but in MS., which you can print and publish in the season. It is the most perfect of my productions.

Southey wrote the article in question, I am well aware. Observe the impudence of the man in speaking of himself. The only remark worth notice in this piece is the assertion that I imitate Wordsworth. It may as well be said that Lord Byron imitates Wordsworth, or that Wordsworth imitates Lord Byron, both being great poets, and deriving from the new springs of thought and feeling which the great events of our age have exposed to view a similar tone of sentiment, imagery, and expression. A certain similarity all the best writers of any particular age inevitably are marked with, from the spirit of that age acting on all. This I had explained in my Preface, which the writer was too disingenuous to advert to. As to the other trash, and particularly that lame attack on my personal character, which was meant so ill, and which I am not the man to feel, 't is all nothing. I am glad, with respect to that part of it which alludes to Hunt, that it should so have happened that I dedicate, as you will see, a work which has all the capacities for being popular to that excellent person. I was amused, too, with the finale; it is like the end of the first act of an opera, when that tremendous concordant discord sets up from the orchestra, and everybody talks and sings at once. It describes the result of my battle with their Omnipotent God; his pulling me under the sea by the hair of my head, like Pharaoh; my calling out like the devil, who was *game* to the last, swearing and cursing in all comic and horrid oaths, like a French postilion on Mont Cenis; entreating everybody to drown themselves; pretending not to be drowned myself when I *am* drowned; and, lastly, *being* drowned.

.   .   .   .

LXII.

TO MR. AND MRS. GISBORNE.

FLORENCE, *November* 6, 1819.

MY DEAR FRIENDS, — I have just finished a letter of five sheets on Carlyle's affair, and am in hourly expectation of Mary's confinement : you will imagine an excuse for my silence.

.   .   .   .

How goes on Portuguese, — and Theocritus? I have deserted the odorous gardens of literature to journey across the great sandy desert of politics; not, as you may imagine, without the hope of finding some enchanted paradise. In all probability, I shall be overwhelmed by one of the tempestuous columns which are forever traversing, with the speed of a storm, and the confusion of a chaos, that pathless wilderness. You meanwhile will be lamenting in some happy oasis that I do not return. This is out-Calderonizing Muley. We have had lightning and rain here in plenty. I like the Cascini very much, where I often walk alone, watching the leaves, and the rising and falling of the Arno. I am full of all kinds of literary plans.

LXIII.

TO LEIGH HUNT.

FLORENCE, *November* 13, 1819.

MY DEAR FRIEND, — Yesterday morning Mary brought me a little boy.[1] She suffered but two hours' pain, and is now so well that it seems a wonder that she stays in bed. The babe is also quite well, and has begun to suck. You may imagine that this is a great relief and a great comfort to me amongst all my misfortunes, past, present, and to come.

Since I last wrote to you, some circumstances have occurred, not necessary to explain by letter, which make my pecuniary condition a very painful one. The physicans absolutely forbid my travelling to England in the winter, but I shall probably pay you a visit in the spring. With what pleasure, among all the other sources of regret and discomfort with which England abounds for me, do I *think* of looking on the original of that kind and earnest face which is now opposite Mary's bed. It will be the only thing which Mary will envy me, or will need to

---

[1] This son was Sir Percy Florence Shelley, who succeeded to the baronetcy on the death of Sir Timothy, in 1844. He died three years ago, after a long life spent in giving everything possible to the world concerning the poet. He furnished the materials for nearly every authentic work ever published about Shelley.

envy me, in that journey, for I shall come alone. Shaking hands with you is worth all the trouble; the rest is clear loss.

I will tell you more about myself and my pursuits in my next letter.

Kind love to Marianne, Bessy, and all the children. Poor Mary begins (for the first time) to look a little consoled; for we have spent, as you may imagine, a miserable five months.

Good by, my dear Hunt.

LXIV.

TO MRS. GISBORNE.

FLORENCE, *November* 16, 1819.

MADONNA, — I have been lately voyaging in a sea without my pilot, and although my sail has often been torn, my boat become leaky, and the log lost, I have yet sailed in a kind of way from island to island; some of craggy and mountainous magnificence, some clothed with moss and flowers and radiant with fountains, some barren deserts. *I have been reading Calderon without you.* I have read the "Cisma de Ingalaterra," the "Cabellos de Absolom," and three or four others. These pieces, inferior to those we read, at least to the "Principe Constante," in the splendor of particular passages, are perhaps superior in their satisfying completeness. The Cabellos de Absolom is full of the deepest and tenderest touches of nature. Nothing can be more pathetically conceived than the character of old David, and the tender and impartial love, overcoming all insults and all crimes, with which he regards his conflicting and disobedient sons. The incest scene of Amnon and Tamar is perfectly tremendous. Well may Calderon say in the person of the former : —

> " Si sangre sin fuego hiere,
> que fara sangre con fuego ? "

Incest is, like many other incorrect things, a very poetical circumstance. It may be the excess of love or hate. It may be the defiance of everything for the sake of another, which clothes itself in the glory of the highest heroism ; or it may be that cynical rage which, confounding the good and the bad in existing opinions, breaks through them for the purpose of rioting in selfishness and antipathy. Calderon, following the Jewish historians, has represented Amnon's action in the basest point of view, — he is a prejudiced savage, acting what he abhors, and abhorring that which is the unwilling party to his crime. Adieu.

LXV.

TO JOHN GISBORNE.

FLORENCE, *November* 16, 1819.

MY DEAR SIr, — I envy you the first reading of Theocritus. Were not the Greeks a glorious people? What is there, as Job says of the leviathan, like unto them? If the army of Nicias had not been defeated under the walls of Syracuse, — if the Athenians had, acquiring Sicily, held the balance between Rome and Carthage, sent garrisons to the Greek colonies in the south of Italy, — Rome might have been all that its intellectual condition entitled it to be, a tributary, not the conqueror, of Greece; the Macedonian power would never have attained to the dictatorship of the civilized states of the world. Who knows whether, under the steady progress which philosophy and social institutions would have made (for, in the age to which I refer, their progress was both rapid and secure) among a people of the most perfect physical organization, whether the Christian religion would have arisen, or the barbarians have overwhelmed the wrecks of civilization which had survived the conquest and tyranny of the Romans? What then should we have been? As it is, all of us who are worth anything spend our manhood in unlearning the follies, or expiating the mistakes, of our youth. We are stuffed full of prejudices; and our natural passions are so managed, that if we restrain them we grow intolerant and precise, because we restrain them not according to reason, but according to error; and if we do not restrain them, we do all sorts of mischief to ourselves and others. Our imagination and understanding are alike subjected to rules the most absurd. So much for Theocritus and the Greeks.

In spite of all your arguments, I wish your money were out of the funds. This middle course which you speak of, and which may probably have place, will amount to your losing not all your income, nor retaining all, but have the half taken away. I feel intimately persuaded, whatever political forms may have place in England, that no party can continue many years, perhaps not many months, in the administration, without diminishing the interest of the national debt. And once having commenced, — and having done so safely, — where will it end?

Give Henry my kindest thanks for his most interesting letter, and bid him expect one from me by the next post.

Mary and the babe continue well. — Last night we had a magnificent thunder-storm, with claps that shook the house like an earthquake. Both Mary and C—— unite with me in kindest remembrances to all.

LXVI.

TO LEIGH HUNT.

FLORENCE, *November* 23, 1819.

MY DEAR HUNT, — *Why* don't you write to us? I was preparing to send you something for your " Indicator," but I have been a drone instead of a bee in this business, thinking that perhaps, as you did not acknowledge any of my late enclosures, it would not be welcome to you, whatever I might send.

What a state England is in ! But you will never write politics. I don't wonder; but I wish, then, that you would write a paper in the Examiner, on the actual state of the country, and what, under all circumstances of the conflicting passions and interests of men, we are to expect ; — not what we ought to expect, nor what, if so and so were to happen, we might expect, but what, as things are, there is reason to believe will come ; — and send it me for my information.   Every word a man has to say is valuable to the public now; and thus you will at once gratify your friend, nay, instruct, and either exhilarate him, or force him to be resigned, and awaken the minds of the people.

I have no spirits to write what I do not know whether you will care much about ; I know well that if I were in great misery, poverty, etc., you would think of nothing else but how to amuse and relieve me.   You omit me if I am prosperous.

I could laugh, if I found a joke, in order to put you in good humor with me after my scolding, — in good humor enough to write to us. . . . Affectionate love to and from all.   This ought not only to be the *Vale* of a letter, but a superscription over the gate of life.

I send you a sonnet.   I don't expect you to publish it, but you may show it to whom you please.

LXVII.

TO LEIGH HUNT.

FLORENCE, *November*, 1819.

MY DEAR FRIEND, — Two letters, both bearing date October 20, arrive on the same day; one is always glad of twins.

.   .   .   .

You do not tell me whether you have received my lines on the Manchester affair.[1] They are of the exoteric species, and are meant not for the Indicator, but the Examiner. I would send for the former, if you like, some letters on such subjects of art as suggest themselves in Italy. Perhaps I will, at a venture, send you a specimen of what I mean next post. I enclose you in this a piece for the Examiner, or let it share the fate, whatever that fate may be, of the " Masque of Anarchy."[2]

I am sorry to hear that you have employed yourself in translating the " Aminta," though I doubt not it will be a just and beautiful translation. You ought to write Amintas. You ought to exercise your fancy in the perpetual creation of new forms of gentleness and beauty.

[1] The " Masque of Anarchy," which Hunt would not publish, " because," he said, " I thought that the public at large had not become sufficiently discerning to do justice to the sincerity and kind-heartedness of the spirit that walked in this flaming robe of verse." He did publish it, however, in 1832.

[2] " Peter Bell the Third." — M. S.

With respect to translation, even *I* will not be seduced by it; although the Greek plays, and some of the ideal dramas of Calderon (with which I have lately, and with inexpressible wonder and delight, become acquainted), are perpetually tempting me to throw over their perfect and glowing forms the gray veil of my own words. And you know me too well to suspect that I refrain from a belief that what I could substitute for them would deserve the regret which yours would, if suppressed. I have confidence in my moral sense alone; but that is a kind of originality. I have only translated the "Cyclops" of Euripides, when I could absolutely do nothing else; and the "Symposium" of Plato, which is the delight and astonishment of all who read it; I mean the original, or so much of the original as is seen in my translation, not the translation itself.

I think I have had an accession of strength since my residence in Italy, though the disease itself in the side, whatever it may be, is not subdued. Some day we shall all return from Italy. I fear that in England things will be carried violently by the rulers, and they will not have learned to yield in time to the spirit of the age. The great thing to do is to hold the balance between popular impatience and tyrannical obstinacy, — to inculcate with fervor both the right of resistance and the duty of forbearance. You know my principles incite me to take all the good I can get in politics, forever aspiring to something more. I am one of those whom nothing will fully satisfy, but who are ready to be partially satisfied in all that is practicable. We shall see.

.   .   .   .

LXVIII.

TO MR. OLLIER.

FLORENCE, *December* 15, 1819.

DEAR SIR, — Pray give Mr. Procter my best
thanks for his polite attention. I read the article
you enclosed with the pleasure which every one feels,
of course, when they are praised or defended ; though
the praise would have given me more pleasure if it
had been less excessive. I am glad, however, to
see the Quarterly cut up, and that by one of their
own people. Poor Southey has enough to endure.
Do you know, I think the article in Blackwood
could not have been written by a favorer of Government and a religionist. I don't believe any such one
could sincerely like my writings. After all, is it not
some friend in disguise, and don't you know who
wrote it?

There is one very droll thing in the Quarterly.
They say that "my chariot wheels are broken."
Heaven forbid! My chariot, you may tell them,
was built by one of the best makers in Bond Street,
and it has gone several thousand miles in perfect
security. What a comical thing it would be to make
the following advertisement: " A report having pre-
vailed, in consequence of some insinuations in the
Quarterly Review, that Mr. Shelley's chariot wheels
are broken, Mr. Charters of Bond Street begs to
assure the public that they, after having carried him

through Italy, France, and Switzerland, still continue in excellent repair."

When the box comes, you may write a note to Mr. Peacock; or it would be better to call on him, and ask *if my tragedy is accepted?* If not, publish what you find in the box. I think it will succeed as a publication. Let " Prometheus " be printed without delay. You will receive the additions, which Mrs. S. is now transcribing, in a few days. It has already been read to many persons. My Prometheus is the best thing I ever wrote.

Pray what have you done with " Peter Bell "? Ask Mr. Hunt for it, and for some other poems of a similar character I sent him to give you to publish. I think Peter not bad in his way; but perhaps no one will believe in anything in the shape of a joke from me.

Of course with my next box you will send me the " Dramátic Sketches." [1] I have only seen the extracts in the Examiner. They have some passages painfully beautiful. When I consider the vivid energy to which the minds of men are awakened in this age of ours, ought I not to congratulate myself that I am a contemporary with names which are great, or will be great, or ought to be great?

Have you seen my poem, " Julian and Maddalo "? Suppose you print that in the manner of Hunt's " Hero and Leander," for I mean to write three other poems, the scenes of which will be laid at Rome, Florence, and Naples, but the subjects of

---

[1] By B. W. Procter.

which will be all drawn from dreadful or beautiful realities, as that of this was.

If I have health — but I will neither boast nor promise. I am preparing an octavo on reform, — a commonplace kind of book, — which, now that I see the passion of party will postpone the great struggle till another year, I shall not trouble myself to finish for this season. I intend it to be an instructive and readable book, appealing from the passions to the reason of men.

LXIX.

TO C. OLLIER.

PISA, *January* 20, 1820.

DEAR SIR, — I send you the " Witch of Atlas," a fanciful poem, which, if its merit be measured by the labor which it cost, is worth nothing ; and the errata of " Prometheus," which I ought to have sent long since, — a formidable list, as you will see.

.   .   .   .

The reviews of my " Cenci " (though some of them, and especially that marked " John Scott," are written with great malignity) on the whole give me as much encouragement as a person of my habits of thinking is capable of receiving from such a source, which is inasmuch as they coincide with and confirm my own decisions. My next attempt (if I should write more) will be a drama, in the composition of which I shall attend to the advice of my

critics, to a certain degree.   But I doubt whether I
shall write more.   I could be content either with
the Hell or the Paradise of poetry ; but the torments
of its Purgatory vex me, without exciting my powers
sufficiently to put an end to the vexation.

I have also to thank *you* for the present of one or
two of your publications.   I am enchanted with your
" Literary Miscellany," although the last article it
contains has excited my polemical faculties so violently that, the moment I get rid of my ophthalmia, I
mean to set about an answer to it, which I will send
to you, if you please.   It is very clever, but, I think,
very false.[1]   Who is your commentator on the German drama ?   He is a powerful thinker, though I
differ from him *toto cœlo* about the Devils of Dante
and Milton.   If you know him personally, pray ask
him from me what he means by receiving the *spirit
into me;*[2] and (if really it is any good) how one is to
get at it.   I was immeasurably amused by the quotation from Schlegel about the way in which the popular faith is destroyed, — first the Devil, then the
Holy Ghost, then God the Father.   I had written a
Lucianic essay to prove the same thing.   There are
two beautiful stories, too, in this " Miscellany."   It
pleased me altogether infinitely.   I was also much

[1] The article (which was written by Mr. Peacock) was an
Essay on Poetry, which the writer regarded as a worn-out
delusion of barbarous times. — L. S.

[2] The writer was the late Archdeacon Hare, who, despite
his orthodoxy, was a great admirer of Shelley's genius.   He
contended that Milton erred in making the Devil a majestical
being, and hoped that Shelley would in time humble his soul,
and " receive the spirit into him." — L. S.

pleased with the "Retrospective Review," — that is, with all the quotations from old books in it ; but it is very ill executed.

When the spirit moves you, write and give me an account of the ill success of my verses.

Who wrote the review in your publication of my "Cenci"? It was written in a friendly spirit, and, if you know the author, I wish you would tell him from me how much obliged I am to him for this spirit, more gratifying to me than any literary laud.

LXX.

TO MR. AND MRS. GISBORNE.

PISA, *February* 9, 1820.

PRAY let us see you soon, or our threat may cost both us and you something, — a visit to Livorno. The stage direction on the present occasion is, Exit Moonshine and enter Wall; or rather four walls, who surround and take prisoners the Gala and Dama.

Seriously, pray do not disappoint us. We shall watch the sky, and the death of the sirocco must be the birth of your arrival.

Mary and I are going to study mathematics. We design to take the most compendious, yet certain methods of arriving at the great results. We believe that your right-angled triangle will contain the solution of the problem of how to proceed.

Do not write, but *come*. Mary is too idle to write, but all that she has to say is *come*. She joins with me in condemning the moonlight plan. Indeed, we ought not to be so selfish as to allow you to come at all, if it is to cost you all the fatigue and annoyance of returning the same night. But it will not be, — so adieu.

LXXI.

TO C. OLLIER.

PISA, *March* 6, 1820.

DEAR SIR, — I do not hear that you have received " Prometheus " and the " Cenci " ; I therefore think it safest to tell you how and when to get them, if you have not yet done so.

.   .   .   .

" Prometheus Unbound," I must tell you, is my favorite poem ; I charge you, therefore, specially to pet him and feed him with fine ink and good paper. " Cenci " is written for the multitude, and ought to sell well. I think, if I may judge by its merits, the " Prometheus " cannot sell beyond twenty copies. I hear nothing either from Hunt, or you, or any one. If you condescend to write to me, mention something about Keats.

Allow me particularly to request you to send copies of whatever I publish to Horace Smith.

Maybe you will see me in the summer ; but in that case I shall certainly return to this " Paradise of Ex- iles " by the ensuing winter.

If any of the Reviews abuse me, cut them out and send them. If they praise, you need not trouble yourself. I feel ashamed if I could believe that I should deserve the latter; the former, I flatter myself, is no more than a just tribute. If Hunt praises me, send it, because that is of another character of thing.

LXXII.

TO C. OLLIER.

PISA, *May* 14, 1820.

DEAR SIR, — I reply to your letter by return of post, to confirm what I said in a former letter respecting a new edition of the " Cenci," which ought by all means to be instantly urged forward.

. . . .

As to the printing of the " Prometheus," be it as you will. But in this case I shall repose or trust in your care respecting the correction of the press; especially in the lyrical parts, where a minute error would be of much consequence. Mr. Gisborne will revise it; he heard it recited, and will therefore more readily seize any error.

If I had even intended to publish " Julian and Maddalo" with my name, yet I would not print it with " Prometheus." It would not harmonize. It is an attempt in a different style, in which I am not yet sure of myself, — a *sermo pedestris* way of treating human nature, quite opposed to the idealisms of that drama. If you print "Julian and Maddalo," I wish it to be printed in some unostentatious form, accompanied with the fragment of "Athanase," and exactly in the manner in which I sent it; and I particularly desire that my name be not annexed to the first edition of it, in any case.

If "Peter Bell" be printed, (you can best judge if it will sell or no, and there would be no other reason for printing such a trifle,) attend, I pray you, particularly to completely concealing the author; and for Emma read Betty, as the name of Peter's sister. Emma, I recollect, is the real name of the sister of a great poet who might be mistaken for Peter. I ought to say that I send you poems in a few posts, to print at the end of "Prometheus," better fitted for that purpose than any in your possession.

Keats, I hope, is going to show himself a great poet; like the sun, to burst through the clouds, which, though dyed in the finest colors of the air, obscured his rising. The Gisbornes will bring me from you copies of whatever may be published when they leave England.

LXXIII.

TO T. L. PEACOCK.

PISA, *May*, 1820.

MY DEAR PEACOCK, — I congratulate you most sincerely on your choice and on your marriage. . . . I was very much amused by your laconic account of the affair. It is altogether extremely like the *dénouement* of one of your own novels, and as such serves to a theory I once imagined, that in everything any man ever wrote, spoke, acted, or imagined is contained, as it were, an allegorical idea of his own future life, as the acorn contains the oak.

.   .   .   .

My friends, the Gisbornes, are now really on their way to London, where they propose to stay only six weeks. I think you will like Mrs. Gisborne. Henry is an excellent fellow, but not very communicative. If you find anything in the shape of dulness or otherwise to endure in Mr. Gisborne, endure it for the lady's sake and mine; but for Heaven's sake do not let him know that I think him stupid. Indeed, perhaps I do him an injustice. Hogg will find it very agreeable (if he postpones his visit so long, or if he visits me at all) to join them on their return. I wish you, and Hogg, and Hunt, and — I know not who besides — would come and spend some months with me together in this wonderful land.

We know little of England here. I take in Galignani's paper, which is filled with extracts from the " Courier," and from those accounts it appears probable that there is but little unanimity in the mass of the people; with on the one side the success of Ministers, and on the other the exasperation of the poor.

I see my tragedy has been republished in Paris; if that is the case, it ought to sell in London, but I hear nothing from Ollier.

I have suffered extremely this winter; but I feel

myself most materially better at the return of spring.
I am on the whole greatly benefited by my residence
in Italy, and but for certain moral causes should probably have been enabled to re-establish my system
completely. Believe me, my dear Peacock, yours
very sincerely.

Pray make my best regards acceptable to your new
companion.

LXXIV.

TO JOHN GISBORNE.

Pisa, *May* 26, 1820.

.   .   .   .

How do you like London, and your journey; the
Alps in their beauty and their eternity; Paris in its
slight and transitory colors; and the wearisome
plains of France, and the *moral* people with whom
you drank tea last night? Above all, *how* are you?
And of the last question, believe me, we are anxiously waiting for a reply, — until which I will say
nothing, nor ask anything. I rely on the journal
with as much security as if it were already written.

I am just returned from a visit to Leghorn, Cas-
ciano, and our old fortress at Sant' Elmo.

.   .   .   .

What a glorious prospect you had from the windows of Sant' Elmo! The enormous chain of the
Apennines, with its many-folded ridges, islanded in
the misty distance of the air; the sea, so immensely

distant, appearing as at your feet ; and the prodigious expanse of the plain of Pisa, and the dark green marshes lessened almost to a strip by the height of the blue mountains overhanging them. Then the wild and unreclaimed fertility of the foreground, and the chestnut trees, whose vivid foliage made a sort of resting-place to the sense before it darted itself to the jagged horizon of this prospect. I was altogether delighted. I had a respite from my nervous symptoms, which was compensated to me by a violent cold in the head. There was a tradition about you at Sant' Elmo, — *an English family that had lived here in the time of the French.* The doctor, too, at the Bagni, knew you.

.   .   .   .

Our anxiety about Godwin is very great, and any information that you could give a day or two earlier than he might, respecting any decisive event in his lawsuit, would be a great relief. Your impressions about Godwin (I speak especially to Madonna mia, who had known him before) will especially interest me. You know that added years only add to my admiration of his intellectual powers, and even the moral resources of his character. Of my other friends I say nothing. To see Hunt is to like him ; and there is one other recommendation which he has to you, he is my friend. To know H——, if any one can know him, is to know something very unlike, and inexpressibly superior, to the great mass of men.

Will Henry write me an adamantine letter, flowing not, like the words of Sophocles, with honey, but

molten brass and iron, and bristling with wheels and
teeth?[1]   I saw his steamboat asleep under the walls.
I was afraid to waken it, and ask it whether it was
dreaming of him, for the same reason that I would
have refrained from awakening Ariadne, after Theseus
had left her — unless I had been Bacchus.

LXXV.

TO T. L. PEACOCK.

LEGHORN, *July* 12, 1820.

MY DEAR PEACOCK, — I remember you said that
when ―――― married you were afraid you would see
or hear but little of him. "There are two voices,"
says Wordsworth, "one of the mountains and one of
the sea, each a mighty voice." So you have two
wives, — one of the mountains, all of whose claims
I perfectly admit, whose displeasure I deprecate, and
from whom I feel assured that I have nothing to fear :
the other of the sea, perhaps, makes you write so
much, that you have not a scrawl to spare. I make
bold to write to you on the news that you are correcting my "Prometheus," for which I return thanks. I
hear of you from Mr. Gisborne, but from you I do
not hear.

Nothing, I think, shows the generous gullibility of
the English nation more than their having adopted

[1] Henry Reveley, an English engineer, was employed in
building a steamboat to ply up and down the Italian coast.

her Sacred Majesty as the heroine of the day, in spite of all their prejudices and bigotry. I, for my part, of course wish no harm to happen to her, even if she has, as I firmly believe, amused herself in a manner rather indecorous with any courier or baron. But I cannot help adverting to it as one of the absurdities of royalty, that a vulgar woman, with all those low tastes which prejudice considers as vices, and a person whose habits and manners every one would shun in private life, without any redeeming virtues, should be turned into a heroine because she is a queen, or, as a collateral reason, because her husband is a king ; and he, no less than his ministers, are so odious that everything, however disgusting, which is opposed to them, is admirable. The Paris paper which I take in copied some excellent remarks from the Examiner about it.

We are just now occupying the Gisbornes' house at Leghorn, and I have turned Mr. Reveley's workshop into my study. The Libecchio here howls like a chorus of fiends all day, and the weather is just pleasant, — not at all hot, the days being very misty, and the nights divinely serene. I have been reading with much pleasure the Greek romances. The best of them is the pastoral of Longus ; but they are all very entertaining, and would be delightful if they were less rhetorical and ornate. I am translating in *ottava rima* the " Hymn to Mercury " of Homer. Of course my stanza precludes a literal translation. My next effort will be that it should be legible, — a quality much to be desired in translations.

I am told that the magazines, etc., blaspheme me

at a great rate. I wonder why I write verses, for
nobody reads them. It is a kind of disorder, for
which the regular practitioners prescribe what is
called a torrent of abuse ; but I fear that can hardly
be considered as a specific.

I enclose two additional poems, to be added to
those printed at the end of " Prometheus " : and I
send them to you, for fear Ollier might not know
what to do in case he objected to some expressions
in the fifteenth and sixteenth stanzas ; and that
you would do me the favor to insert an asterisk or
asterisks, with as little expense to the sense as may
be. The other poem I send to you, not to make
two letters.

.   .   .   .

Believe me, my dear Peacock, sincerely and affectionately yours.

LXXVI.

TO MARY SHELLEY.

(Leghorn.)

CASA SILVA, Sunday Morning,
July 23, 1820.

MY DEAR LOVE, — I believe I shall have taken a
very pleasant and spacious apartment at the Bagni
for three months. It is as all the others are, — dear.
I shall give forty or forty-five sequins for the three
months, but as yet I do not know which. I could
get others something cheaper, and a great deal

worse ; but if we would write, it is requisite to have space.

To-morrow evening, or the following morning, you will probably see me. T—— is planning a journey to England to secure his property in the event of a revolution, which, he is persuaded, is on the eve of exploding. I neither believe that, nor do I fear that the consequences will be so immediately destructive to the existing forms of social order. Money will be delayed, and the exchange reduced very low, and my annuity and Mrs. M.'s, on account of these being *money*, will be in some danger ; but land is quite safe. Besides, it will not be so rapid. Let us hope we shall have a reform. T—— will be lulled into security, while the slow progress of things is still flowing on, after this affair of the Queen may appear to be blown over.

There is bad news from Palermo : the soldiers resisted the people, and a terrible slaughter, amounting, it is said, to four thousand men, ensued. The event, however, was as it should be. Sicily, like Naples, is free. By the brief and partial accounts of the Florence paper, it appears that the enthusiasm of the people was prodigious, and that the women fought from the houses, raining down boiling oil on the assailants.

.   .   .   .

I have no thought of leaving Italy. The best thing we can do is to save money, and, if things take a decided turn, (which I am convinced they will at last, but not perhaps for two or three years,) it will be time for me to assert my rights, and preserve my

annuity.   Meanwhile, another event may decide us.
Kiss sweet babe, and kiss yourself for me. — I love
you affectionately.

LXXVII.

TO MARY SHELLEY.
(Bagni di San Giuliano.)

[LEGHORN,] CASA RICCI, *September* 1, 1820.

I AM afraid, my dearest, that I shall not be able
to be with you so soon as to-morrow evening, though
I shall use every exertion.   Del Rosso I have not
seen, nor shall until this evening.   Jackson I have,
and he is to drink tea with us this evening, and bring
the " Constitutionnel."

You will have seen the papers, but I doubt that they
will not contain the latest and most important news.
It is certain, by private letters from merchants, that
a serious insurrection has broken out at Paris, and
the reports last night are, that an attack made by the
populace on the Tuileries still continued when the
last accounts came away.   At Naples the constitutional party have declared to the Austrian Minister,
that, if the Emperor should make war on them, their
first action would be to put to death all the members
of the royal family, — a necessary and most just measure, when the forces of the combatants, as well as
the merits of their respective causes, are so unequal.
That kings should be everywhere the hostages for
liberty were admirable.

What will become of the Gisbornes, or of the English at Paris? How soon will England itself, and perhaps Italy, be caught by the sacred fire? And what, to come from the solar system to a grain of sand, shall we do?

Kiss babe for me, and your own self. I am somewhat better, but my side still vexes me — a little.

LXXVIII.

TO CLAIRE CLAIRMONT.

PISA, *October* 29, 1820.

I WROTE you a kind of scrawl the other day merely to show that I had not forgotten you. . . . Mrs. Mason has just given me your letter brought by the Tantinis. I called on the Tantinis last night, and am pained to find that they confirm the intelligence of your letter. They tell me you looked very melancholy and desolate, which they imputed to the weather; you must indeed be very uncomfortable for it to become visible to them. Keep up your spirits, my best girl, until we meet at Pisa. But for Mrs. Mason I should say come back immediately, and give up a plan so inconsistent with your feelings; as it is, I fear you had better endure at least until you come here. You know, however, whatever you shall determine on, where to find one ever affectionate friend, to whom your absence is too painful for your return ever to be unwelcome.

.   .   .   .

I have read or written nothing lately, having been much occupied by my sufferings, and by Medwin, who relates wonderful and interesting things of the interior of India. We have also been talking of a plan to be accomplished with a friend of his, a man of large fortune, who will be at Leghorn next spring, and who designs to visit Greece, Syria, and Egypt in his own ship. This man has conceived a great admiration for my verses, and wishes above all things that I could be induced to join his expedition. How far all this is practicable, considering the state of my finances, I know not yet. I know that if it were, it would give me the greatest pleasure, and the pleasure might be either doubled or divided by your presence or absence. . . . I am going to study Arabic — for a purpose and a motive as you may conceive. I wish you would inquire for me at Florence whether there is an Arabic grammar or dictionary, and any other Arabic books, either printed or in manuscript, to be bought. You can ask Dr. Bojti, and if he knows nothing go to Molini's Library, and inquire of him. At all events, go to Molini's, and send me all the information you can pick up. I trust this to your kind love. If I buy and pay for any, I can send you scudi at the same time, which I have made some ineffectual efforts to convey to Florence. Pardon me, my dear, for mentioning scudi, and do not love me less because they are a portion of the inevitable dross of life which clings to our friendship.

LXXIX.

TO JAMES OLLIER.

PISA, *November* 10, 1820.

DEAR SIR, — Mr. Gisborne has sent me a copy of the "Prometheus," which is certainly most beautifully printed. It is to be regretted that the errors of the press are so numerous, and in many respects so destructive of the sense of a species of poetry which, I fear, even without this disadvantage, very few will understand or like. I shall send you the list of errata in a day or two.

I send some poems to be added to the pamphlet of "Julian and Maddalo." I think you have some other smaller poems belonging to that collection, and I believe you know that I do not wish my name to be printed on the title-page, though I have no objection to my being known as the author.

I enclose also another poem, which I do not wish to be printed with "Julian and Maddalo," but at the end of the second edition of "The Cenci," or of any other of my writings to which my name is affixed, if any other should at present have arrived at a second edition, which I do not expect. I have a purpose in this arrangement, and have marked the poem I mean by a cross.

. . . .

My friend Captain Medwin is with me, and has shown me a poem on Indian hunting, which he has sent you to publish. It is certainly a very elegant and classical composition, and, even if it does not belong to the highest style of poetry, I should be surprised if it did not succeed. May I challenge your kindness to do what you can for it?

You will hear from me again in a post or two. The "Julian and Maddalo," and the accompanying poems, are all my saddest verses raked up into one heap. I mean to mingle more smiles with my tears in future.

LXXX.

TO T. L. PEACOCK.

PISA, *November* [probably 15], 1820.

MY DEAR PEACOCK, — I delayed to answer your last letter, because I was waiting for something to say: at least something that should be likely to be interesting to you. The box containing my books, and consequently your Essay against the cultivation of poetry, has not arrived; my wonder, meanwhile, in what manner you support such a heresy in this matter-of-fact and money-loving age, holds me in suspense. Thank you for your kindness in correcting "Prometheus," which I am afraid gave you a great deal of trouble. Among the modern things which have reached me is a volume of poems by Keats: in other respects insignificant enough, but containing the fragment of a poem called "Hyperion." I dare say you have not time to read it; but it is certainly an astonishing piece of writing, and gives me a conception of Keats which I confess I had not before.

I hear from Mr. Gisborne that you are surrounded with papers — a chaos of which you are the god; a sepulchre which encloses in a dormant state the chrysalis of the Pavonian Psyche. May you start into life some day, and give us another " Melincourt." Your Melincourt is exceedingly admired, and I think much more so than any of your other writings. In this respect the world judges rightly. There is more of the true spirit, and an object less indefinite, than in either " Headlong Hall " or Scythrop.

I am, speaking literarily, infirm of purpose. I have great designs, and feeble hopes of accomplishing them. I read books, and, though I am ignorant enough, they seem to teach me nothing. To be sure, the reception the public have given me might go far enough to damp any man's enthusiasm. They teach you, it may be said, only what is true. Very true, I doubt not, and the more true the less agreeable. I can compare my experience in this respect to nothing but a series of wet blankets. I have been reading nothing but Greek and Spanish. Plato and Calderon have been my gods. A schoolfellow of mine from India is staying with me, and we are beginning Arabic together. Mary is writing a novel, illustrative of the manners of the Middle Ages in Italy, which she has raked out of fifty old books. I promise myself success from it; and certainly, if what is wholly original will succeed, I shall not be disappointed.

Adieu. *In publica commoda peccem, si longo sermone.*

LXXXI.

TO JOHN GISBORNE.

(At Leghorn.)

PISA, Oggi [*November*, 1820].

MY DEAR SIR, — I send you the Phædon and
Tacitus. I congratulate you on your conquest of the
Iliad. You must have been astonished at the per-
pectually increasing magnificence of the last seven
books. Homer there truly begins to be himself.
The battle of the Scamander, the funeral of Patroclus,
and the high and solemn close of the whole bloody
tale in tenderness and inexpiable sorrow, are wrought
in a manner incomparable with anything of the same
kind. The Odyssey is sweet, but there is nothing
like this.

I am bathing myself in the light and odor of the
flowery and starry Autos. I have read them all more
than once. Henry will tell you how much I am in
love with Pacchiani. I suffer from my disease considerably. Henry will also tell you how much, and
how whimsically, he alarmed me last night.

My kindest remembrances to Mrs. Gisborne, and
best wishes for your health and happiness.

I have a new Calderon coming from Paris.

LXXXII.

TO CLAIRE CLAIRMONT.

Tuesday Evening, [*January* 16,] 1821.

MANY thanks for your kind and tender letter. which Mrs. M. gave me to-day, several days after it had arrived. I had been very ill, and had not seen her for a fortnight. I had several times been going to write to you to request you to love me better than you do, when meanwhile your letter arrives. I shall punctually follow all such portions of the advice it contains which are practicable.

I write to-night that I may not seem to neglect you, though I have little time. I am delighted to hear of your recovered health. May I entreat you to be cautious in keeping it? Mine is far better than it has been, and the relapse, which I now suffer, into a state of ease from one of pain, is attended with such an excessive susceptibility of nature that I suffer equally from pleasure and from pain. You will ask me naturally enough where I find any pleasure. The wind, the light, the air, the smell of a flower, affects me with violent emotions. There needs no catalogue of the causes of pain.

I see Emily,[1] and, whether her presence is the source of pain or pleasure to me, I am equally ill-fated in both. I am deeply interested in her destiny, and that interest can in no manner influence it. She

---

[1] Emilia Viviani, the subject of " Epipsychidion."

is not, however, insensible to my sympathy, and she counts it among her alleviations.   As much comfort as she receives from my attachment to her, I lose. There is no reason that you should fear any mixture of that which you call love.   My conception of Emilia's talents augments every day.   Her moral nature is fine, but not above circumstances; yet I think her tender and true, which is always something. How many are only one of these at a time !

So much for sentiment and ethics.   The Williamses are come, and Mrs. W. dined here to-day, — an extremely pretty and gentle woman, apparently not *very* clever.   I like her very much.   I have only seen her for an hour, but I will tell you more another time.   Mary will write you sheets of gossip.   I have not seen Mr. W.   The Greek expedition appears to be broken up.   No news of any kind that I know of.

You delight me with your progress in German, in spite of the reproach which accompanies the account of it. . . . I wish to Heaven, my dear girl, that I could be of any avail to add to your pleasure or diminish your pain, — how ardently, you cannot know; you only know — as you frequently take care to tell me — how vainly. . . . I took up my pen for an instant only to thank you, and, if you will, to kiss you for your kind attention to me, and I find I have written in ill spirits, which may infect you. Let them not do so.   I will write again to-morrow. Meanwhile yours most tenderly.

LXXXIII.

TO T. L. PEACOCK.

PISA, *February* 15, 1821.

MY DEAR PEACOCK, — The last letter I received from you, nearly four months from the date thereof, reached me by the boxes which the Gisbornes sent by sea. I am happy to learn that you continue in good external and internal preservation. I received at the same time your printed denunciations against general, and your written ones against particular poetry; and I agree with you as decidedly in the latter as I differ in the former. The man whose critical gall is not stirred up by such rhymes as ——'s, may safely be conjectured to possess no gall at all. The world is pale with the sickness of such stuff. At the same time, your anathemas against poetry itself excited me to a sacred rage, or *cacoëthes scribendi* of vindicating the insulted Muses. I had the greatest possible desire to break a lance with you, within the lists of a magazine, in honor of my mistress Urania; but God willed that I should be too lazy, and wrested the victory from your hope: since first having unhorsed poetry, and the universal sense of the wisest in all ages, an easy conquest would have remained to you in me, the knight of the shield of shadow and the lance of gossamere. Besides, I was at that moment reading Plato's "Ion," which I recommend you to reconsider. Perhaps in the comparison of Platonic and Malthusian doctrines, the *mavis errare* of Cicero is a justifiable argument; but I have a whole quiver of arguments on such a subject.

Have you seen Godwin's answer to the apostle of the rich? And what do you think of it? It has not yet reached me, nor has your box, of which I am in daily expectation.

We are now in the crisis and point of expectation in Italy. The Neapolitan and Austrian armies are rapidly approaching each other, and every day the news of a battle may be expected. The former have advanced into the Ecclesiastical States, and taken hostages from Rome, to assure themselves of the neutrality of that power, and appear determined to try their strength in open battle. I need not tell you how little chance there is that the new and undisciplined levies of Naples should stand against a superior force of veteran troops. But the birth of liberty in nations abounds in reversals of the ordinary laws of calculation: the defeat of the Austrians would be the signal of insurrection throughout all Italy.

I am devising literary plans of some magnitude. But nothing is more difficult and unwelcome than to write without a confidence of finding readers; and if my plan of " The Cenci " found none or few, I despair of ever producing anything that shall merit them.

Among your anathemas of the modern attempts in poetry, do you include Keats's " Hyperion "? I think it very fine. His other poems are worth little; but if the Hyperion be not grand poetry, none has been produced by our contemporaries.

I suppose *you* are writing nothing but Indian laws, etc.   I have but a faint idea of your occupation ; but I suppose it has something to do with pen and ink.

Mary desires to be kindly remembered to you ; and I remain, my dear Peacock, yours very faithfully.

LXXXIV.

TO C. OLLIER.

PISA, *February* 16, 1821.

DEAR SIR, — I send you three poems, — " Ode to Naples," a sonnet, and a longer piece, entitled "Epipsychidion."   The two former are my own ; and you will be so obliging as to take the first opportunity of publishing according to your own discretion.   The longer poem, I desire, should not be considered as my own ; indeed, in a certain sense, it is a production of a portion of me already dead ; and in this sense the advertisement is no fiction.[1]   It is to be published simply for the esoteric few ; and I make its author a secret, to avoid the malignity of those who turn sweet food into poison, transforming all they touch into the corruption of their own natures.   My wish with

---

[1] In his Preface he speaks of the poem as having been written by a person who " died at Florence, as he was preparing for a voyage to one of the wildest of the Sporades, which he had bought, and where it was his hope to have realized a scheme of life suited perhaps to that happier and better world of which he is now an inhabitant, but hardly practicable in this."   The Preface is signed " S." — L. S.

respect to it is, that it should be printed immediately in the simplest form, and merely one hundred copies : those who are capable of judging and feeling rightly with respect to a composition of so abstruse a nature certainly do not arrive at that number, among those, at least, who would ever be excited to read an obscure and anonymous production ; and it would give me no pleasure that the vulgar should read it. If you have any bookselling reason against publishing so small a number as a hundred, merely, distribute copies among those to whom you think the poetry would afford any pleasure, and send me, as soon as you can, a copy by the post. I have written it so as to give very little trouble, I hope, to the printer, or to the person who revises. I would be much obliged to you if you would take this office on yourself.

Is there any expectation of a second edition of the " Revolt of Islam "? I have many corrections to make in it, and one part will be wholly remodelled. I am employed in high and new designs in verse ; but they are the labors of years, perhaps.

. . . .

Pray send me news of my intellectual children. For "Prometheus" I expect and desire no great sale. "The Cenci" ought to have been popular. I remain, dear Sir, your very obedient servant.

LXXXV.

TO CLAIRE CLAIRMONT.

Sunday [*February* 18, 1821].

.   .   .   .

Your predilection for Germany, German literature and manners, and for an attempt at forming some connections there, still continues. There can be no harm in making the attempt, should you succeed in finding a fit occasion for it, because you can always recede in case it should not answer your expectations. The situation of *dame de compagnie* is one indeed in which there is little to be hoped, compared with what is to be feared, calculating on common cases ; but I am willing to believe that yours is an exception to these, and that every one who knows you intimately must find a necessity of interesting themselves deeply in you. But what are your opportunities, that you so confidently discuss the merits of the question, as if the determination of it were in your power? Has the Princess engaged to interest herself in your affairs, or any other of your acquaintances at Florence? If indeed it be in your power to accompany some German lady of rank to her own country, I think, under the impressions you seem to have conceived, you ought not to delay putting it into effect.

.   .   .   .

You are indeed Germanizing very fast, and the remark you made of the distinction between the manner in which the mind is expressed upon the physiognomy, or the entire figure, of the Italian or the Austrian, is in the choicest style of the *criticism of pure reason*. There is a great deal of truth in it; of truth surrounded and limited by so many exceptions as entirely to destroy its being, as a practical law of pathognomy. I hope you will find Germany and the Germans answer your expectations. I have had no opportunity of forming an idea of them. Their philosophy, as far as I understand it, contemplates only the silver side of the shield of truth; better in this respect than the French, who saw only the narrow edge of it.

You send no news of Naples and Neapolitan affairs; we know nothing of them except what we hear from Florence. Every post may be expected to bring decisive news, for even the news that they defend themselves against so immense and well appointed a force is decisive. I hate the cowardly envy which prompts such base stories as Sgricci's about the Neapolitans; a set of slaves who dare not to imitate the high example of clasping even the shadow of freedom, allege the ignorance and excesses of a populace whom oppression has made savages in sentiment and understanding. That the populace of the city of Naples are brutal, who denies to be true; they cannot improvise tragedies as Sgricci can, but is it certain that under no excitement they would be incapable of more enthusiasm for their country? Besides, it is not of them we speak, but of the people of the kingdom of Naples, the cultivators of the soil, whom a sudden and great impulse might awaken into

citizens and men, as the French and Spaniards have
been awakened, and may render instruments of a system of future social life before which the existing an-
archism of Europe will be dissolved and absorbed.
This feeling is base among the Tuscans about Naples.
As to the Austrians, I doubt not they are strong men,
well disciplined, obeying the master motion like the
wheels of a perfect engine ; they may even have as
men more individual excellence and perfection (not
that I believe it) than the Neapolitans ; but all these
things, if the spirit of Regeneration is abroad, are
chaff before the storm ; the very elements and events
will fight against them ; indignation and shameful
repulse will burn after them to the valleys of the Alps.
Lombardy will renew the league against the Imperial
power ; Germany itself will wrest from its oppressors
a power confided to them under stipulations which,
after having assumed, they refused to carry into effect.
You have seen or heard, I suppose, of the note sent
by the British ministry to the Allied sovereigns. Even
the unprincipled Castlereagh dared not join them
against Naples, and ventured to condemn the principles of their alliance, saying as much as to forbid
them to touch Spain and Portugal. If the Austrians
meet with any serious check, they may as well at
once retire, for the good spirit of the world is out
against them. If they march to Naples at once, let
us hide our heads in sorrow, for our hopes of political
good are vain.

.   .   .   .

What pleasure it gives me to hear that you are
well ! Health is the greatest possession, health of

body and mind, as the writer, weak enough in both, too well knows.   Tell me particularly how you get on with your Italian friends.   Study German ; I will give you a dictionary if I can find one at Leghorn.   " Be strong, live happy, and love," says Milton.   Adieu, dear girl ; confide and persuade yourself of my eternal and tender regard.

Yours with deepest affection.

Keats is very ill at Naples.   I have written to him to ask him to come to Pisa, without, however, inviting him into our own house.   We are not rich enough for that sort of thing.   Poor fellow ! [1]

.   .   .   .

LXXXVI.

TO C. OLLIER.

PISA, *February* 22, 1821.

DEAR SIR, — Peacock's essay is at Florence at present.   I have sent for it, and will transmit to you my paper [on Poetry [2]] as soon as it is written, which will be in a very few days.   Nevertheless, I should be sorry that you delayed your magazine through any dependence on me.   I will not accept anything for this paper, as I had determined to write it, and

[1] On the same page of the MS. of this letter can be read the cancelled words in Shelley's handwriting . —

" My dear Keats, — I learn this moment that you are at Naples and that — "

See Dowden, II. 393.

[2] The " Defence of Poetry."

promised it you, before I heard of your liberal arrangements; but perhaps in future, if I think I have any thoughts worth publishing, I shall be glad to contribute to your magazine on those terms. Meanwhile, you are perfectly at liberty to publish the "Ode to Naples," the Sonnet, or any short piece you may have of mine.

I suppose "Julian and Maddalo" is published. If not, do not add the "Witch of Atlas" to that peculiar piece of writing; you may put my name to the Witch of Atlas, as usual. The piece I last sent you, I wish, as I think I told you, to be printed immediately, and that anonymously. I should be very glad to receive a few copies of it by the box, but I am unwilling that it should be any longer delayed.

I doubt about Charles the First; but if I do write it, it shall be the birth of severe and high feelings. You are very welcome to it, on the terms you mention, and, when once I see and feel that I can write it, it is already written. My thoughts aspire to a production of a far higher character; but the execution of it will require some years. I write what I write chiefly to inquire, by the reception which my writings meet with, how far I am fit for so great a task or not. And I am afraid that your account will not present me with a very flattering result in this particular.

You may expect to hear from me within a week, with the answer to Peacock. I shall endeavor to treat the subject in its elements, and unveil the inmost idol of the error.

If any Review of note abuses me excessively, or the contrary, be so kind as to send it me by post.

LXXXVII.

TO T. L. PEACOCK.

PISA, *March* 21, 1821.

MY DEAR PEACOCK, — I despatch by this post the first part of an essay, intended to consist of three parts, which I design for an antidote to your " Four Ages of Poetry." [1] You will see that I have taken a more general view of what is poetry than you have, and will perhaps agree with several of my positions, without considering your own touched. But read and judge ; and do not let us imitate the great founders of the picturesque, Price and Payne Knight, who, like two ill-trained beagles, began snarling at each other when they could not catch the hare.

I hear the welcome news of a box from England announced by Mr. Gisborne. How much new poetry does it contain? The Bavii and Mævii of the day are fertile ; and I wish those who honor me with boxes would read and inwardly digest your " Four Ages of Poetry" ; for I had much rather, for my own private reading, receive political, geological, and moral treatises, than this stuff in *terza, ottava,* and *tremillesima rima,* whose earthly baseness has attracted the lightning of your undiscriminating censure upon the temple of immortal song. These

---

[1] The "Four Ages of Poetry," here alluded to, was published in Ollier's " Literary Miscellany." Shelley wrote the " Defence of Poetry " as an answer to it.

verses enrage me far more than those of Codrus did Juvenal, and with better reason. Juvenal need not have been stunned, unless he had liked it; but my boxes are packed with this trash, to the exclusion of better matter. But your box will make amends.

We are surrounded here in Pisa by revolutionary volcanoes, which as yet give more light than heat: the lava has not yet reached Tuscany. But the news in the papers will tell you far more than it is prudent for me to say; and for this once I will observe your rule of political silence. The Austrians wish that the Neapolitans and Piedmontese would do the same.

We have seen a few more people than usual this winter, and have made a very interesting acquaintance with a Greek Prince,[1] perfectly acquainted with ancient literature, and full of enthusiasm for the liberties and improvement of his country. Mary has been a Greek student several months, and is reading " Antigone " with our turbaned friend, who in return is taught English.

.   .   .   .

I have had a severe ophthalmia, and have read or written little this winter; and have made acquaintance in an obscure convent with the only Italian for whom I ever felt any interest.[2]

.   .   .   .

---

[1] Prince Alexander Mavrocordato, to whom Shelley dedicated his drama, " Hellas."

[2] Emilia Viviani, to whom " Epipsychidion " was addressed.

LXXXVIII.

TO MR. AND MRS. GISBORNE.

BAGNI, Tuesday Evening
[*June* 5, 1821].

MY DEAR FRIENDS, — We anxiously expect your arrival at the Baths; but as I am persuaded that you will spend as much time with us as you can save from your necessary occupations before your departure, I will forbear to vex you with importunity. My health does not permit me to spend many hours from home. I have been engaged these last days in composing a poem on the death of Keats,[1] which will shortly be finished; and I anticipate the pleasure of reading it to you, as some of the very few persons who will be interested in it and understand it. It is a highly wrought *piece of art*, and perhaps better, in point of composition, than anything I have written.

.   .   .   .

My unfortunate box! it contained a chaos of the elements of "Charles I." If the idea of the *creator* had been packed up with them, it would have shared the same fate; and that, I am afraid, has undergone another sort of shipwreck.

Very faithfully and affectionately yours.

[1] "Adonais."

LXXXIX.

TO C. OLLIER.

PISA, *June* 8, 1821.

DEAR SIR, — You may announce for publication a poem entitled "Adonais." It is a lament on the death of poor Keats, with some interposed stabs on the assassins of his peace and of his fame; and will be preceded by a criticism on " Hyperion," asserting the due claims which that fragment gives him to the rank which I have assigned him. My poem is finished, and consists of about forty Spenser stanzas. I shall send it you, either printed at Pisa, or transcribed in such a manner as it shall be difficult for the reviser to leave such errors as *assist* the obscurity of the " Prometheus." But, in case I send it printed, it will be merely that mistakes may be avoided ; [so] that I shall only have a few copies struck off in the cheapest manner.

If you have interest enough in the subject, I could wish that you would inquire of some of the friends and relations of Keats respecting the circumstances of his death, and could transmit me any information you may be able to collect, and especially as to the degree in which, as I am assured, the brutal attack in the Quarterly Review excited the disease by which he perished.

I have received no answer to my last letter to you. Have you received my contribution to your magazine ? Dear Sir, yours very sincerely.

XC.

TO JOHN GISBORNE.

Pisa, Saturday, *June* 16, 1821.

My dear Friend, — I have received the heart-rending account of the closing scene of the great genius whom envy and ingratitude scourged out of the world.[1] I do not think that, if I had seen it before, I could have composed my poem. The enthusiasm of the imagination would have overpowered the sentiment.

As it is, I have finished my Elegy; and this day I send it to the press at Pisa. You shall have a copy the moment it is completed. I think it will please you. I have dipped my pen in consuming fire for his destroyers; otherwise the style is calm and solemn.

Pray, when shall we see you? Or are the streams of Helicon less salutary than sea-bathing for the nerves? Give us as much as you can before you go to England, and rather divide the term than not come soon.

.　　.　　.　　.　　.　　.　　.

A droll circumstance has occured. "Queen Mab," a poem written by me when very young, in the most furious style, with long notes against Jesus Christ, and God the Father, and the King, and bishops, and marriage, and the devil knows what, is just published

------

[1] Referring to Keats.

by one of the low booksellers in the Strand, against my wish and consent, and all the people are at loggerheads about it. H. S. gives me this account. You may imagine how much I am amused. For the sake of a dignified appearance, however, and really because I wish to protest against all the bad poetry in it, I have given orders to say that it is all done against my desire, and have directed my attorney to apply to Chancery for an injunction, which he will not get.[1]

I am pretty ill, I thank you, just now; but I hope you are better.

XCI.

TO MR. AND MRS. GISBORNE.

MY DEAREST FRIENDS, — I am fully repaid for the painful emotions from which some verses of my poem sprang by your sympathy and approbation, which is all the reward I expect. and as much as I desire. It is not for me to judge whether, in the high praise your feelings assign me, you are right or wrong. The poet and the man are two different natures; though they exist together, they may be unconscious of each other, and incapable of deciding on each other's powers and efforts by any reflex act.

---

[1] Shelley, a few days later, addressed a letter to the Examiner, repudiating this poem, much of which. it will be remembered, was written when he was but eighteen years of age.

The decision of the cause, whether or no *I* am a poet, is removed from the present time to the hour when our posterity shall assemble ; but the court is a very severe one, and I fear that the verdict will be, " Guilty, — death ! "

I shall be with you on the first summons. I hope that the time you have reserved for us, " this bank and shoal of time," is not so short as you once talked of.

In haste, most affectionately yours.

XCII.

TO CLAIRE CLAIRMONT.

PISA, Saturday [*June* 16, 1821].

.   .   .   .   .   .

I have received a most melancholy account of the last illness of poor Keats, which I will neither tell you nor send you, for it would make you too low-spirited. My Elegy on him is finished. I have dipped my pen in consuming fire to chastise his destroyers ; otherwise the tone of the poem is solemn and exalted. I send it to the press here, and you will soon have a copy. Horace Smith tells me of a curious circumstance, which, were I in England, would work me much annoyance. A low bookseller has got hold of " Queen Mab," and published it, and says he will defy all prosecutions, and is selling them by thousands. Horace Smith applied for an injunction on my part, but, like Southey in " Wat Tyler," was refused. The abuse which all the government prints are pouring forth on me, and, as Horace Smith says, the " diabolical calumnies which they invent, and which religion alone could inspire," is boundless. I enjoy, and am amused with, the turmoil of these poor people ; but perhaps it is well for me that the Alps and the ocean are between us.

XCIII.

TO THE EDITOR OF THE "QUARTERLY REVIEW."

SIR, — Should you cast your eye on the signature of this letter before you read the contents, you might imagine that they related to a slanderous paper which appeared in your Review some time since. I never notice anonymous attacks. The wretch who wrote it has doubtless the additional reward of a consciousness of his motives, besides the thirty guineas a sheet, or whatever it is that you pay him. Of course you cannot be answerable for all the writings which you edit, and *I* certainly bear you no ill-will for having edited the abuse to which I allude, — indeed, I was too much amused by being compared to Pharaoh not readily to forgive editor, printer, publisher, stitcher, or any one, except the despicable writer, connected with something so exquisitely entertaining. Seriously speaking, I am not in the habit of permitting myself to be disturbed by what is said or written of me, though I dare say I may be condemned sometimes justly enough. But I feel, in respect to the writer in question, that " I am there sitting, where he durst not soar."

The case is different with the unfortunate subject of this letter, the author of " Endymion," to whose feelings and situation I entreat you to allow me to call your attention. I write considerably in the dark ; but if it is Mr. Gifford that I am addressing, I am persuaded that in an appeal to his humanity and justice he will acknowledge the *fas ab hoste doceri.* I am aware that the first duty of a reviewer is towards the public, and I am willing to confess that the Endymion is a poem considerably defective, and that perhaps it deserved as much censure as the pages of your Review record against it ; but, not to mention that there is certain contemptuousness of phraseology from which it is difficult for a critic to abstain, in the review of Endymion, I do not think that the writer has given it its due praise. Surely the poem, with all its faults, is a very remarkable production for a man of Keats's age, and the promise of ultimate excellence is such as has rarely been afforded even by such as has afterwards attained high literary eminence. Look at Book II., line 833, etc., and Book III., line 113 to 120, — read down that page, and then again from line 193. I could cite many other passages to convince you that it deserved milder usage. Why it should have been reviewed at all, excepting for the purpose of bringing its excellences into notice, I cannot conceive, for it was very little read, and there was no danger that it should become a model to the age of that false taste with which I confess that it is replenished.

Poor Keats was thrown into a dreadful state of mind by this review, which, I am persuaded, was not written with any intention of producing the effect, to which it has at least greatly contributed, of embittering his existence, and inducing a disease from which there are now but faint hopes of his recovery. The first effects are described to me to have resembled insanity, and it was by assiduous watching that he was restrained from effecting purposes of suicide. The agony of his sufferings at length produced the rupture of a blood-vessel in the lungs, and the usual process of consumption appears to have begun. He is coming to pay me a visit in Italy; but I fear that unless his mind can be kept tranquil, little is to be hoped from the mere influence of climate.

But let me not extort anything from your pity. I have just seen a second volumne, published by him evidently in careless despair. I have desired my bookseller to send you a copy, and allow me to solicit your special attention to the fragment of a poem entitled " Hyperion," the composition of which was checked by the review in question. The great proportion of this piece is surely in the very highest style of poetry. I speak impartially, for the canons of taste to which Keats has conformed in his other compositions are the very reverse of my own. I leave you to judge for yourself: it would be an insult to you to suppose that from motives, however honorable, you would lend yourself to a deception of the public.

XCIV.

TO A LADY.

[Exact date unknown.]

IT is probable that you will be earnest to employ the sacred talisman of language. To acquire these you are now necessitated to sacrifice many hours of the time, when, instead of being conversant with particles and verbs, your nature incites you to contemplation and inquiry concerning the objects which they conceal. You desire to enjoy the beauties of eloquence and poetry, — to sympathize in the original language with the institutors and martyrs of ancient freedom. The generous and inspiriting examples of philosophy and virtue you desire intimately to know and feel; not as mere facts detailing names, and dates, and motions of the human body, but clothed in the very language of the actors, — that language dictated by and expressive of the passions and principles that governed their conduct. Facts are not what we want to know in poetry, in history, in the lives of individual men, in satire, or panegyric. They are the mere divisions, the arbitrary points on which we hang, and to which we refer those delicate and evanescent hues of mind, which language delights and instructs us in precise proportion as it expresses. What is a translation of Homer into English? A person who is ignorant of Greek need only look at "Paradise Lost," or the tragedy of "Lear," translated into French, to obtain an analogical conception of its worthless and miserable inadequacy. Tacitus, or Livius, or Herodotus, are equally undelightful and uninstructive in translation. You require to know and to be intimate with those persons who have acted a distinguished part to benefit, to enlighten, or even to pervert and injure humankind. Before you can do this, four years are yet to be consumed in the discipline of the ancient languages, and those of modern Europe which you only imperfectly know, and which conceal from your intimacy such names as Ariosto, Tasso, Petrarch, and Machiavelli; or Goethe, Schiller, Wieland, etc. The French language you, like every other respectable woman, already know; and if the great name of Rousseau did not redeem it, it would have been perhaps as well that you had remained entirely ignorant of it.

XCV.

TO MR. AND MRS GISBORNE.

BAGNI, Friday Night
[*July* 13, 1821].

MY DEAR FRIENDS, — I have been expecting every day a writ to attend at your court at Guebhard's, whence you know it is settled that I should conduct you hither to spend your last days in Italy. A thousand thanks for your maps; in return for which I send you the only copy of " Adonais " the printer has yet delivered.   I wish I could say, as Glaucus could, in the exchange for the arms of Diomed, — ἑκατόμ-βιοι ἐννεαβοίων.

I will only remind you of " Faust," my desire for the conclusion of which is only exceeded by my desire to welcome you.   Do you observe any traces of him in the poem I send you?   Poets, the best of them, are a very chameleonic race; they take the color not only of what they feed on, but of the very leaves under which they pass.

Mary is just on the verge of finishing her novel; but it cannot be in time for you to take to England.— Farewell.

XCVI.

TO MRS. SHELLEY.

(Bagni di Pisa.)

LIONE BIANCO, FLORENCE, Tuesday
[*August* 1, 1821].

MY DEAREST LOVE, — I shall not return this evening; nor, unless I have better success, to-morrow. I have seen many houses, but very few within the compass of our powers; and, even in those which seem to suit, nothing is more difficult than to bring the proprietors to terms.   I congratulate myself on having taken the season in time, as there is great expectation of Florence being full next winter.   I shall do my utmost to return to-morrow evening.   You may expect me about ten or eleven o'clock, as I shall purposely be late, to spare myself the excessive heat.

The Gisbornes (four o'clock, Tuesday) are just set out in a diligence and four, for Bologna. They have promised to write from Paris. I spent three hours this morning principally in the contemplation of the Niobe, and of a favorite Apollo; all worldly thoughts and cares seem to vanish from before the sublime emotions such spectacles create; and I am deeply impressed with the great difference of happiness enjoyed by those who live at a distance from these incarnations of all that the finest minds have conceived of beauty, and those who can resort to their company at pleasure. What should we think if we were forbidden to read the great writers who have left us their works? And yet to be forbidden to live at Florence or Rome is an evil of the same kind, of scarcely less magnitude.

I am delighted to hear that the W.'s are with you. I am convinced that Williams must persevere in the use of the doccia. Give my most affectionate remembrances to them. I shall know all the houses in Florence, and can give W. a good account of them all. You have not sent my passport, and I must get home as I can. I suppose you did not receive my note.

.   .   .   .

Kiss little babe, and how is he? But I hope to see him fast asleep to-morrow night. And pray, dearest Mary, have some of your novel prepared for my return.

XCVII.

TO MARY SHELLEY.

(Bagni di Pisa.)

BOLOGNA, *Agosto* 6 [1821].

DEAREST MINE, — I am at Bologna, and the Caravella is ordered for Ravenna. I have been detained, by having made an embarrassing and inexplicable arrangement, more than twelve hours, or I should have arrived at Bologna last night instead of this morning. Though I have travelled all night at the rate of two miles and a half an hour in a little open calesso, I am perfectly well in health. One would think that I were the Spaniel of Destiny, for the more she knocks me about, the more I fawn on her. I had an overturn about daybreak; the old horse stumbled and threw me and the fat vetturino into a slope of meadow, over the hedge. My angular figure struck where it was pitched, but my vetturino's spherical form rolled fairly to the bottom of the hill, and that with so few symptoms of reluctance in the life that animated it that my ridicule (for it was the drollest sight in the world) was suppressed by my fear that the poor devil had been hurt. But he was very well, and we continued our journey with great success. My love to the Williamses. Kiss my pretty ones, and accept an affectionate one for yourself from me. The chaise waits. I will write the first night from Ravenna at length.

XCVIII.

TO MARY SHELLEY.

RAVENNA, *August* 7, 1821.

MY DEAREST MARY, — I arrived last night at ten o'clock, and sat up talking with Lord Byron until five this morning. I then went to sleep, and now awake at eleven, and, having despatched my breakfast as quick as possible, mean to devote the interval until twelve, when the post departs, to you.

Lord Byron is very well, and was delighted to see me. He has in fact completely recovered his health, and lives a life totally the reverse of that which he led at Venice. He has a permanent sort of *liaison* with Contessa Guiccioli, who is now at Florence, and seems from her letters to be a very amiable woman. She is waiting there until something shall be decided as to their emigration to Switzerland or stay in Italy; which is yet undetermined on either side. She was compelled to escape from the Papal territory in great haste, as measures had already been taken to place her in a convent, where she would have been unrelentingly confined for life. The oppression of the marriage contract, as existing in the laws and opinions of Italy, though less frequently exercised, is far severer than that of England. I tremble to think of what poor Emilia is destined to.

Lord Byron had almost destroyed himself in Venice :

his state of debility was such that he was unable to digest any food, he was consumed by hectic fever, and would speedily have perished, but for this attachment, which has reclaimed him from the excesses into which he threw himself from carelessness and pride, rather than taste.   Poor fellow ! he is now quite well, and immersed in politics and literature.   He has given me a number of the most interesting details on the former subject, but we will not speak of them in a letter.   Fletcher is here, and as if, like a shadow, he waxed and waned with the substance of his master; Fletcher also has recovered his good looks, and from amidst the unseasonable gray hairs a fresh harvest of flaxen locks put forth.

We talked a great deal of poetry, and such matters, last night; and as usual differed, and I think more than ever.   He affects to patronize a system of criticism fit for the production of mediocrity, and although all his fine poems and passages have been produced in defiance of this system, yet I recognize the pernicious effects of it in "The Doge of Venice"; and it will cramp and limit his future efforts, however great they may be, unless he gets rid of it.   I have read only parts of it, or rather he himself read them to me, and gave me the plan of the whole.

Lord Byron has also told me of a circumstance that shocks me exceedingly; because it exhibits a degree of desperate and wicked malice for which I am at a loss to account.   When I hear such things my patience and my philosophy are put to a severe proof, whilst I refrain from seeking out some obscure hiding-place where the countenance of man may never meet me more.[1]

. . . .

Imagine my despair of good, imagine how it is possible that one of so weak and sensitive a nature as mine can run further the gauntlet through this hellish society of men. *You* should write to the Hoppners a letter refuting the charge, in case you believe, and know, and can prove that it is false; stating the grounds and proofs of your belief. I need not dictate what you should say, nor, I hope, inspire you with warmth to rebut a charge which you only can effectually rebut. If you will send the letter to me here, I will forward it to the Hoppners. Lord Byron is not up, I do not know the Hoppners' address, and I am anxious not to lose a post.

XCIX.

TO MARY SHELLEY.

Thursday, *August* 8.

MY DEAREST MARY, — I wrote to you yesterday, and I begin another letter to-day, without knowing

---

[1] The subject referred to here was a slander circulated regarding Shelley and Mary by the Hoppners, an English family that had professed great friendship for them. Mrs. Julian Marshall, in her recent " Life and Letters of Mary Shelley," deduces evidence which proves conclusively the falsity of this and other similar stories which were circulated about the Shelleys during their residence in Italy.

exactly when I can send it, as I am told the post only goes once a week. I dare say the subject of the latter half of my letter gave you pain, but it was necessary to look the affair in the face, and the only satisfactory answer to the calumny must be given by you, and could be given by you alone. This is evidently the source of the violent denunciations of the Literary Gazette, in themselves contemptible enough, and only to be regarded as effects, which show us their cause, which, until we put off our mortal nature, we never despise, — that is, the belief of persons who have known and seen you that you are guilty of crimes.

.   .   .   .

After having sent my letter to the post yesterday, I went to see some of the antiquities of this place, which appear to be remarkable. This city was once of vast extent, and the traces of its remains are to be found more than four miles from the gate of the modern town. The sea, which once came close to it, has now retired to the distance of four miles, leaving a melancholy extent of marshes, interspersed with patches of cultivation, and towards the sea-shore with pine forests, which have followed the retrocession of the Adriatic, and the roots of which are actually washed by its waves.

.   .   .   .

I went in L. B.'s carriage, first to the Chiesa San Vitale, which is certainly one of the most ancient churches in Italy. It is a rotunda, supported upon buttresses and pilasters of white marble ; the ill effect of which is somewhat relieved by an interior row of columns. The dome is very high and narrow. The whole church, in spite of the elevation of the soil, is very high for its breadth, and is of a very peculiar and striking construction. In the section of one of the large tables of marble with which the church is lined, they showed me the *perfect figure*, as perfect as if it had been painted, of a Capuchin friar, which resulted merely from the shadings and the position of the stains in the marble. This is what may be called a pure anticipated cognition of a Capuchin.

I then went to the tomb of Theodosius, which has now been dedicated to the Virgin, without, however, any change in its original appearance. It is about a mile from the present city. This building is more than half overwhelmed by the elevated soil, although a portion of the lower story has been excavated, and is filled with brackish and stinking waters, and a sort of vaporous darkness, and troops of prodigious frogs. It is a remarkable piece of architecture, and without belonging to a period when the ancient taste yet survived, bears, nevertheless, a certain impression of that taste. It consists of two stories ; the lower supported on Doric arches and pilasters, and a simple entablature ; the other circular within, and polygonal outside, and roofed with one single mass of ponderous stone, for it is evidently one, and Heaven alone knows how they contrived to lift it to that height. It is a sort of flattish dome, rough-wrought within by the chisel, from which the Northern conquerors tore the plates of silver that adorned it, and polished without, with things like handles appended to it, which were also wrought out of the solid stone, and to which I suppose the ropes were applied to draw it up. You ascend externally into the second story by a flight of stone steps, which are modern.

The next place I went to was a church called *la Chiesa di Sant' Appollinare*, which is a basilica, and built by one, I forget whom, of the Christian Emperors. It is a long church, with a roof like a barn, and supported by twenty-four columns of the finest marble, with an altar of jasper, and four columns of jasper, and giallo antico, supporting the roof of the tabernacle, which are said to be of immense value. It is something like that church (I forget the name of it) we saw at Rome fuore delle mura. I suppose the Emperor stole these columns, which seem not at all to belong to the place they occupy. Within the city, near the church of San Vitale, there is to be seen the tomb of the Empress Galla Placidia, daughter of Theodosius the Great, together with those of her husband Constantius, her brother Honorius, and her son Valentinian, — all Emperors.

.   .   .   .

Friday.

We ride out in the evening, through the pine forests which divide this city from the sea. Our way of life is this, and I have accommodated myself to it without much difficulty : — L. B. gets up at two, breakfasts; we talk, read, etc., until six; then we ride, and dine at eight; and after dinner sit talking till four or five in the morning. I get up at twelve, and am now devoting in the interval between my rising and his to you.

L. B. is greatly improved in every respect. In

genius, in temper, in moral views, in health, in happiness. The connection with La Guiccioli has been an inestimable benefit to him. He lives in considerable splendor, but within his income, which is now about £4,000 a year; £100 of which he devotes to purposes of charity. He has had mischievous passions, but these he seems to have subdued, and he is becoming what he should be, a virtuous man. The interest which he took in the politics of Italy, and the actions he performed in consequence of it, are subjects not fit to be *written*, but are such as will delight and surprise you. He is not yet decided to go to Switzerland, — a place, indeed, little fitted for him : the gossip and the cabals of those Anglicized coteries would torment him, as they did before, and might exasperate him into a relapse of libertinism, which he says he plunged into, not from taste, but despair. La Guiccioli and her brother (who is L. B.'s friend and confidant, and acquiesces perfectly in her connection with him) wish to go to Switzerland; as L. B. says, merely from the novelty of the pleasure of travelling. L. B. prefers Tuscany or Lucca, and is trying to persuade them to adopt his views. He has made *me* write a long letter to her to engage her to remain, — an odd thing enough for an utter stranger to write on subjects of the utmost delicacy to his friend's mistress. But it seems destined that I am always to have some active part in everybody's affairs whom I approach. I have set down, in lame Italian, the strongest reasons I can think of against the Swiss emigration. To tell you truth, I should be very glad to accept, as my fee, his establishment in

Tuscany.   Ravenna is a miserable place; the people are barbarous and wild, and their language the most infernal patois that you can imagine.   He would be, in every respect, better among the Tuscans.   I am afraid he would not like Florence, on account of the English there.   There is Lucca, Florence, Pisa, Siena, and I think nothing more.   What think you of Prato, or Pistoia, for him? — no Englishman approaches those towns; but I am afraid no house could be found good enough for him in that region.

He has read to me one of the unpublished cantos of " Don Juan," which is astonishingly fine.   It sets him not only above, but far above, all the poets of the day, — every word is stamped with immortality. I despair of rivalling Lord Byron, as well I may, and there is no other with whom it is worth contending. This canto is in the style, but totally, and sustained with incredible ease and power, like the end of the second canto.   There is not a word which the most rigid asserter of the dignity of human nature would desire to be cancelled.   It fulfils, in a certain degree, what I have long preached of producing, — something wholly new and relative to the age, and yet surpassingly beautiful.   It may be vanity, but I think I see the trace of my earnest exhortations to him to create something wholly new.   He has finished his Life up to the present time, and given it to Moore, with liberty for Moore to sell it for the best price he can get, with condition that the bookseller should publish it after his death.   Moore has sold it to Murray for *two thousand pounds*.   I have spoken to him of Hunt, but not with a direct view of demanding a contribution; and, though I am sure that if asked it would not be refused, yet there is something in me that makes it impossible. Lord Byron and I are excellent friends, and were I reduced to poverty, or were I a writer who had no claims to a higher station than I possess, or did I possess a higher than I deserve, we should appear in all things as such, and I would freely ask him any favor. Such is not the case. The demon of mistrust and pride lurks between two persons in our situation, poisoning the freedom of our intercourse. This is a tax, and a heavy one, which we must pay for being human. I think the fault is not on my side, nor is it likely, I being the weaker. I hope that in the next world these things will be better managed. What is passing in the heart of another rarely escapes the observation of one who is a strict anatomist of his own.

Write to me at Florence, where I shall remain a day at least, and send me letters, or news of letters. How is my little darling? And how are you, and how do you get on with your book? Be severe in your corrections, and expect severity from me, your sincere admirer. I flatter myself you have composed something unequalled in its kind, and that, not content with the honors of your birth and your hereditary aristocracy, you will add still higher renown to your name. Expect me at the end of my appointed time. I do not think I shall be detained. Is C. with you, or is she coming? Have you heard anything of my poor Emilia, from whom I got a letter the day of my departure, saying that her marriage was deferred for a *very short* time, on account of the illness of her sposo? How are the Williamses, and Williams especially? Give my very kindest love to them.

Lord B. has here splendid apartments in the house of his mistress's husband, who is one of the richest men in Italy. *She* is divorced, with an allowance of twelve hundred crowns a year, a miserable pittance from a man who has a hundred and twenty thousand a year. Here are two monkeys, five cats, eight dogs, and ten horses, all of whom (except the horses) walk about the house like the masters of it. *Tita* the Venetian is here, and operates as my valet; a fine fellow, with a prodigious black beard, and who has stabbed two or three people, and is one of the most good-natured looking fellows I ever saw.

We have good rumors of the Greeks here, and a Russian war. I hardly wish the Russians to take any part in it. My maxim is with Æschylus: τὸ δυσσεβὲς — μετὰ μεν πλείονα τίκτει, σφετέρᾳ δείκοτα γεννᾷ. There is a Greek exercise for you. How should slaves produce anything but tyranny, — even as the seed produces the plant?

Adieu, dear Mary.

C.

TO T. L. PEACOCK.

RAVENNA, *August* [probably 10], 1821.

MY DEAR PEACOCK, — I received your last letter just as I was setting off from the Bagni on a visit to

Lord Byron at this place. Many thanks for all your kind attention to my accursed affairs. . . .

I have sent you by the Gisbornes a copy of the "Elegy on Keats." The subject, I know, will not please you ; but the composition of the poetry, and the taste in which it is written, I do not think bad. You and the enlightened public will judge. Lord Byron is in excellent cue both of health and spirits. He has got rid of all those melancholy and degrading habits which he indulged at Venice. He lives with one woman, a lady of rank here, to whom he is attached, and who is attached to him, and is in every respect an altered man. He has written three more cantos of "Don Juan." I have yet only heard the fifth, and I think that every word of it is pregnant with immortality. I have not seen his late plays, except "Marino Faliero," which is very well, but not so transcendently fine as Don Juan. Lord Byron gets up at two. I get up — quite contrary to my usual custom, but one must sleep or die, like Southey's sea-snake in Kehama — at twelve. After breakfast, we sit talking till six. From six to eight we gallop through the pine forests which divide Ravenna from the sea ; then come home and dine, and sit up gossiping till six in the morning. I do not think this will kill me in a week or fortnight, but I shall not try it longer.

.   .   .   .

I write nothing, and probably shall write no more. It offends me to see my name classed among those who have no name. If I cannot be something better, I had rather be nothing. My motive was never the infirm desire of fame ; and if I should continue an author, I feel that I should desire it. This cup is justly given to one only of an age ; indeed, participation would make it worthless : and unfortunate they who seek it and find it not.

. . . .

CI.

TO MARY SHELLEY.

RAVENNA, Saturday.

MY DEAR MARY, — You will be surprised to hear that L. B. has decided upon coming to Pisa, in case he shall be able, with my assistance, to prevail upon his mistress to remain in Italy, of which I think there is little doubt. He wishes for a large and magnificent house, but he has furniture of his own, which he would send from Ravenna. Inquire if any of the large palaces are to be let. We discussed Prato, Pistoia, Lucca, etc., but they would not suit him so well as Pisa, to which, indeed, he shows a decided preference. So let it be ! Florence he objects to, on account of the prodigious influx of English.

I don't think this circumstance ought to make any difference in our own plans with respect to this winter in Florence, because we could easily reassume our station with the spring, at Pugnano or the baths, in order to enjoy the society of the noble lord. But do you consider this point, and write to me your full opinion, at the Florence post-office.

I suffer much today from the pain in my side, brought on, I believe, by this accursed water. In other respects, I am pretty well, and my spirits are much improved; they had been improving, indeed, before I left the baths, after the deep dejection of the early part of the year.

I am reading " Anastasius." One would think that L. B. had taken his idea of the three last cantos of Don Juan from this book. That, of course, has nothing to do with the merit of this latter, poetry having nothing to do with the invention of facts. It is a very powerful, and very entertaining novel, and a faithful picture, they say, of modern Greek manners. I have read L. B.'s Letter to Bowles; some good things, — but he ought not to write prose criticism.

You will receive a long letter, sent with some of L. B.'s express to Florence. I write this in haste.

CII.

TO MARY SHELLEY.

RAVENNA, *August* 15, 1821.

.   .   .   .

I went the other day to see Allegra [1] at her convent, and stayed with her about three hours. She is grown tall and slight for her age, and her face is somewhat altered. The traits have become more delicate, and she is much paler, probably from the effect of im-

[1] A natural daughter of Byron's.

proper food.   She yet retains the beauty of her deep blue eyes, and of her mouth; but she has a contemplative seriousness which, mixed with her excessive vivacity, which has not yet deserted her, has a very peculiar effect in a child.   She is under very strict discipline, as may be observed from the immediate obedience she accords to the will of her attendants. This seems contrary to her nature, but I do not think it has been obtained at the expense of much severity. Her hair, scarcely darker than it was, is beautifully profuse, and hangs in large curls on her neck.   She was prettily dressed in white muslin, and an apron of black silk, with trousers.   Her light and airy figure and her graceful motions were a striking contrast to the other children there.   She seemed a thing of a finer and a higher order.   At first she was very shy, but after a little caressing, and especially after I had given her a gold chain which I had bought at Ravenna for her, she grew more familiar, and led me all over the garden, and all over the convent, running and skipping so fast that I could hardly keep up with her.   She showed me her little bed, and the chair where she sat at dinner, and the carozzina in which she and her favorite companions drew each other along a walk in the garden.   I had brought her a basket of sweetmeats, and before eating any of them she gave her companions and each of the nuns a portion.   This is not much like the old Allegra.   I asked her what I should say from her to her mamma, and she said, " Che mi manda un bacio e un bel vestituro."

" E come vuoi il vestituro sia fatto ? "

" Tutto di seta e d' oro," was her reply.

Her predominant foible seems the love of distinction and vanity, and this is a plant which produces good or evil according to the gardener's skill. I then asked what I should say to papa? " Che venga farmi un visitino e che porta seco la *mammina*." Before I went away, she made me run all over the convent, like a mad thing. The nuns, who were half in bed. were ordered to hide themselves, and on returning Allegra began ringing the bell which calls the nuns to assemble. The tocsin of the convent sounded, and it required all the efforts of the prioress to prevent the spouses of God from rendering themselves, dressed or undressed, to the accustomed signal. Nobody scolded her for these *scappature*, so I suppose she is well treated, so far as temper is concerned. Her intellect is not much cultivated. She knows certain *orazioni* by heart, and talks and dreams of *Paradiso* and all sorts of things, and has a prodigious list of saints, and is always talking of the Bambino. This will do her no harm, but the idea of bringing up so sweet a creature in the midst of such trash till sixteen !

CIII.

TO MARY SHELLEY.

RAVENNA, Wednesday.

MY DEAREST LOVE, — I write, though I doubt whether I shall not arrive before this letter, as the post only leaves Ravenna once a week, on Saturdays, and as I hope to set out to-morrow evening by the courier. But as I must necessarily stay a day at Florence, and as the natural incidents of travelling may prevent me from taking my intended advantage of the couriers, it is probable that this letter will arrive first. Besides, as I will explain, I am not *yet* quite my own master. But that by and by. I do not think it necessary to tell you of my impatience to return to you and my little darling, or the disappointment with which I have prolonged my absence from you. I am happy to think that you are not quite alone.

Lord Byron is still decided upon Tuscany; and such is his impatience, that he has desired me — as if I should not arrive in time — to write to you to inquire for the best unfurnished palace in Pisa, and to enter upon a treaty for it. It is better not to be on the Lung' Arno; but, in fact, there is no such hurry, and as I shall see you so soon it is not worth while to trouble yourself about it.

I told you I had written by L. B.'s desire to La Guiccioli, to dissuade her and her family from Switzerland. Her answer is this moment arrived, and my representation seems to have reconciled them to the unfitness of that step. At the conclusion of a letter, full of all the fine things she says she has heard of me, is this request, which I transcribe: " Signore — la vostra bontà mi fa ardita di chiedervi un favore — me lo accorderete voi? Non partite da Ravenna senza Milord." Of course, being now, by all the laws of knighthood, captive to a lady's request, I shall only be at liberty on *my parol*, until Lord Byron is settled at Pisa. I shall reply, of course, that the *boon* is granted, and that, if her lover is reluctant to quit Ravenna after I have made arrangements for receiving him at Pisa, I am bound to place myself in the same situation as now, to assail him with importunities to rejoin her. Of this there is, fortunately, no need; and I need not tell you there is no fear that this chivalric submission of mine to the great general laws of antique courtesy, against which I never rebel, and which is my religion, should interfere with my quick returning, and long remaining with you, dear girl.

I have seen Dante's tomb, and worshipped the sacred spot. The building and its accessories are comparatively modern, but the urn itself, and the tablet of marble, with his portrait in relief, are evidently of equal antiquity with his death. The countenance has all the marks of being taken from his own; the lines are strongly marked, far more than the portraits, which, however, it resembles; except, indeed, the eye, which is half closed, and reminded me of Pacchiani. It was probably taken after death. I saw the library, and some specimens of the earliest illuminated printing from the press of Faust. They are on vellum, and of an execution little inferior to that of the present day.

We ride out every evening as usual, and practise pistol-shooting at a pumpkin; and I am not sorry to observe that I approach towards my noble friend's exactness of aim. The water here is villanous, and I have suffered tortures; but I now drink nothing

but alcalescent water, and am much relieved.   I
have the greatest trouble to get away; and L. B., as
a reason for my stay, has urged that, without either
me or the Guiccioli, he will certainly fall into his old
habits.   I then talk, and he listens to reason; and I
earnestly hope that he is too well aware of the terrible and degrading consequences of his former mode
of life to be in danger from the short interval of
temptation that will be left him.   L. B. speaks with
great kindness and interest of you, and seems to wish
to see you.

RAVENNA, Thursday.

.   .   .   .

Lord Byron is immediately coming to Pisa.   He
will set off the moment I can get him a house.   Who
would have imagined this?   Our first thought ought
to be ——, our second our own plans.   The hesita-
tion in your letter about Florence has communicated
itself to me; although I hardly see what we can do
about Horace Smith, to whom our attentions are so
due, and would be so useful.   If I do not arrive before this long scrawl, write something to Florence to
decide me.   I shall certainly, not without strong
reasons, at present *sign* the agreement for the old
codger's house; although the extreme beauty and
fitness of the place, should we decide on Florence,
might well overbalance the objection of your deaf
visitor.   One thing, — with Lord Byron and the people we know at Pisa, we should have a security and
protection, which seems to be more questionable at
Florence.   But I do not think that this consideration
ought to weigh.   What think you of remaining at

Pisa? The Williamses would probably be induced to stay there if we did; Hunt would certainly stay, at least this winter, near us, should he emigrate at all; Lord Byron and his Italian friends would remain quietly there; and Lord Byron has certainly a great regard for us; — the regard of such a man is worth — *some* of the tribute we must pay to the base passions of humanity in any intercourse with those within their circle; he is better worth it than those on whom we bestow it from mere custom.

.   .   .   .

My greatest content would be utterly to desert all human society. I would retire with you and our child to a solitary island in the sea, would build a boat, and shut upon my retreat the floodgates of the world. I would read no reviews, and talk with no authors. If I dared trust my imagination, it would tell me that there are one or two chosen companions besides yourself whom I should desire. But to this I would not listen, — where two or three are gathered together, the devil is among them. And good far more than evil impulses, love far more than hatred, has been to me, except as you have been its object, the source of all sorts of mischief. So on this plan I would be alone, and would devote either to oblivion or to future generations the overflowings of a mind which, timely withdrawn from the contagion, should be kept fit for no baser object. But this it does not appear that we shall do.

The other side of the alternative (for a medium ought not to be adopted) is to form for ourselves a society of our own class, as much as possible, in intellect, or in feelings; and to connect ourselves with the interests of that society. Our roots never struck so deeply as at Pisa, and the transplanted tree flourishes not. People who lead the lives which we led until last winter are like a family of Wahabee Arabs pitching their tent in the midst of London. We must do one thing or the other, — for yourself, for our child, for our existence. The calumnies, the sources of which are probably deeper than we perceive, have ultimately for object the depriving us of the means of security and subsistence. You will easily perceive the gradations by which calumny proceeds to pretext, pretext to persecution, and persecution to the ban of fire and water. It is for this, and not because this or that fool, or the whole court of fools, curse and rail, that calumny is worth refuting or chastising.

CIV.

TO LEIGH HUNT.

PISA, *August* 26, 1821.

MY DEAREST FRIEND, — Since I last wrote to you, I have been on a visit to Lord Byron at Ravenna. The result of this visit was a determination, on his part, to come and live at Pisa; and I have taken the finest palace on the Lung' Arno for him. But the material part of my visit consists in a message which he desires me to give you, and which, I think, ought to add to your determination, — for such a one

I hope you have formed, of restoring your shattered health and spirits by a migration to these " regions mild of calm and serene air."

He proposes that you should come and go shares with him and me in a periodical work, to be conducted here; in which each of the contracting parties should publish all their original compositions, and share the profits. He proposed it to Moore, but for some reason it was never brought to bear. There can be no doubt that the *profits* of any scheme in which you and Lord Byron engage must, from various, yet co-operating reasons, be very great. As for myself, I am, for the present, only a sort of link between you and him, until you can know each other, and effectuate the arrangement; since (to entrust you with a secret which, for your sake, I withhold from Lord Byron) nothing would induce me to share in the profits, and still less in the borrowed splendor of such a partnership. You and he, in different manners, would be equal, and would bring, in a different manner, but in the same proportion, equal stocks of reputation and success. Do not let my frankness with you, nor my belief that you deserve it more than Lord Byron, have the effect of deterring you from assuming a station in modern literature which the universal voice of my contemporaries forbids me either to stoop or to aspire to. I am, and I desire to be, nothing.

I did not ask Lord Byron to assist me in sending a remittance for your journey; because there are men, however excellent, from whom we would never receive an obligation, in the worldly sense of the word; and I am as jealous for my friend as for myself; but I suppose that I shall at last make up an impudent face, and ask Horace Smith to add to the many obligations he has conferred on me. I know I need only ask.

I think I have never told you how very much I like your "Amyntas"; it almost reconciles me to translations. In another sense I still demur. You might have written another such poem as the "Nymphs," with no great access of efforts. I am full of thoughts and plans, and should do something, if the feeble and irritable frame which encloses it was willing to obey the spirit. I fancy that then I should do great things. Before this, you will have seen "Adonais." Lord Byron, I suppose from modesty, on account of his being mentioned in it, did not say a word of "Adonais," though he was loud in his praise of "Prometheus," and, what you will not agree with him in, censure of "The Cenci." Certainly, if "Marino Faliero" is a drama, "The Cenci" is not, — but that between ourselves. Lord Byron is reformed, as far as gallantry goes, and lives with a beautiful and sentimental Italian lady, who is as much attached to him as may be. I trust greatly to his intercourse with you, for his creed to become as pure as he thinks his conduct is. He has many generous and exalted qualities, but the canker of aristocracy wants to be cut out.

.   .   .   .

CV.

TO HORACE SMITH.

PISA, *September* 14, 1821.

MY DEAR SMITH, — I cannot express the pain and disappointment with which I learn the change in your plans, no less than the afflicting cause of it. Florence will no longer have any attractions for me this winter, and I shall contentedly sit down in this humdrum Pisa, and refer to hope and to chance the pleasure I had expected from your society this winter.

.   .   .   .

I had marked down several houses in Florence, and one especially on the Arno, a most lovely place, though they asked rather more than perhaps you would have chosen to pay, — yet nothing approaching to an English price. I do not yet entirely give you up. Indeed, I should be sorry not to hope that Mrs. Smith's state of health would not soon become such as to remove your principal objection to this delightful climate. I have not, with the exception of three or four days, suffered in the least from the heat this year. Though it is but fair to confess that my temperament approaches to that of the salamander.

We expect Lord Byron here in about a fortnight. I have just taken the finest palace in Pisa for him, and his luggage, and his horses, and all his train, are, I believe, already on their way hither. I dare say you have heard of the life he led at Venice, rivalling the wise Solomon almost in the number of his concubines. Well, he is now quite reformed, and is leading a most sober and decent life, as *cavaliere servente* to a very pretty Italian woman, who has already arrived at Pisa with her father and her brother (such are the manners of Italy), as the jackals of the lion. He is occupied in forming a new drama, and, with views which I doubt not will expand as he proceeds, is determined to write a series of plays, in which he will follow the French tragedians and Alfieri, rather than those of England and Spain, and produce something new, at least to England. This seems to me the wrong road; but genius like his is destined to lead, and not to follow. He will shake off his shackles as he finds they cramp him. I believe he will produce something very great; and that familiarity with the dramatic power of human nature will soon enable him to soften down the severe and unharmonizing traits of his " Marino Faliero." I think you know Lord Byron personally, or is it your brother? If the latter, I know that he wished particularly to be introduced to you, and that he will sympathize in some degree in this great disappointment which I feel in the change, or, as I yet hope, in the prorogation of your plans.

I am glad you like " Adonais," and, particularly, that you do not think it metaphysical, which I was afraid it was. I was resolved to pay some tribute of sympathy to the unhonored dead, but I wrote, as usual, with a total ignorance of the effect that I should produce. — I have not yet seen your pastoral drama ;

if you have a copy, could you favor me with it?   It
will be six months before I shall receive it from England.   I have heard it spoken of with high praise,
and I have the greatest curiosity to see it.

All public attention is now centred on the wonderful revolution in Greece.   I dare not, after the events
of last winter, hope that slaves can become freemen
so cheaply; yet I know one Greek of the highest
qualities, both of courage and conduct, the Prince
Mavrocordato, and if the rest be like him, all will go
well. — The news of this moment is, that the Russian
army has orders to advance.

Mrs. S. unites with me in the most heartfelt regret.
And I remain, my dear Smith, most faithfully yours.

If you happen to have brought a copy of Clarke's
edition of " Queen Mab " for me, I should like very
well to see it. — I really hardly know what this poem
is about.   I am afraid it is rather rough.

CVI.

TO C. OLLIER.

PISA, *September* 25, 1821.

DEAR SIR, — It will give me great pleasure if I can
arrange the affair of Mrs. Shelley's novel with you to
her and your satisfaction.   She has a specific purpose
in the sum which she instructed me to require.

.   .   .   .

The romance is called "Castruccio, Prince of Lucca," and is founded (not upon the novel of Machiavelli

under that name, which substitutes a childish fiction
for the far more romantic truth of history, but) upon
the actual story of his life.   He was a person who,
from an exile and an adventurer, after having served
in the wars of England and Flanders in the reign of
our Edward the Second, returned to his native city,
and, liberating it from its tyrants, became himself its
tyrant, and died in the full splendor of his dominion,
which he had extended over the half of Tuscany.
He was a little Napoleon, and, with a dukedom instead of an empire for his theatre, brought upon the
same all the passions and the errors of his antitype.
The chief interest of this romance rests upon Euthanasia, his betrothed bride, whose love for him is
only equalled by her enthusiasm for the liberty of the
republic of Florence, which is in some sort her country, and for that of Italy, to which Castruccio is a
devoted enemy, being an ally of the party of the
Emperor.   This character is a masterpiece ; and the
keystone of the drama, which is built up with admirable art, is the conflict between these passions and
these principles.   Euthanasia, the last survivor of a
noble house, is a feudal countess, and her castle is
the scene of the exhibition of the knightly manners
of the time.   The character of Beatrice, the prophet-
ess, can only be done justice to in the very language
of the author.   I know nothing in Walter Scott's
novels which at all approaches to the beauty and
sublimity of this — creation, I may almost say, for it
is perfectly original ; and, although founded upon the
ideas and manners of the age which is represented, is
wholly without a similitude in any fiction I ever read.

Beatrice is in love with Castruccio, and dies ; for the romance, although interspersed with much lighter matter, is deeply tragic, and the shades darken and gather as the catastrophe approaches. All the manners, customs, opinions, of the age are introduced ; the superstitions, the heresies, and the religious persecutions are displayed ; the minutest circumstance of Italian manners in that age is not omitted ; and the whole seems to me to constitute a living and a moving picture of an age almost forgotten. The author visited the scenery which she describes in person ; and one or two of the inferior characters are drawn from her own observation of the Italians, for the national character shows itself still in certain instances under the same forms as it wore in the time of Dante.[1]

. . . .

It may be printed on thin paper, like that of this letter, and the expense shall fall upon me. Lord Byron has his works sent in this manner ; and no person who has either fame to lose or money to win ought to publish in any other manner.

By the by, how do I stand with regard to these two

[1] The book here alluded to was ultimately published under the title of "Valperga." Mrs. Shelley received £400 for the copyright ; and this sum was generously devoted to the relief of Godwin's pecuniary difficulties. In a letter to Mrs. Gisborne, dated June 30, 1821, Mrs. Shelley says that she first formed the conception at Marlow ; that this took a more definite shape at Naples ; that the work was delayed several times ; and that it was "a child of a mighty slow growth." It was also, she says, a work of labor, as she had read and consulted a great many books. — L. S.

great objects of human pursuit? I *once* sought something nobler and better than either; but I might as
well have reached at the moon, and now, finding that
I have grasped the air, I should not be sorry to know
what substantial sum, especially of the former, is in
your hands on my account. The gods have made
the reviewers the almoners of this worldly dross, and
I think I must write an ode to flatter them to give
me some, — if I would not that they put me off with a
bill on posterity, which, when my ghost shall present,
the answer will be, " No effects."

Charles the First is conceived, but not born. Unless I am sure of making something good, the play
will not be written. Pride, that ruined Satan, will
kill Charles the First, for his midwife would be only
less than him whom thunder has made greater. I
am full of great plans; and, if I should tell you them,
I should add to the list of these riddles.

I have not seen Mr. Procter's " Mirandola." Send
it me in the box, and pray send me the box immediately. It is of the utmost consequence; and, as
you are so obliging as to say you will not neglect
my commissions, pray send this without delay. I
hope it *is* sent, indeed, and that you have recol-
lected to send me several copies of " Prometheus,"
" The Revolt of Islam," and " The Cenci," etc., as I
requested you. Is there any chance of a second
edition of the Revolt of Islam? I could materially
improve that poem on revision. The " Adonais," in
spite of its mysticism, is the least imperfect of my
compositions, and, as the image of my regret and
honor for poor Keats, I wish it to be so. I shall

write to you, probably, by next post on the subject of that poem, and should have sent the promised criticism for the second edition, had I not mislaid, and in vain sought for, the volume that contains " Hyperion."   Pray give me notice against what time you want the second part of my " Defence of Poetry." I give you this Defence, and you may do what you will with it.

Pray give me an immediate answer about the novel.

CVII.

TO JOHN GISBORNE.

PISA, *October* 22, 1821.

MY DEAR GISBORNE, — At length the post brings a welcome letter from you, and I am pleased to be assured of your health and safe arrival.   I expect with interest and anxiety the intelligence of your progress in England, and how far the advantages there compensate the loss of Italy.   I hear from Hunt that he is determined on emigration, and, if I thought the letter would arrive in time, I should beg you to suggest some advice to him.   But you ought to be incapable of forgiving me in the fact of depriving England of what it must lose when Hunt departs.

Did I tell you that Lord Byron comes to settle at Pisa, and that he has a plan of writing a periodical work in connection with Hunt?   His house, Madame Felichi's is already taken and fitted up for him, and he has been expected every day these six weeks. La Guiccioli, who awaits him impatiently, is a very pretty, sentimental, innocent Italian, who has sacrificed an immense fortune for the sake of Lord Byron, and who, if I know anything of my friend, of her, and of human nature, will hereafter have plenty of leisure and opportunity to repent her rashness. Lord Byron is, however, quite cured of his gross habits, as far as habits; the perverse ideas on which they were formed are not yet eradicated.

We have furnished a house at Pisa, and mean to make it our head-quarters. I shall get all my books out, and intrench myself like a spider in a web. If you can assist P. in sending them to Leghorn, you would do me an especial favor ; but do not buy me Calderon, Faust, or Kant, as H. S. promises to send them me from Paris, where I suppose you had not time to procure them. Any other books you or Henry think would accord with my design, Ollier will furnish you with.

I should like very much to hear what is said of my " Adonais," and you would oblige me by cutting out, or making Ollier cut out, any respectable criticism on it and sending it me ; you know I do not mind a crown or two in postage. The " Epipsychidion " is a mystery ; as to real flesh and blood, you know that I do not deal in those articles ; you might as well go to a gin-shop for a leg of mutton, as expect anything human or earthly from me. I desired Ollier not to circulate this piece except to the $\sigma\upsilon\nu\epsilon\tauο\acuteι$, and even they, it seems, are inclined to approximate me to the circle of a servant girl and her sweetheart. But

I intend to write a Symposium of my own to set all this right.

I am just finishing a dramatic poem, called Hellas, upon the contest now raging in Greece, — a sort of imitation of the Persæ of Æschylus, full of lyrical poetry. I try to be what I might have been, but am not successful. I find that (I dare say I shall quote wrong)

> "Den herrlichsten, den sich der Geist emprängt
>   Drängt immer fremd und fremder Stoff sich an."

The Edinburgh Review lies. Godwin's answer to Malthus is victorious and decisive ; and that it should not be generally acknowledged as such is full of evidence of the influence of successful evil and tyranny. What Godwin is compared to Plato and Lord Bacon, we well know ; but compared with these miserable sciolists, he is a vulture to a worm.

I read the Greek dramatists and Plato forever. You are right about Antigone ; how sublime a picture of a woman ! and what think you of the choruses, and especially the lyrical complaints of the godlike victim? and the menaces of Tiresias, and their rapid fulfilment? Some of us have, in a prior existence, been in love with an Antigone, and that makes us find no full content in any mortal tie. As to books, I advise you to live near the British Museum, and read there. I have read, since I saw you, the " Jungfrau von Orleans " of Schiller, — a fine play if the fifth act did not fall off. Some Greeks, escaped from the defeat in Wallachia, have passed through Pisa to re-embark at Leghorn for the Morea ;

and the Tuscan Government allowed them, during their stay and passage, three lire each per day and their lodging; that is good. Remember me and Mary most kindly to Mrs. Gisborne and Henry, and believe me yours most affectionately.

.

CVIII.

TO C. OLLIER.

PISA, *November* 11, 1821.

DEAR SIR, — I send you the drama of " Hellas," relying on your assurance that you will be good enough to pay immediate attention to my literary requests. What little interest this poem may ever excite depends upon its immediate publication; I entreat you, therefore, to have the goodness to send the MS. instantly to a printer, and the moment you get a proof despatch it to me by the post. The whole might be sent at once. Lord Byron has his poem sent to him in this manner, and I cannot see that the inferiority in the composition of a poem can affect the powers of a printer in the matter of despatch, etc. If any passages should alarm you in the notes, you are at liberty to suppress them; the poem contains nothing of a tendency to danger.

Do not forget my other questions. I am especially curious to hear the fate of " Adonais." I confess I should be surprised if *that* poem were born to an immortality of oblivion.

Within a few days I may have to write to you on a subject of greater interest. Meanwhile, I rely on your kindness for carrying my present request into immediate effect.

CIX.

TO JOSEPH SEVERN.[1]

PISA, *November* 29, 1821

DEAR SIR,—I send you the elegy on poor Keats, and I wish it were better worth your acceptance. You will see, by the preface, that it was written before I could obtain any particular account of his last moments; all that I still know was communicated to me by a friend who had derived his information from Colonel Finch; I have ventured to express, as I felt, the respect and admiration which *your* conduct towards him demands.

In spite of his transcendent genius, Keats never was, nor ever will be, a popular poet; and the total neglect and obscurity in which the astonishing remnants of his mind still lie was hardly to be dissipated by a writer who, however he may differ from Keats in more important qualities, at least resembles him in that accidental one, a want of popularity.

[1] Severn was a young English artist, who ministered to Keats's dying hours with the tenderest care. He died in Rome in 1879, and was buried beside Keats in the English cemetery. His "Life, Friendship, and Letters," edited by William Sharp, has just been published.

I have little hope, therefore, that the poem I send you will excite any attention, nor do I feel assured that a critical notice of his writings would find a single reader.   But for these considerations, it had been my intention to have collected the remnants of his compositions, and to have published them with a life and criticism. — Has he left any poems or writings of whatsoever kind, and in whose possession are they? Perhaps you would oblige me by information on this point.

Many thanks for the picture you promised me.   I shall consider it among the most sacred relics of the past.

For my part, I little expected, when I last saw Keats at my friend Leigh Hunt's, that I should survive him.

Should you ever pass through Pisa, I hope to have the pleasure of seeing you, and of cultivating an acquaintance into something pleasant, begun under such melancholy auspices.

Accept, my dear sir, the assurances of my sincere esteem, and, believe me, your most sincere and faithful servant.

CX.

TO CLAIRE CLAIRMONT.

PISA, *December* 11, 1821.

.   .   .   .

The Exotic, as you are pleased to call me, droops in this frost, — a frost both moral and physical, — a solitude of the heart. These late days I have been un-able to ride, the cold towards sunset is so excessive, and my side reminding me that I am mortal. Medwin rides almost constantly with Lord Byron, and the party sometimes consists of Gamba, Taaffe, Medwin, and the Exotic, who, unfortunately belonging to the order of Mimosa, thrives ill in so large a society. I cannot endure the company of many persons, and the society of one is either great pleasure, or great pain.

We expect the Hunts every day, but I suppose the tramontana is a great wind at sea, and detains them. I think I told you they are to live at Lord Byron's.

The news of the Greeks continues to be more and more glorious. It may be said that the Peloponnesus is entirely free, and Mavrocordato has been acting a distinguished part, and will probably fill a high rank in the magistracy of the infant republic.

.   .   .   .

CXI.

TO CLAIRE CLAIRMONT.

Pisa, *December* 31 [1821].

I RETURNED from Leghorn on Friday evening, but too late for the post, or you would have heard from me. The expected person has not arrived, having been detained by the tremendous weather. I hope soon to have more satisfactory intelligence. Your desires on this subject are the object of my anxious thought. . . . The weather has been frightful here. Torrents of rain have swollen the Arno to a greater degree than has been known for many years; the fury of the torrent is inconceivably great. The wind was beyond anything I ever remember, and all the shores of the Mediterranean are strewn with wrecks. The damage sustained at Genoa, and the number of lives lost, has been immense; the ships suspected of pestilence have been driven from their moorings into the town, and everything coming from Genoa has been subjected to a strict quarantine. Three mails from France are due, and a thousand contradictory rumors are afloat as to the cause. You may imagine, and I am sure you will share, our anxiety about poor Hunt. I wonder, and am shocked at my own insensibility, that I can sleep or enjoy one moment of peace until I hear of his safety. I shall, of course, write to tell you the moment of his arrival. I know you will be anxious about these poor people. The ship in which they sail was spoken with in the Bay of Biscay, and was then quite safe. We have little new in politics. You will have heard of the amphibious state of things in France, and the establishment of the ultra Ministry by the preponderance afforded to that party by the coalition of the Liberals with it. The Greeks are going on evidently, and those massacres at Smyrna and Constantinople import nothing to the stability of the cause. There is no such thing as a rebellion in Ireland, or anything that looks like it. The people are indeed stung to madness by the oppression of the Irish system, and there is no such thing as getting rents or taxes even at the

point of the bayonet throughout the southern prov-
inces. But there are no regular bodies of men in
opposition to the government, nor have the people
any leaders. In England all bears for the moment
the aspect of a sleeping volcano.

.   .   .   .

CXII.

TO T. L. PEACOCK.

PISA, *January* [probably 11], 1822.

MY DEAR PEACOCK, — I am still at Pisa, where I
have at length fitted up some rooms at the top of a
lofty palace that overlooks the city and the surrounding region, and have collected books and plants
about me, and established myself for some indefinite
time, which, if I read the future, will not be short.
I wish you to send my books by the very first opportunity, and I expect in them a great augmentation
of comfort. Lord Byron is established here, and we
are constant companions. No small relief this, after
the dreary solitude of the understanding and the
imagination in which we passed the first years of our
expatriation, yoked to all sorts of miseries and dis-
comforts. Of course you have seen his last volume,
and if you before thought him a great poet, what is
your opinion now that you have read " Cain " ?   " The
Foscari " and " Sardanapalus " I have not seen ; but as
they are in the style of his later writings, I doubt not
they are very fine. We expect Hunt here every

day, and remain in great anxiety on account of the heavy gales which he must have encountered at Christmas. Lord Byron has fitted up the lower apartments of his palace for him, and Hunt will be agreeably surprised to find a commodious lodging prepared for him after the fatigues and dangers of his passage. I have been long idle, and, as far as writing goes, despondent; but I am now engaged on " Charles the First," [1] and a devil of a nut it is to crack.

M. and C., who is not with us just at present, are well, and so is our little boy, the image of poor William. We live, as usual, tranquilly. I get up, or at least wake, early; read and write till two; dine; go to Lord B.'s, and ride, or play at billiards, as the weather permits; and sacrifice the evening either to light books or whoever happens to drop in. Our furniture, which is very neat, cost fewer shillings than that at Marlow did pounds sterling; and our windows are full of plants, which turn the sunny winter into spring. My health is better, my cares are lighter; and although nothing will cure the consumption of my purse, yet it drags on a sort of life in death, very like its master, and seems, like Fortunatus's, always empty, yet never quite exhausted. You will have seen my " Adonais," and perhaps my "Hellas," and I think, whatever you may think of the subject, the composition of the first poem will not wholly displease you. I wish I had something better to do than furnish this jingling food for the hunger of oblivion, called verse, but I have not; and

---

[1] The drama that Shelley left as a fragment.

since you give me no encouragement about India, I
cannot hope to have.

How is your little star, and the heaven which contains the milky way in which it glimmers?   Adieu.

CXIII.

TO HORACE SMITH.

PISA, *January* 25, 1822.

MY DEAR SMITH, — I have delayed this fortnight
answering your kind letter, because I was in treaty
for a Calderon, which at last I have succeeded in
procuring at a tolerably moderate price.   All the
other books you mention I should be glad to have ;
together with whatever others might fall in your way
that you might think interesting.

Will you not think my exactions upon your kindness interminable if I ask you to execute another
commission for me?   It is to buy a good pedal harp,
without great ornament or any appendage that would
unnecessarily increase the expense, — but good ; nor
should I object to its being second-hand, if that were
equally compatible with its being despatched immediately.   Together with the harp I should wish for
five or six napoleons' worth of harp music, at your
discretion.   I do not know the price of harps at
Paris, but I suppose that from seventy to eighty
guineas would cover it, and I trust to your accustomed kindness, as I want it for a present, to make

the immediate advance, as, if I were to delay, the grace of my compliment would be lost. Do not take much trouble about it, but simply take what you find, if you are so exceedingly kind as to oblige me. It had better be sent by Marseilles, through some merchant, or in any other manner you think best, addressed to me at Messrs. Guebhard & Co., merchants, Leghorn; the books may be sent together with it.

Our party at Pisa is the same as when I wrote last. Lord Byron unites us at a weekly dinner, when my nerves are generally shaken to pieces by sitting up contemplating the rest making themselves vats of claret, etc., till three o'clock in the morning. We regret *your* absence exceedingly, and Lord Byron has desired me to convey his best remembrances to you. I imagine it is *you*, and not your brother, for whom they are intended. Hunt was expected, and Lord Byron had fitted up a part of his palace for his accommodation, when we heard that the late violent storms had forced him to put back; and that nothing could induce Marianne to put to sea again. This, for many reasons that I cannot now explain, has produced a chaos of perplexities. . . . The reviews and journals, they say, continue to attack me, but I value neither the fame they can give nor the fame they can take away, therefore blessed be the name of the reviews.

CXIV.

TO JOHN GISBORNE.

PISA, *April* 10, 1822.

MY DEAR GISBORNE, — I have received Hellas, which is prettily printed, and with fewer mistakes than any poem I ever published. Am I to thank you for the revision of the press? or who acted as mid-wife to this last of my orphans, introducing it to oblivion, and me to my accustomed failure? May the cause it celebrates be more fortunate than either! Tell me how you like "Hellas," and give me your opinion freely. It was written without much care, and in one of those few moments of enthusiasm which now seldom visit me, and which make me pay dear for their visits. I know what to think of "Adonais," but what to think of those who confound it with the many bad poems of the day, I know not.

I have been reading over and over again "Faust," and always with sensations which no other composition excites. It deepens the gloom and augments the rapidity of ideas, and would therefore seem to me an unfit study for any person who is a prey to the reproaches of memory and the delusions of an imagination not to be restrained. And yet the pleasure of sympathizing with emotions known only to few, although they derive their sole charm from despair, and the scorn of the narrow good we can attain in our present state, seems more than to ease the pain which belongs to them.   Perhaps all discontent with the *less* (to use a Platonic sophism) supposes the sense of a just claim to the *greater*, and that we admirers of Faust are on the right road to Paradise. Such a supposition is not more absurd, and is certainly less demoniacal, than that of Wordsworth, where he says :

> " This earth,
> Which is the world of all of us, and where
> *We find our happiness, or not at all.*"

.   .   .   .

Have you read Calderon's " Magico Prodigioso "? I find a striking singularity between Faust and this drama, and if I were to acknowledge Coleridge's distinction, should say Goethe was the *greatest* philosopher, and Calderon the *greatest* poet. Cyprian evidently furnished the *germ* of Faust, as Faust may furnish the germ of other poems ; although it is as different from it in structure and plan as the acorn from the oak.   I have — imagine my presumption — translated several scenes from both, as the basis of a paper for our journal.   I am well content with those from Calderon, which in fact gave me very little trouble ; but those from Faust — I feel how imperfect a representation, even with all the license I assume to figure to myself how Goethe would have written in English, my words convey.   No one but Coleridge is capable of this work.

We have seen here a translation of some scenes, and indeed the most remarkable ones, accompanying those astonishing etchings which have been published in England from a German master.   It is not bad, —

and faithful enough; but how weak! how incompe-
tent to represent Faust! I have only attempted the
scenes omitted in this translation, and would send you
that of the *Walpurgisnacht,* if I thought Ollier would
place the postage to my account. What etchings
those are! I am never satiated with looking at them;
and, I fear, it is the only sort of translation of which
Faust is susceptible. I never perfectly understood
the Hartz Mountain scene until I saw the etching;
and then Margaret in the summer-house with Faust!
The artist makes one envy his happiness that he can
sketch such things with calmness, which I only dared
look upon once, and which made my brain swim
round only to touch the leaf on the opposite side of
which I knew that it was figured. Whether it is that
the artist has surpassed Faust, or that the pencil sur-
passes language in some subjects, I know not, or that
I am more affected by a visible image, but the etching certainly excited me far more than the poem it
illustrated. Do you remember the fifty-fourth letter
of the first part of the " Nouvelle Héloïse "? Goethe, in a subsequent scene, evidently had that letter
in his mind, and this etching is an idealism of it. So
much for the world of shadows!

What think you of Lord Byron's last volume? In
my opinion it contains finer poetry than has appeared
in England since the publication of Paradise Re-
gained. "Cain" is apocalyptic,—it is a revelation
not before communicated to man. I write nothing
but by fits. I have done some of Charles I.; but although the poetry succeeded very well, I cannot seize
on the conception of the subject as a whole, and sel-

dom now touch the canvas.   You know I don't think much about Reviews, nor of the fame they give, nor that they take away.   It is absurd in any Review to criticise " Adonais," and still more to pretend that the verses are bad. " Prometheus" was never intended for more than five or six persons.

.   .   .   .

CXV.

TO HORACE SMITH.

PISA, *April* 11, 1822.

MY DEAR SMITH, — I have, as yet, received neither the . . ., nor his metaphysical companions. *Time, my Lord, has a wallet on his back*, and I suppose he has bagged them by the way.   As he has had a good deal of *alms* for oblivion out of me, I think he might as well have favored me this once ; I have, indeed, just dropped another mite into his treasury, called " Hellas," which I know not how to send to you ; but I dare say, some fury of the Hades of authors will bring one to Paris.   It is a poem written on the Greek cause last summer, — a sort of lyrical, dramatic, non-descript piece of business.

Lord Byron has read me one or two letters of Moore to him, in which Moore speaks with great kindness of me ; and of course I cannot but feel flattered by the approbation of a man, my inferiority to whom I am proud to acknowledge.   Amongst other things, however, Moore, after giving Lord B. much good advice about public opinion, etc., seems to deprecate MY influence on his mind on the subject of religion, and to attribute the tone assumed in "Cain" to my suggestions. Moore cautions him against my influence on this particular, with the most friendly zeal; and it is plain that his motive springs from a desire of benefiting Lord B., without degrading me.

. . . .

Where are you? We settle this summer near Spezia; Lord Byron at Leghorn. May not I hope to see you, even for a trip in Italy? I hope your wife and little ones are well. Mine grows a fine boy, and is quite well.

I have contrived to get my musical coals at Newcastle itself.

My dear Smith, believe me, faithfully yours.

CXVI.

TO HORACE SMITH.

(Versailles.)

LERICI, *May*, 1822.

MY DEAR SMITH, — It is some time since I have heard from you; are you still at Versailles? Do you still cling to France, and prefer the arts and conveniences of that over-civilized country to the beautiful nature and mighty remains of Italy? As to me, like Anacreon's swallow, I have left my Nile, and have taken up my summer quarters here, in a lonely house, close by the seaside, surrounded by the soft and sub-

lime scenery of the gulf of Spezia.   I do not write ;
I have lived too long near Lord Byron, and the sun
has extinguished the glowworm ; for I cannot hope,
with St. John, that "*the light came into the world,
and the world knew it not.*"

.   .   .   .

CXVII.

TO HORACE SMITH.

LERICI, *June* 29, 1822.

.   .   .   .

England appears to be in a desperate condition,
Ireland still worse ; and no class of those who subsist
on the public labor will be persuaded that *their* claims
on it must be diminished. But the government
must content itself with less in taxes, the landholder
must submit to receive less rent, and the fundholder
a diminished interest, or they will all get nothing.   I
once thought to study these affairs, and write or act in
them.   I am glad that my good genius said, *Refrain.*
I see little public virtue, and I foresee that the contest will be one of blood and gold, two elements
which, however much to my taste in my pockets and
my veins, I have an objection to out of them.

Lord Byron continues at Leghorn, and has just received from Genoa a most beautiful little yacht, which
he caused to be built there.   He has written two new
cantos of " Don Juan," but I have not seen them.   I
have just received a letter from Hunt, who has ar-

rived at Genoa. As soon as I hear that he has sailed, I shall weigh anchor in my little schooner, and give him chase to Leghorn, when I must occupy myself in some arrangements for him with Lord Byron. Between ourselves, I greatly fear that this alliance will not succeed; for I, who could never have been regarded as more than the link of the two thunderbolts, cannot now consent to be even that; and how long the alliance may continue, I will not prophesy. Pray do not hint my doubts on the subject to any one, or they might do harm to Hunt; and they *may* be groundless.

I still inhabit this divine bay, reading Spanish dramas, and sailing, and listening to the most enchanting music. We have some friends on a visit to us, and my only regret is that the summer must ever pass, or that Mary has not the same predilection for this place that I have, which would induce me never to shift my quarters. Farewell.

CXVIII.

TO MRS. E. E. WILLIAMS.

(Casa Magni.)

PISA, *July* 4, 1822.

You will probably see Williams before I can disentangle myself from the affairs with which I am now surrounded. I return to Leghorn to-night, and shall urge him to sail with the first fair wind, without expecting me. I have thus the pleasure of contributing to your happiness when deprived of every other, and of leaving you no other subject of regret but the absence of one scarcely worth regretting. I fear you are solitary and melancholy at Villa Magni, and, in the intervals of the greater and more serious distress in which I am compelled to sympathize here, I figure to myself the countenance which had been the source of such consolation to me, shadowed by a veil of sorrow.

How soon those hours passed, and how slowly they return, to pass so soon again, perhaps forever, in which we have lived together so intimately, so happily! Adieu, my dearest friend! I only write these lines for the pleasure of tracing what will meet your eyes. Mary will tell you all the news.

CXIX.

TO MARY SHELLEY.

PISA, *July* 4, 1822.

MY DEAREST MARY, — I have received both your letters, and shall attend to the instructions they convey. I did not think of buying the Bolivar; Lord B. wishes to sell her, but I imagine would prefer ready money. I have as yet made no inquiries about houses near Pugnano, — I have no moment of time to spare from Hunt's affairs; I am detained unwillingly here, and you will probably see Williams in the boat before me, — but that will be decided to-morrow.

Things are in the worst possible situation with re-spect to poor Hunt. I find Marianne in a desperate state of health, and on our arrival at Pisa sent for Vacca. He decides that her case is hopeless, and that, although it will be lingering, must inevitably end fatally. This decision he thought proper to commu-nicate to Hunt; indicating at the same time, with great judgment and precision, the treatment neces-sary to be observed for availing himself of the chance of his being deceived. This intelligence has extin-guished the last spark of poor Hunt's spirits, low enough before. The children are well, and much improved.

Lord Byron is at this moment on the point of leaving Tuscany. The Gambas have been exiled, and he declares his intention of following their for-tunes. His first idea was to sail to America, which was changed to Switzerland, then to Genoa, and last to Lucca. Everybody is in despair, and everything in confusion. Trelawny was on the point of sailing to Genoa for the purpose of transporting the Bolivar overland to the Lake of Geneva, and had already whispered in my ear his desire that I should not in-fluence Lord Byron against this terrestrial navigation. He next received *orders* to weigh anchor and set sail for Lerici. He is now without instructions, moody and disappointed. But it is the worst for poor Hunt, unless the present storm should blow over. He places his whole dependence upon the scheme of a journal, for which every arrangement has been made. Lord Byron must of course furnish the requisite funds at present, as I cannot; but he seems inclined to depart without the necessary explanations and arrangements due to such a situation as Hunt's. These, in spite of delicacy, I must procure; he offers him the copyright of "The Vision of Judgment" for the first number. This offer, if sincere, is *more* than enough to set up the journal, and, if sincere, will set everything right.

How are you, my best Mary? Write especially how is your health and how your spirits are, and whether you are not more reconciled to staying at Lerici, at least during the summer.

You have no idea how I am hurried and occupied; I have not a moment's leisure, but will write by next post.

Ever, dearest Mary, yours affectionately.

9 783337 135553